"I'm sorry. I just don't believe..."

Abby looked at Brad before continuing. "I don't believe people go through some magic tunnel when they die and encounter lights and angels."

"Do you think I'm lying, Abby? If you honestly believe death is the end of everything," Brad asked quietly, "then what do you think has been going on with Aaron's toys?"

She stared at him, then looked away.

"Haven't you been half believing in ghosts, sweetheart? Hoping that maybe part of Aaron is still around?"

"It's been almost a year," Abby whispered. "And it's Christmas again. Sometimes, Brad, I wonder if I can stand it. He seems so close."

Brad took her in his arms. "Abby," he whispered. "I *know* who's been moving Aaron's toys...."

Dear Reader,

We're wrapping up the holiday season for you with four romantic delights!

Our final Women Who Dare title for 1993 is by **Sharon Brondos**. In *Doc Wyoming,* Dr. Dixie Sheldon is enthusiastic about opening her new medical office in the small community of Seaside, Wyoming... until she meets the taciturn local sheriff, Hal Blane. Blane seems determined to prevent her from doing her job. And he especially doesn't want Dixie treating his mother, for fear she'll unearth family secrets he'd prefer to keep buried.

Longtime favorite author **Margaret Chittenden** has penned a charming tale of a haunted house and a friendly spirit in *When the Spirit is Willing.* Laura Daniels, needing to start over after the death of her husband, moves to picturesque Port Dudley to raise her daughter in peace. But peace eludes her when she discovers that her new home is haunted, and the resident ghost appears to be an aggressive matchmaker!

Two of our December Superromance titles will evoke the sort of emotions the holidays are all about. The moving *Angels in the Light,* by **Margot Dalton**, focuses on Abby Malone, who is decidedly unenthusiastic about her latest story assignment. She absolutely does not believe in near-death experiences. But she has no idea how to explain the new Brad Carmichael. He is no longer the selfish, immature boy who'd simply taken off when she'd needed him most, but a sensitive, gentle man who wants Abby to believe anything is possible.

New author **Maggie Simpson** will charm you with *Baby Bonus.* Susan Montgomery's life is turned upside down from the moment Andrew Bradley knocks on her door to inform her that she has a grandson to care for—courtesy of her runaway daughter and his irresponsible son. Even worse, Andrew is determined to stick around to make sure the baby is raised according to the Andrew Bradley School of Grandparenting!

In January, Lynn Erickson, Peg Sutherland, Judith Arnold and Risa Kirk will take you to the Caribbean, North Carolina, Boston and Rodeo Drive! Be sure to come along for the ride!

Holiday Greetings!

Marsha Zinberg,
Senior Editor

Margot Dalton

ANGELS in the Light

Harlequin Books

TORONTO • NEW YORK • LONDON
AMSTERDAM • PARIS • SYDNEY • HAMBURG
STOCKHOLM • ATHENS • TOKYO • MILAN
MADRID • WARSAW • BUDAPEST • AUCKLAND

ISBN 0-373-70576-X

ANGELS IN THE LIGHT

ABOUT THE AUTHOR

This is the first time Margot Dalton, author of eleven Superromance novels, has set a story in her adopted province of British Columbia. "I've always written about the Prairies," says Margot. "An area I love very much. But there is a beautiful—almost ethereal—quality to the Okanagan Valley, particularly in the autumn, which makes it uniquely suited to the rather magical tone of this Christmas story."

Note to readers: Margot Dalton welcomes your letters and will try to answer each one personally. Letters can be sent to her c/o Harlequin Reader Service, P.O. Box 1397, Buffalo, NY 14240, U.S.A.

Books by Margot Dalton

HARLEQUIN SUPERROMANCE

511—JUNIPER
533—DANIEL AND THE LION
558—ANOTHER WOMAN

HARLEQUIN CRYSTAL CREEK

2—COWBOYS AND CABERNET
5—EVEN THE NIGHTS ARE BETTER
11—NEW WAY TO FLY (coming next month)

CHAPTER ONE

"THAT'S WHAT *I* think, Abby."

Abby Malone, who had been daydreaming over a tossed salad, raised her head and gazed at her lunch companion. She struggled to recapture the thread of the conversation. "I guess I didn't . . . Joan, what did you say?"

"I *said*," the other woman repeated, leaning forward, "that I think he's an angel."

"An angel," Abby repeated blankly. "This guy's . . . like from heaven, you mean?"

"Yes," her friend breathed, settling back in her chair and giving Abby a significant look.

Abby returned the look, her face solemn. She wondered how she and Joan appeared to the other people in the trendy restaurant. Did they look alike, these two thirty-year-old women having lunch together? Would anybody who glanced casually in their direction be at all interested in what they did or thought?

Probably not, Abby decided.

She and Joan weren't the kind to invite interested second looks from the men dining nearby. They looked like what they were—a pair of working women on their lunch hour, loaded down with obligations and responsibilities, about as far removed from glamour and romance, from any kind of whimsy, as it was possible to get.

And yet here was Joan, talking in hushed tones about an angel she'd met on a downtown street corner.

"Joan, the man's a vagrant. He's a *panhandler,* for God's sake," Abby said. "What makes you think he's some kind of celestial being?"

"His eyes," Joan said with a dreamy smile. "He has the most gorgeous eyes, Abby. Like pools of purest aquamarine. You can't imagine what it's like to gaze into those eyes. I could just drown in them. And he's so incredibly gentle. He's...he's *otherworldly.* I just know it."

Abby shook her head in disbelief, then smiled automatically as the waitress arrived with a fresh pot of coffee.

"You're crazy," she said fondly when they were alone again. "Absolutely certifiable. What happened exactly? You stopped to give the guy a dollar and he mentioned that his last address was in the Milky Way, or what?"

Joan looked up with a reproving expression in her gentle blue eyes. "Go ahead, laugh. You always laugh. You've been laughing at me since we were in the third-grade Christmas pageant together."

"Anybody would have laughed. Your halo fell down around your neck and got caught on one of your wings and you almost strangled. Talk about an angel," Abby said with a grin.

Joan giggled at the memory, then sobered. "Maybe I *am* being silly. But, Abby, there's still something special about him. There really is. I want you to come and see him."

"See him? How? Like an exhibit in the zoo, or what?"

"I mean, just look into his eyes. Talk to him for a minute and see what you think."

"I've *seen* him, Joan," Abby said patiently. "He's on that corner every morning. He sits there in his dirty ragged clothes and plays that old harmonica, and people drop coins in his cup. He's a fixture. Why should I go and see him again?"

"Because you've never really *looked* at him," Joan said earnestly, her face suddenly vivid with emotion as she leaned across the table. "If you ever really looked into his eyes, Abby..."

"All right, all right. On my way down to the newspaper I'll go by his corner, gaze deep into his eyes and ask him if he's heard any good harp tunes lately."

"Abby..."

"Just kidding. Actually, I could use an angel these days."

"Why?" Joan asked. "What's bothering you?"

Abby shook her head. "Nothing much. Just Lorna's latest brain wave."

"Your editor?"

"Yeah. She called yesterday," Abby said. "I was planning to do my next article on the sterile insect program, you know?"

Joan nodded. "I remember. You told me you'd get it done before Christmas."

"Well, I won't," Abby said gloomily. "Christmas is just three months away, and Lorna's got a completely different assignment for me to do in the meantime."

"Really? What is it?"

Abby felt a resurgence of the troubled unhappiness that had dogged her ever since the conversation with her editor the previous evening.

"NDE," she said reluctantly. "They want me to do an article on NDE."

Joan stared at her blankly. "What's that?"

"Near-death experience. You know, those people who are clinically dead and see blinding lights and angels and all that, then come back? They want a research article taking an objective look at the whole phenomenon."

"That's strange. I mean, this magazine you write for—it specializes in really dry scientific stuff, doesn't it?"

"That's what I wondered about, too. I would have thought the whole business of near-death experience was parapsychology at best. But Lorna disagrees. She says there are scientists who believe the experience arises out of chemical changes in the brain at the time of death, oxygen deprivation, that sort of thing. There's quite a lot of interest in it," Abby said, keeping her voice deliberately casual.

Joan looked at her friend in sympathy. "Doesn't she understand that something like this might be really hard for you? After all, it's only been . . ."

"She's not concerned about my personal life," Abby said briefly.

"But why you? I mean, you had the other article all planned and researched. Can't somebody else do this one?"

"Lorna says I have something of a local advantage on this story. Apparently there's an active chapter of NDE survivors who meet regularly up here in our area. The editorial staff thought I could sit in on a few of the meetings, do some interviews, that sort of thing."

"They *meet?*" Joan asked incredulously. "What for?"

"To share the experience, I guess. Lorna tells me that it's a very powerful thing. Even life altering in some cases."

"Still," Joan murmured, "it seems really insensitive of them, asking you to do this."

"Lorna did say that if I was reluctant for personal reasons, they'd probably understand. But I was specifically requested to do the article and she reminded me that it's not really wise to turn that kind of thing down, if you know what I mean."

Abby tensed again when she recalled the implied threat, knowing how many people coveted her job and how little concern the professional staff at the Los Angeles-based magazine would have with a writer's "personal reasons" for turning down an important assignment.

"How?" Joan asked. "I mean, how were you specifically requested?"

"Somebody in this area gave the idea to the magazine and recommended me as a person who'd be competent to write the article. Lorna thinks it's going to attract a whole lot of national attention."

"Well, that's good, anyway. Will it be really hard for you, Abby?"

"I hate it," Abby said slowly. "I hate the thought of doing it. I'm repelled by the whole idea of near-death experience."

"But, Abby..." Joan began.

"The whole thing just seems so cowardly. Why do people always feel such a tremendous need to delude themselves? Why do they want to keep pretending that nothing ever ends, and there's always a happy ending?"

"So what do *you* believe? About death, I mean."

"I believe that when you're dead, you're dead. Life ceases to exist, in any form. I have to believe that or I'd go crazy."

"No heaven? No afterlife?" Joan asked gently.

"No!" Abby said, then reached out to touch her friend's hand. "Sorry, Joannie. I didn't mean to yell at you. I just..." She leaned forward, gazing into Joan's sympathetic eyes. "I can't allow myself to believe in any of that harps-and-angels stuff, Joan. If I did, I'd probably be running around to spiritualists, paying them huge amounts of money to summon Aaron up for me and let me talk to him just one more time. I'm afraid to let myself believe that he still exists in any form. I don't think I could bear it, having him exist somewhere but not being able to see him and touch him."

As she spoke, Abby felt a stab of pain that was wearily familiar, even after all these months. She gazed at the salad on her plate without seeing it, flooded with vivid memories of that terrible day last Christmas.

She could feel Aaron clutching her hand, trotting along beside her. She saw his fat cheeks and sparkling eyes, his shy radiant smile, his sturdy plump legs and arms, the sweet rounded baby look that was just beginning to fade into the slim legginess of childhood. She squeezed his small hand in hers and listened to the endless stream of chatter that drifted around her knees, the questions and observations and delighted chuckles with which Aaron rejoiced in his world.

They had been on their way to cut their Christmas tree that day, she and Aaron, but they'd stopped off for a few minutes at the old heritage house by the lake. Abby had been writing an article on the building's restoration and she'd wanted some more pictures of the wooden wainscoting and moldings before the paint was stripped away.

Aaron had his toy farm to play with, in its little carrier shaped like a barn. He wandered into the dark closet under the old curved staircase, leaving the door open just enough to let a ray of sunlight fall across his cozy hiding place.

Abby paused to lean inside and check that there was nothing to hurt him, nothing that might fall on him or tangle in his clothes. She gave him a smile and a kiss, watched for a moment while he began solemnly to line up his plastic chickens on the fence posts, then took out her camera. She was deeply absorbed in her work, when she heard him cry out, a scream of fear and pain that made her catch her breath.

She ran back and pulled him out from under the stairs. His eyes were wide with terror as he held out his hand. Abby gasped and brushed at the spider, a big black glistening thing that was lodged near his chubby wrist.

When the spider fell to the floor and flipped over to expose the red hourglass shape on its abdomen, Abby's whole world began to spin crazily and her mind filled with a choking cloud of terror. But Aaron was whimpering and rubbing fretfully at his hand, and it was already beginning to swell.

Abby forced herself to breathe deeply, to stay calm, to kiss him and murmur gentle words of reassurance as she bundled him into his snowsuit and rushed outside to the car.

By the time they reached the hospital emergency room Aaron's small arm was swollen and tender all the way to the shoulder, warm to the touch. His cheeks were flushed and his bright dark eyes were glassy with pain.

"Hold on, sweetheart," Abby whispered, cuddling his little body on her knee as the young doctor had examined him. "Just hold on."

She kissed his hair tenderly, aching with waves of love as she tried to draw his pain into her own body, to shield him from anything that might ever hurt him.

"It's all right, darling," she murmured as he cried. "It's all right, baby. Everything's going to be all right."

But it wasn't all right.

"Ounce for ounce, the black widow spider is probably one of the most toxic animals on earth," the young doctor told Abby quietly as she gazed over the child's head at him, dry mouthed with terror.

"But isn't there . . . there must be some kind of antitoxin."

"Yes, there is, but he seems to be having an ana-phylactic reaction to the venom. Some kind of severe allergic response...."

Later, of course, Abby learned all there was to know about allergic reactions to animal toxins. But that day she knew nothing at all except that her child's dear little body was swelling, growing blotchy and dis-torted before her horrified eyes. His breathing pas-sages were swelling, as well, inexorably choking off the air that he needed so desperately.

And just as the sun slipped below the hills and soft twilight spread across the lake, Aaron died.

Abby looked vacantly at Joan, then at the waitress who brought their sandwiches. She struggled to pull herself back to reality, but her eyes were faraway and dark with pain, remembering that gray silent evening.

She just hadn't been able to grasp it. She'd held him in her arms and kept whispering to him, kissing him and cuddling him while they'd tried with such gentle-ness to make her understand.

"But...but he can't be," she'd faltered, staring wildly up at them. "Just a few minutes ago he was...he was putting his chickens on the fence posts. We were going to cut our Christmas tree. He's going to his friend's birthday party on Saturday. He has his first dentist's appointment next week. He can't...he can't *possibly* be..."

"Abby," Joan said gently, breaking into her rev-erie. "Are you all right, dear?"

"Sure," Abby said, forcing a smile. "I'm fine. What do you think, Joannie? Do these sandwiches look edible?"

Banishing her unhappy thoughts, Abby focused on her lunch. "So," she said, swallowing a bite of her sandwich, "how's your mom?"

Joan's face clouded. "Not very good. Her arthritis is just terrible these days. I was up most of the night wringing cloths in hot water and putting them on her knees."

Abby looked at her friend's weary face and fought to keep her voice calm and detached. "Maybe she should go back into the hospital for a while so you can get some rest, Joannie."

"Oh, no," Joan said in horror. "She hates being in there, Abby. You know how she gets."

"Yeah. I know how she gets," Abby said in a flat tone.

There was an uncomfortable silence while Abby sipped coffee and Joan toyed with the last of her dill pickle. "So," Abby said finally, "I guess tonight's off, then?"

"Tonight?"

"You were going to come over to my place for supper, then we were going down to the park to listen to the string quartet. Remember?"

Joan's eyes widened and took on a faraway, wistful look. "Oh, yes, I remember. And you said what's-his-name might be coming along with us?"

"Mitch. His name is Mitchell Flanagan. He edits the fine-arts pages down at the paper. I thought you two might get along really well together."

"But..." Joan murmured helplessly, "but, Abby, I don't think Mom would... I mean, she's home alone all day, and in such awful pain. If I just go home for a few minutes after work and then leave again right away, I think she'll be so—"

"Joan, listen to me," Abby said, interrupting her friend's faltering words. This time, she was unable to keep the impatient edge from her voice. "This last big flare-up of your mother's arthritis... could it by any chance have anything to do with the concert in the park tonight? Did you mention that you might be going with me?"

"I think maybe I... It's possible that I mentioned it. I've really been looking forward to it."

"And did you by any chance mention the possibility of Mitch joining us?"

"I could have," Joan said after a moment's thought. "Mom enjoys his column so much, especially the book reviews. I probably mentioned to her that I was going to be meeting him."

"I see," Abby said dryly, setting her cup down and looking at the dinner check. "Do you have a ten?"

Joan ignored the question, looking directly at her friend, a bright spot of color appearing in each pale cheek. "Abby, I know what you're thinking."

"Really? What am I thinking?"

"You're thinking that this is all some kind of phony act. That she's pretending to be in pain to keep me from going out and having a good time, maybe meeting a really nice man."

"Wow," Abby said with a brief sardonic grin. "You are psychic. That's exactly what I'm thinking."

"I know you've never liked her," Joan began stiffly, "but she is my mother, Abby."

"Sure," Abby said, unmoved by her friend's tone. "She's also your jailer, it seems to me."

"Oh, come on, Abby."

"No, *you* come on. How many times has this happened, Joan? How many times have we made plans, gotten all excited about doing something together and then had to cancel because your mother suddenly has a gallbladder attack, or her heart starts palpitating again, or her arthritis flares up?"

Joan paused, her flush deepening. "We do lots of things together, you and I," she said in a low defensive tone. "*Lots* of things, Abby. We go shopping, and out for bike rides, and sometimes we—"

"Yeah," Abby interrupted briskly. "We do. But never in the evening, right? And how many times do we get to include anybody else, like a couple of men, for instance, without your mother having some kind of fit?"

"She just..." Joan paused helplessly.

Abby gazed at her friend's gentle, worried face, the lines of weariness etched around her eyes and mouth, the slight tremble of her hands.

"It's okay, Joannie," she murmured with quick sympathy, regretting her own bullying. "I know what she's like and I guess you have to live with her, so there's not much you can do about it."

"But I just hate having you think I'm some kind of..."

"Joannie, I think you're some kind of saint," Abby said with a smile. "No wonder you're attracted to this guy who's an angel. You two belong together."

Joan smiled wanly at the mention of the mysterious street-corner man, then immediately looked worried again. "But your friend..."

"Mitch? He'll be fine. I'll just tell him something came up. He still really wants to meet you, though. I told him you could play Vivaldi's entire *Four Seasons* on the violin from memory and he says you sound like his kind of woman."

Joan turned pink with pleasure and waved a modest hand. "Oh, goodness, you shouldn't tell him that. I haven't played for ages, Abby. I'd make a hundred mistakes."

"It's not your virtuosity. It's the principle of the thing, kid. I think what Mitch likes most is the idea of—"

Abby paused abruptly, her heart thundering, her face turning white with shock as she stared down at the colorful sunlit throng on the street below.

"Abby," Joan asked in alarm, gazing at her friend's pale cheeks and wide, staring eyes. "Abby, what is it?"

"Nothing," Abby said in small tight voice, turning away after a moment to pick the check up again, trying to control her shaking hands.

"Abby, come on. What did you see down there?"

"It's so silly," Abby murmured, still struggling to regain control of herself. "I just... I thought I saw somebody, that's all."

"Who?"

"Brad," Abby whispered, gazing directly at the other woman. "I thought it was Brad."

Joan stared back at her. "Is he in town?" she asked finally.

"Last I heard he was in Los Angeles, learning to bodysurf," Abby said in a quiet, bitter voice. "No, I don't think he's back."

"When did you see him last, Abby?"

"Oh, ages ago. Almost a year," she said briskly, wondering in despair if this terrible wound in her heart was ever going to heal.

Just the sight of that stranger's dark head shining in the sunlight, his broad shoulders and lithe springing walk had been enough to make her whole body tingle and set her soul on fire. And it wasn't Brad at all, just some handsome executive on his way back to the office. She didn't even know why the sight of the man had triggered her memory so powerfully. Brad never wore a suit and tie....

"I remember now," Joan was saying. "He left not long after Aaron...after he..." She paused, floundering awkwardly.

"Died," Abby supplied in a cold mechanical tone. "Aaron died, Joan. He didn't pass away or go to sleep or slip off to heaven, or any of that other crap. He died. He was three years old, and I loved him, and he died. End of story."

"Oh, Abby," Joan murmured, her gentle face twisting with sympathy.

"Aaron died on December 10 when we were getting ready to go out and cut our Christmas tree. Brad left the week after New Year's."

"I remember," Joan whispered.

"And I fell apart," Abby said. "I fell completely to pieces, but now I'm finally starting to recover, Joan. The last thing I want is to see Brad Carmichael again, or think about him, or talk about him, or even see men who look like him. Ever."

"If you fell apart," Joan said loyally, "it was certainly a well-concealed breakdown, Abby. I'll bet most people in your life didn't even realize how you were suffering."

"Oh, I'm a very controlled person," Abby said with a bitter smile. "When I go to pieces I do it in a very tidy, well-disciplined manner so as to make the least possible mess. But," she added after a brief silence, "*you* knew, didn't you, Joannie? You knew just what I was going through."

"Of course I did," Joan said. "I felt so awful because there was nothing I could do to help."

"You helped more than you'll ever know, just by staying close and caring about me. I'll always be grateful to you for that, as long as I live."

Joan's cheeks turned pink again and she gave an awkward little laugh. "It was nothing. We've been friends since forever, Abby. I really care about you. And," she added with sudden anger, "that man can never, ever come back! After the way he hurt you, I'd *kill* him if he ever tried to upset your life again."

Abby smiled, beginning to recover from her earlier shock. "You just look so damn fierce," she said, gazing fondly at the woman across the table. "Like an enraged bunny."

Joan chuckled and dug into her handbag for money to pay her half of the check.

"Don't forget to stop and see the angel," she said as they parted in the street below.

"I wouldn't dream of it," Abby said solemnly. "Like I told you, I could use an angel these days."

But she did forget, after all, and was hurrying into the last block before the newspaper office, when she remembered her promise.

"Oh, damn," she muttered.

She paused, considering how long it would take to retrace her steps back to the corner that was the acknowledged turf of Joan's mysterious vagrant.

Still hesitant, Abby glanced at her watch and finally decided to stop by the man's corner later in the afternoon after she'd finished work.

Which just served to prove, she thought with a brief wintry smile, that deadlines really were more important than angels.

ABBY SQUARED HER shoulders, clutched her briefcase and walked into the newspaper building, nodding with forced cheerfulness at the young receptionist behind the long counter.

"Hi, Trudy. How's the arm?"

The tiny blond receptionist grimaced at a plaster cast on her right arm, which rested inside a sling.

"I'm getting pretty sick of it, let me tell you. Although you know, Abby, it's amazing what you can do with your left hand if you have to."

"That'll teach you to be such an aggressive baseball player. Trying to steal *home*, of all things."

Trudy grinned wickedly. "Yeah, but you should see the other girl. Their catcher, I mean. I mowed her down and ran right over her. She needed a whole week off work to recover."

"My, what brutality. And I thought baseball was supposed to be a gentle, civilized sport."

The receptionist smiled back at her, then reached for the big manila envelope that Abby was taking from her briefcase. "Press releases?"

Abby nodded. "Just one for the tourism association. If you could manage to run this on Friday I'd be eternally grateful."

"I'll see what we can do," Trudy promised. "Anything else?"

"Not today. I'll have a bunch of things for you on Thursday, though. Everybody seems to be gearing up for fall and Christmas."

Trudy shook her head and grinned. "God, what a woman," she said in awe.

It was an old joke between the two of them, this matter of Abby's work ethic and productivity. Abby was a free-lance writer who handled public relations for a number of firms and organizations in the Okanogan Valley in British Columbia. But she also did some writing and proofreading for the paper on a casual basis and wrote articles for other local publications.

And as if all that wasn't enough, her major source of income was the standing assignment to supply quarterly research articles for a glossy international scientific magazine. Articles like the one on . . .

"Is Mitch around?" Abby asked hastily.

"In the back," Trudy said. "He left a pile of stuff on your desk to go through."

"My *desk?*" Abby echoed in disbelief. "Since when did they give me a desk?"

"Since Tim moved all his old cameras and darkroom stuff down to the basement. Mitch says that corner is going to be yours on a permanent basis."

"I'm not even officially a staff member," Abby marveled, "and they give me a *desk*."

"Don't get too excited," Trudy warned her with an amiable grin. "It's not much of a desk. Most of the drawers are missing and it's covered with grunge so ancient that nobody can even identify it."

"Who cares? A desk's a desk," Abby said, moving around behind the counter and into the warren of cubicles where the newspaper was assembled each day. "Hi, Mitch," she added as a stocky young man with horn-rimmed glasses and a pleasant freckled face strolled around a corner with a sheaf of papers in his hand.

"Hi, Abby. May I come in?"

"Come in where?"

"To your office," Mitch said with a grin, indicating the battered old wooden desk shoved into a dark corner of the composing room.

Abby grinned back. "Imaginary walls, right?"

"Right. And a really impressive imaginary door," Mitch said, making knocking motions. "Look at those solid oak panels."

Abby dumped her briefcase on the desk and made a great show of straightening her hair in an invisible mirror. Then she seated herself behind the old desk.

"Come in," she called in a lofty tone. "It's not *locked,* you know."

Mitch grinned and straddled a wobbly ladder-backed chair next to Abby's desk. "So, kid, are we still on for tonight?"

"Tonight?"

"The concert," Mitch said patiently. "In the park, remember? You were going to bring your friend along?"

"Oh, that," Abby said, paging through piles of galley prints on her desk, frowning in concentration. "Mitch, this stuff is getting worse all the time. Can't *anybody* spell anymore?"

"A few people can, but they're usually the ones who can't type. Abby, pay attention. I asked you about the concert, remember?"

Abby looked up at him, her eyes clearing slowly. "Mitch . . . I'm sorry."

"Uh-oh," the young man said in a fatalistic tone. "I knew it. Another rejection, right?"

"Mitch, it's not a rejection. Joan really wants to meet you. She was so excited about the concert all week, but then her mother . . ."

"I keep hearing about this mother." Mitch removed the heavy glasses and rubbed his temples. "What kind of dragon is she, anyhow?"

"The very worst kind," Abby said, surprised at how attractive Mitch looked without his glasses, gentle and boyishly vulnerable. "She's one of those big heavy women who's always complaining that her appetite is just terrible and she couldn't possibly eat a single thing, you know?"

"And the whole family has to rush around trying to tempt her with little delicacies so she won't fade away, right?"

"Right," Abby said with a grimace. "Except there isn't a whole family—there's just poor Joan. Her father died when she was six years old, and ever since she's borne the entire brunt of that woman's selfishness."

"Why doesn't she move away?"

"Oh, God, she couldn't," Abby said. "Several times Joan and I have discussed renting a house or apartment together. And every time, her mother has some kind of medical crisis that makes it impossible for Joan to leave her."

Mitch replaced his glasses and looked at Abby with an uncharacteristically shrewd expression on his pleasant round face. "And," he began slowly, "I suppose Mama would take a pretty dim view of a man in her daughter's life, wouldn't she, now?"

"She always has," Abby said. "As far back as high school, if a boy showed any kind of interest in Joan there was big trouble on the home front. Never directly, mind you. Just little emotional breakdowns or mysterious illnesses that came along and demanded Joan's whole attention."

"Plus some fairly massive guilt trips," Mitch suggested dryly.

"Right," Abby said, glancing at him in surprise. "How did you know? I've never told you all this stuff, have I?"

"Just a good guess. Families are much the same all over the world, you know."

"You're right. And I guess I really shouldn't be so hard on Vera Holland. I know she's just terrified of being old and lonely and that's why she behaves the way she does. It's all kind of sad, actually."

"But hard on Joan."

"Yes," Abby agreed. "It's certainly hard on Joan."

They were both silent for a moment. Abby gazed at the stocky young man across the desk, thinking what a truly nice person he was and what an ideal companion he would be for Joan if she could ever manage to get the two of them together.

"How about you, Abby?" Mitch asked suddenly.

"Me?"

"Do you have any family?"

My family died last Christmas, Abby thought with another searing wave of pain.

She could see by his sudden taut look that Mitch knew what she was thinking and regretted his casual question, so she forced herself to shake her head and smile. "Oh, I have a family, all right. But they're all living far away."

"How far?"

"My mother met a nice man on a cruise ship a few years after my dad died, and married him after a whirlwind courtship. They live in Pennsylvania. And my kid sister is married to a career soldier who gets exotic postings all over the world. So I don't see much of them."

"I see."

Mitch was silent a moment as he carefully straightened the edges of a ragged pile of advertising paste-ups on Abby's desk.

"Well," Abby said, hanging her jacket over the chair back and rummaging in her handbag for her reading glasses, "this stuff isn't going to correct itself, is it?"

"It never does," Mitch agreed dryly. "Abby..." he added.

She paused, caught by something in his tone, and lowered her glasses so she could gaze at him over the rims. "What?"

"I went over this morning to have a look at the new performing-arts center they're building."

"Really?" Abby asked with interest. "Are they working on it already? I thought the whole thing existed only on paper."

"They've just started. The footings and foundations are in, and the walls will be going up soon. It's going to be a beautiful building. Lots of glass, a kind of soaring, airy structure...interesting lines."

"Oh, good," Abby said fervently. "I was really afraid they might be planning another of those concrete-block monstrosities."

"So was I, but this architectural firm obviously has some imagination. That's why I went over there, actually. I wanted to talk to one of the architects and do a story on the plans, you know, and how they set about the job of designing a performing-arts center."

"That's a great idea. And I'm jealous. I wish I'd thought of it first. Did you get to see one of them?"

"I talked to an associate in the firm. I take it he's the one who's been responsible for most of the design."

"I don't even know who's doing the work. Is it a local firm?"

"No, they're out of Vancouver, but this associate is going to be on-site till the job is done."

"I see." Abby looked up quickly, caught once more by something in her friend's tone. "Mitch, you sound a little . . ."

"What?"

"I don't know. A little strange. Is something bothering you?"

"This architect . . ." He hesitated awkwardly.

"Yes? What about him?"

"Abby, the architect is Brad."

CHAPTER TWO

ABBY'S FACE DRAINED of color and her mind reeled with shock. She stared at the young man's troubled face, trying to grasp his words. "Brad?" she whispered finally. "Brad *Carmichael?*"

"Yes. That's who it is."

Abby shook her head, feeling dizzy and disoriented. "But that's... Mitch, that's just crazy! Brad wasn't an... an *architect.* He was a... he dug ditches and pounded nails. He was a construction worker."

"I made an appointment to interview the architect on the site, and the man who came into the office was Brad Carmichael."

Abby shook her head, trying to make sense of this bizarre conversation. She was shocked enough to learn that Brad was back in the valley. But to hear that he was passing himself off as a trained professional...

"I lived with the man for almost a year, Mitch," Abby said bluntly. "Don't you think I'd probably know about a little tiny detail like a degree in architecture?"

"I know what you're saying, Abby. I met Brad a couple of times while you two were together, and I always thought he was just what he seemed to be...what you've just indicated. A blue-collar worker with a wild, high-living outlook."

"Well, you were right," Abby said grimly. "That's exactly what he is, Mitch. He's certainly not an architect. You've made some kind of mistake. Or else," she added, struck by a sudden thought, "maybe the whole thing is just Brad's idea of a joke. He heard you were coming over to the site so he set his hammer down, grabbed some blueprints and pretended to be the architect on the job, just to get you going. That's really his style, Mitch."

The young editor shook his head. "I checked, Abby," he said gently.

"Checked?" Abby echoed. "How?"

"Come on, kid. You know how research is done. I called the company in Vancouver and verified that Brad was the consultant on this job. Then I called a local guy I know to see if he had any information on our man."

"And?" Abby said tensely when Mitch paused.

"And my friend here in town says Brad's one of the brightest architects on the western seaboard. Says his work is brilliant, but it's been sporadic over the past ten years because he keeps dropping out of the picture for extended periods of time. He started working for the firm in Vancouver last spring, I guess, but nobody had heard anything from him for a couple of years before that."

Abby stared at her friend, eyes dark with emotion. "No wonder they hadn't heard from him," she muttered finally. "He was living with me, working for the municipality as a ditchdigger while the new sewer system was being installed."

"And he never hinted at his background? You never had a clue?"

"That's for sure," Abby said bitterly. "I never had a clue about anything where Brad was concerned. I certainly never suspected that he had more than a high school diploma, if that. But," she added in a low voice, "he was so appealing. I'd never met a man like him."

"He wasn't Aaron's father, was he?" Mitch asked.

"Oh, goodness, no," Abby said with a bleak smile. "Aaron's father is my ex-husband. Jim's a dentist in Edmonton. We parted amiably when Aaron was nine months old and Jim finally realized that I was never going to be the kind of wife to stay home in a ruffled apron, whipping up goodies for the members of the dental association and their wives. I was a great disappointment to him," she added thoughtfully. "I kept shocking him by having ideas and goals of my own."

"He sure doesn't sound like your type," Mitch said, giving her a sympathetic smile.

"Oh, he wasn't. But neither was Brad, although I sure fell for him hard. It's embarrassing when I look back on it."

Abby paused, a faraway look in her eyes, then continued. "I remember when we met. I'd been alone for over a year. One hot day in the fall I went to a construction site to do a story on the new miracle building materials. And here was this gorgeous, barechested hunk in jeans and boots and hard hat, lounging on a beam about fifteen feet in the air and grinning down at me. He started carrying on a conversation as if we were sitting across a cocktail table. I just couldn't resist him. Three months later he moved in with me."

"And?" Mitch prodded her gently.

Abby gave him a wintry smile. "And he was the most unstable, erratic, inconsiderate... But, my God, he was charming," she finished in a soft voice. "One look from him would get me, every single time. I kept forgiving him and making excuses for him, trying again and again... until Aaron..."

Again she paused, biting her lip.

"What happened, Abby?" Mitch asked gently. "I mean, after you lost Aaron. Was Brad just too insensitive, or what?"

"It wasn't that," Abby said after a moment's thought. "My grief made him frantic somehow. And his own grief, too, I guess, because he really loved Aaron. I thought afterward that maybe Brad had always been afraid of death, and that's why he lived so high and wild, you know? When Aaron died and the reality was right there in front of him, and I was so stunned and drowning in suffering... Well, he just couldn't deal with it. One day I came home and he was gone. Just vanished without a trace."

"Did you ever hear from him again?"

"Not for several months. Then he started sending letters from a Vancouver address, but by then I was so angry I sent all of them back unopened. After a while they stopped coming."

"That must have been about the same time he started working as an architect again."

"I suppose so. I still can't grasp it, Mitch. I can't see Brad Carmichael as anything other than a blue-collar guy with a wild life-style."

"I have his card," Mitch offered tentatively, "if you'd like...."

"No!" Abby said, and then smiled to temper the harshness of her tone. "Sorry, Mitch, but I have no desire to see him, ever again. Absolutely none."

Mitch was silent. Abby gave him a sharp glance.

"Mitch?" she said finally. "What is it?"

"He asked about you, Abby," he said awkwardly. "He seemed really concerned. He said he hoped everything was all right in your life."

"I wish he'd expressed that sentiment a year ago," she said coldly, "when he left me with a broken heart, a handful of unpaid bills and a child to mourn."

"Abby..."

"It's all right, Mitch. Thanks for your concern, but I really just want to get on with my life."

"Okay," Mitch said, lifting himself from the chair and moving toward the door. "What about the concert? Shall we go by ourselves?"

"Oh, Mitch..." Abby looked at his pleasant face with regret. "I don't think so, if it's all right with you. I've had a couple of shocks today and I just feel really wiped out. I'd rather have a hot bath and an early night and wait till sometime when I can talk Joan into coming along. Okay?"

"Sure thing. By the way," Mitch added with an apologetic grin, "those galleys, Abby..."

"Yes? When do you need them?"

Mitch consulted his watch. "About two hours ago," he said cheerfully, then ducked around the corner with a chuckle when Abby tossed a wad of paper at him.

Alone at her desk, she began to work her way through the mountain of proofreading, finding it increasingly difficult to keep her mind on her work.

First there was the disturbing knowledge that Brad Carmichael was back in the valley, so close that she might well see him at any turn. Abby wondered how she'd cope, how she'd control herself if she suddenly rounded a corner and he was there, standing in front of her.

She drew a deep breath, forcing herself to summon Brad's image, trying to look at him with cool detachment.

It just wasn't possible. Abby still shivered at the thought of those remarkable eyes shading from steel gray to dark green with the play of his emotions, the rugged tanned face with its warm crooked grin, the sensuous, sculpted lips.

And his body...

Abby almost moaned aloud, remembering Brad's powerful shoulders, his flat hard stomach and broad chest covered with little curling dark hairs, his square callused hands and bulging muscles...

"Oh, God," she whispered, drowning in pain and a flood of pure sexual desire that she hadn't felt for months. "Oh, Brad..." Horrified at herself, Abby shook off her scarf to run a trembling hand through her straight, dark hair, then retied it carefully. She drew a deep breath and returned to her work. But despite her firm resolve she soon found herself thinking about him again.

Brad Carmichael was a licensed architect. Could she possibly have been fooled for so long?

Of course, Abby had learned almost nothing about Brad's background during the time they'd lived together. He wasn't close to his family, who lived somewhere on the East Coast, and he always gave the impression that they disapproved of him.

Maybe that had all been lies, too, Abby thought. Maybe he'd grown up right in the valley. Maybe he had a couple of wives and a whole string of little green-eyed kids scattered around, and that was why he'd been so secretive.

And he'd hurt her so terribly.

Even Brad's magical charm could wear thin when you'd been waiting for him on an icy street corner for over an hour. Or, Abby recalled grimly, when he disappeared from a party and left you humiliated in front of your friends, having to make arrangements to find your own way home.

Brad Carmichael was the most careless, irresponsible, unreliable man she'd ever met. And yet the mere thought of him was still enough to make her throat tighten and her heart begin to thud in her chest, make her whole body go soft and moist with yearning.

"He asked about you," Mitch had said. "He sounded really concerned...."

Abby moaned again and dropped her head onto her folded arms, so buffeted by waves of loneliness that she wondered if she could survive the rest of the day.

ABBY NODDED at the ragged man who sat on the curb, a harmonica in his big tanned hands. She stepped back from the old tin cup where she'd tossed a handful of coins and glanced at him casually as she turned away, trying to determine what it was about the man that had captured Joan's interest so powerfully.

He looked like any other vagrant, in a pair of ancient, patched blue jeans held up at the waist with a length of twine and a torn denim shirt so faded that it was almost white. On his feet were battered hiking boots with one sole flapping dangerously. An old baseball cap covered his mass of tangled golden hair.

Probably about thirty or forty years old, Abby thought, moving aside to listen as a few people gathered and he launched into a gentle sobbing rendition of "Red River Valley." He was thin, but big and muscular. Clothes ancient and stained, though they looked reasonably clean and were carefully mended by hand with small, even stitches.

She paused, still partly hidden behind the silent group clustered on the sidewalk, and gazed with sudden interest at the man's hands. He looked as if he'd been living on the road for most of his life, but his hands were beautiful. His long fine fingers cradled the battered old harmonica with grace and strength. And he was so clean. Even his fingernails were as clean as Abby's, in spite of his ragged appearance.

Abby smiled, picturing this vagabond standing at the lakeshore by moonlight, scrubbing his clothes on a flat rock, washing his thin hard-muscled body and his shining golden hair....

Suddenly she realized that the music had stopped and the little group of onlookers had drifted away. She was alone with the mysterious stranger, and he was looking directly at her.

Abby stared into the man's weathered face and felt her world slipping into confusion. Just as Joan had said, his eyes were a deep pure aquamarine, so serene and gentle that a sense of peace came stealing into Abby's mind as she gazed at him, along with a tentative glimmer of happiness and optimism unlike anything she'd known for months.

Strangest of all, she felt a powerful sense of Aaron's nearness, as if the little boy might be waiting for her just around the corner. And for the first time, Abby's memories of her lost child weren't painful at all, but warm and healing.

The ragged man on the curb returned Abby's gaze with calm interest. He didn't shift awkwardly or turn away, just went on looking directly into her eyes with that gentle, benign expression. Suddenly, Abby felt the need to speak with him, to hear his voice, to understand who he was and why his presence brought Aaron so near.

"My friend..." she began awkwardly, and paused, flushed with nervousness. "My friend told me about your... your music. She comes to listen to you on her lunch hour."

The stranger nodded tranquilly and smiled, waiting.

"She... her name's Joan Holland. She works at an insurance office a few blocks away. She has light brown hair pulled straight back, about this long." Abby indicated a level just below her chin. "And... and blue eyes, and she's about my height. We went to school together."

Again the man nodded and gave her a sweet luminous smile, then paused to incline his head politely at a well-dressed businessman who dropped a coin into the cup as he hurried past.

Maybe he was mute, Abby thought with sudden embarrassment. Or simpleminded, although there seemed to be a glow of intelligence in those wonderful jewel-like eyes.

"She is very sad," the man said quietly, startling Abby. His voice was deep and resonant, with a strange, indefinable lilt that was both haunting and appealing. "She feels that life is passing her by."

Abby stared at the man in surprise. "Joan? Did she tell you that?"

Again she felt the mild warmth of his smile. "I can tell," he said simply.

"How?" Abby asked, feeling awkward and clumsy.

The vagrant ignored her question, glancing down at the silver harmonica in his hands. "She has music in her soul," he commented softly. "Your friend is like a songbird trapped in a cage. She needs to be set free so she can sing."

"Yes, she does," Abby agreed, marveling at this outlandish conversation. "Please, I want to know how you know these things. Who are you?"

Again he failed to answer Abby's question. Instead he looked straight up into her face so that she felt the tranquil light of his eyes penetrating all the way to her soul, flowing though her with a healing warmth.

"Who are you mourning?" he asked, his voice soft and quiet.

"My little boy," Abby said simply, no longer even bothering to be amazed at the conversation. "He died last Christmas."

"He was very small," the man said. It was not a question but a statement.

"Just three years old," Abby said with a catch in her voice. "His name was . . . was Aaron. And I loved him so much."

Her mouth began to quiver and tears burned in her throat. The man on the curb looked up at her gravely but made no move to touch or comfort her, just watched her with those calm sea blue eyes.

"Why do you grieve?" he asked finally.

"I keep thinking..." Abby paused and took a deep ragged breath, staring into the vivid depths of his eyes. "I keep worrying that he might be scared or lonely wherever he is. He doesn't have any of his toys or his little blanket... he could never go to sleep without his blanket. And what if they don't know how he likes to be held, or what he wants to eat, or..." Almost overcome with emotion, she gazed at the man's quiet face like a drowning person looking for a lifeline.

"But I know that's ridiculous," Abby went on, forcing her voice to sound cold and steady. "When you're dead, you're dead. That's why I hate myself for these ridiculous fantasies I have all the time. I just... I miss him so much," she concluded simply, with a painful catch in her throat.

"You have no need to grieve," the man said softly. "He is surrounded by love. Your little boy lives in love, and he is happy."

Abby felt a sudden wondrous surge of disbelieving hope and an urgent need to learn more about the enigmatic presence in front of her.

"How do you know?" she demanded, moving closer to him and staring down at him. "How do you know about Aaron? Who are you?"

Suddenly she became aware of people gathering around them once more, a pair of young office workers on their way home, a mother pushing her baby in a stroller, three older ladies with metal shopping carts.

The man nodded at her and smiled gently, then picked up his harmonica and began to play "Greensleeves." There was such a haunting wistful lilt to the song that two of the white-haired ladies wiped tears from their eyes.

Abby stepped back and watched as he played, wondering if she'd imagined the whole strange interlude. Already the sense of Aaron's nearness was fading and the vagabond sitting on the curb was once again just a wandering tramp in ragged clothes, playing his tunes to a scattered group of bystanders for the coins they dropped into his tin cup.

The whole scene was normal—a city street washed by the late-summer sunlight, nothing unusual about it.

Abby turned aside and walked slowly back to the parking lot where she'd left her car, shaking her head at her foolishness.

And yet, she realized as she unlocked the door and tossed her briefcase into the back seat, there was something different about the day. She had a feeling of warm confusion, and a flare of yearning that caused both pain and pleasure.

She pulled out onto the street and headed for home, humming under her breath. The tune that kept going through her head was "Greensleeves," with its ancient lilting cadence.

By the time she neared her own street, though, Abby's natural skepticism was fully restored. She alternated between rueful amusement at her confused feelings and annoyance with herself for having behaved so carelessly.

Abby shifted restlessly on the seat of the car and frowned into the rearview mirror, uncomfortable at her memory of the conversation. It was bad enough that she'd revealed so much of her emotions to a man she didn't even know, prattling on about Aaron's death and listening to the vagrant's fairy tales about a place where Aaron was "happy."

Abby's mouth set in a firm line.

She hated those sugary-sweet fantasies about "heaven" and all the other platitudes and euphemisms that people used to mask the harsh, inexorable reality of death.

"When you're dead, you're dead," Abby muttered once again, glaring into the rearview mirror as she shifted into the turning lane.

No matter what opinion was held by mysterious tramps on street corners.

Worse than her indiscretions about Aaron, though, was the fact that she'd told the vagrant quite a lot about Joan...her name, where she worked.... Had she even mentioned the name of Joan's employer?

Abby grimaced in concern and pulled up the long, curving drive toward her house. For a moment her uneasiness ebbed away and she felt the same small glow of involuntary pleasure that always came with her first sight of the rustic brick-and-cedar building nestled among towering pines.

She'd bought this house when she'd first moved back to the valley after her divorce, using her meager cash settlement as a down payment. It was frequently a struggle to pay the mortgage each month, but the house was still a good investment, because real estate was skyrocketing all over the southern half of the province. Besides, Abby had wanted a house for Aaron to grow up in, a place where he could feel at home while he built happy childhood memories, a yard where he could play in safety, have a puppy and cat and treehouse.

There hadn't been time to build the tree house, although Brad had often talked about it during those idyllic early months. And the puppy had vanished in the miserable, confused weeks just after Aaron had died. She'd slipped her leash and run off one morning, and they'd both been too distracted and unhappy to search for her. Of all their dreams only the cat was left, a massive, slow-moving calico tomcat who was powerful enough to come and go through the sturdy little pet flap Brad had installed in the kitchen door and who treated Abby with icy disdain.

Wilbur certainly wasn't the most cuddly and delightful of pets, Abby reflected, getting out of her car and walking through the carport to the front door, passing the big cat, who crouched on the veranda, gazing at her through slitted eyes. But at least he was company of a sort. Better than coming home to a completely empty house.

And the cat reminded her of happier times when she would return after a day of research or work at the paper to find the puppy playing on the lawn, the cat sleeping on the veranda railing, Brad and Aaron involved in some boisterous game in Aaron's room.

Abby swallowed hard, remembering. She still hadn't been able to part with any of Aaron's toys or clothes, no matter how she tried. She knew that it probably wasn't healthy to keep them, that she should pack everything up and give it to some charity. But she just couldn't bring herself to do it.

The small bed was still neatly made, with Aaron's battered old stuffed lion and his blanket on the pillow. The toys stood in orderly rows on the shelves. The room echoed with ghostly shouts of laughter, with Aaron's high-pitched eager questions and Brad's deep quiet voice in response. . . .

Abby shook herself and looked down at the big cat who waited for her at the top of the steps. "Hi, Wilbur," she said, forcing herself to sound bright and cheerful. "Did you have a nice day? My goodness, Wilbur, don't jump all over me like that. Try to restrain yourself."

Wilbur ignored her, squatting contemptuously on the edge of the step, still watching with cold yellow eyes as Abby unlocked the door. One whisker twitched, then stilled.

"Coming in?" Abby asked, holding the door for him.

She knew that Wilbur used the little pet flap on the back door during the day when she was gone. But he refused to let himself in and out when Abby was home, demanding instead that she drop whatever she was doing and open the door for him.

The big cat hesitated, eyeing the interior of the house with cold appraisal, then turned to gaze out across the yard and down the sunlit hillside toward the lake, shimmering in the distance. He watched a white butterfly flitting among the chrysanthemums along the driveway and gazed thoughtfully at a swallow darting into the pine tree at the edge of the carport. Finally, with a huge yawn of lofty boredom, he turned and stalked past Abby into the house.

"Wilbur," she said with a grin, following him inside, "you are just such a—"

She stopped short and caught her breath in alarm.

Someone was in the house. She could sense the whisper of a presence, a breath of movement in the still air.

Wilbur, too, stopped abruptly on his way to the kitchen, one paw delicately raised, his ears pointed alertly. The hair lifted slightly along the back of his neck and his big body quivered.

Abby drew a deep breath to steady herself and looked around at the quiet living room. Like the exterior of the house, it had a pleasant rustic atmosphere, with a hardwood floor covered by big hooked rugs, a roomy couch with a woven Navaho blanket thrown over one arm, a pair of overstuffed chairs and a comfortable wooden rocker that Brad had made during the winter down in his basement workshop.

A big stone fireplace covered most of one wall and was flanked by wooden shelves—also Brad's handiwork—filled with books.

Everything was quiet and untouched. Abby scanned the room, looking at the stereo, her computer table in one corner, the VCR and the television in their handmade cabinet. Even the tapes and compact disks were intact, arranged in tidy rows.

She tiptoed through the living room and into the kitchen, where the door was still locked and bolted from the inside, then slipped back outside to check the basement. All the windows were closed, their grills bolted to the window frames. The dead bolt on the front door, she recalled, had also been firmly in place when she'd unlocked it.

Abby stood for a moment in the sunlight by the back door, shivering with apprehension, trying to compose herself. She had no proof that somebody was in the house, nothing but a feeling. And those raised hackles on Wilbur's neck.

But that could mean anything. Wilbur was a notoriously ill-tempered cat. His hackles went up over almost anything, including what he considered to be inferior grades of cat food.

Abby leaned briefly against the rose trellis, trying to smile at her foolishness.

"Ghosts and angels," she murmured to Wilbur, who had appeared on the back step and was looking up at her with scorn. "I wonder what's happening to me, Wilbur. Am I losing it completely, do you think?"

She forced herself to move back inside, trying not to think about the locked doors, the chain bolts still in place, the barred windows... and the knowledge that if intruders had somehow broken into the house, they were undoubtedly still there.

Nevertheless she leaned down to sweep Wilbur into her arms, cuddling his heavy, inert body against her chest as she edged down the hall to her bedroom. Wilbur stiffened in outrage at this indignity, but Abby clung to the cat, holding the warm comforting mass of him tightly in her arms.

She stood in her quiet room and looked around at the brass bedstead covered by a lovely handmade quilt, the old wooden steamer trunk, the antique dresser with its ornate swinging mirror.

No drawers stood open, nothing had been moved, nothing looked different.

And yet there was that sense of a presence, of something wafting in the still air of the room, as if a person had just passed by so close that Abby could sense the nearness. The hair prickled on her arms and icy fingers crept along her spine.

She set Wilbur on the floor, where he stared up at her bitterly for a moment and then stalked away down the hallway, his tail waving high in the air.

Abby followed him, pausing at the door to Aaron's room.

She glanced inside, then stood stock-still, frozen in position, the color draining slowly from her face.

The room had been rearranged, but was still orderly. The little table had been carefully set for tea, with Aaron's tiny set of dishes and pots. His dolls and stuffed animals sat on the small wooden chairs, smiling blandly at one another. Curious George gazed across the table at the Cabbage Patch baby, while the old stuffed lion from Aaron's pillow stared unblinkingly at the cheerful Indian doll in buckskin and feathers who graced the opposite chair.

Choking with emotion, Abby stumbled into the room and looked down at the table. The little cups brimmed with water, and a plate in the center of the table contained tiny pieces of something that Abby recognized as crumbled oatmeal cookies from the tin in the kitchen.

She heard Aaron's voice, soft and coaxing. "C'mon, lion, eat your dinner. *That's* a good boy. Eat it all gone...."

Abby choked back a rending sob and glanced around wildly. Aaron's train set was carefully arranged in the corner near the toy shelves, the little boxcars loaded with wooden blocks. A rag doll lay beside the tiny wooden rocking chair, which still swayed almost imperceptibly in the afternoon stillness, as if its small occupant had just gotten up to run across the room.

The sight of that little rocking chair was more than Abby could bear. She screamed aloud and rushed out into the hallway, forgetting her earlier fear, forgetting everything but the numbing shock and bewilderment that flooded her whole being.

She ran blindly through the silent house, calling his name aloud, looking in closets, in cupboards, under the stairs, through the basement and the back porch.

"Aaron!" she shouted frantically. "Aaron, is that you, baby? Where are you? Who's here? Is there anybody in the house?"

At last, still sobbing, she moved back toward the little boy's room, half expecting to find that the tea party and the train had just been figments of her imagination.

It didn't happen, she told herself. *I'm just overwrought. When I look in there again the toys will be on the shelves and the lion will be in his place on the pillow, just like always.*

But when she entered the room the dolls and toys remained frozen in position, smiling at one another across the little table, while the train carried its load of blocks to an invisible destination.

Abby began to shiver. She crossed the room and sat on the bed, lifting the old stuffed lion from his chair and cradling him in her arms, gazing over his tufted head with dark brooding eyes.

And then she saw the toy farm.

It was laid out neatly at the foot of the bed, a sprawling tidy array of pens and barns, of buildings and animals and farm implements. A white plastic fence stood neatly along the edge. On the fence, plump yellow-and-red plastic chickens were perched in cheerful rows.

Abby gazed at the chickens for a long time, an eternity of breathless silence. She heard music ringing in her ears and felt the dark waters closing over her head. Then, abruptly, she remembered a pair of aquamarine blue eyes, a gentle face, a quiet tranquil voice.

"He is surrounded by love. Your little boy lives in love and he is happy...."

"Oh, dear God," Abby whispered, holding the old stuffed lion in a spasmodic grip, her eyes wide and staring. "Oh, *Aaron*..."

CHAPTER THREE

AUTUMN CREPT OVER the valley, touching the hillsides with vivid fingers of gold, shining in the gentle waves that lapped against the lakeshore, glowing through the misty haze of twilight. Woodsmoke drifted on the warm, still air and the harvest moon rose huge and golden above the treetops, spilling radiance onto the shimmering dark waters of the lake.

By late September the sun at midday was still rich and warm, beaming down on city streets that seemed empty and slow moving now that the crush of summer tourists had finally departed.

Joan Holland walked along the curving lakeshore boulevard, drawing in great breaths of tangy golden air as rich and sparkling as fine wine. Her steps quickened as she neared the corner, and her blue eyes darkened with anticipation.

She paused to remove the pins from her hair and shake it loose, letting the limp strands fluff and lift gently on the breeze. Then she took a final deep breath and rounded the corner, her heart beating crazily with excitement and fear.

Joan was always afraid when she approached this corner, terrified that the mysterious vagabond might have slipped away during the night, leaving her whole world cold and empty.

She knew, of course, that his disappearance was inevitable. He couldn't stay all winter on the street corner, playing his harmonica and silently presenting his tin cup for handouts. Even in this sheltered valley the Canadian winter could sometimes be harsh, with sudden heavy snowfalls and sharp killing frosts.

I wonder if he even has a coat, Joan thought. *I wonder where he sleeps at night, and whether he ever gets—*

All thoughts were suspended abruptly when she saw him. Her throat tightened with emotion as she looked down at that familiar denim-clad form, his big thin body and golden hair shining in the light.

The man's old baseball cap and battered harmonica lay on the sidewalk beside him. He sat quietly on the curb with his arms wrapped around his knees, eyes closed, weathered face lifted to the sun. Joan gazed at him in silence, drinking in the fine sculpted line of cheek and brow and chin, the classic profile, the gentleness of his mouth.

"Hello," he murmured without opening his eyes. "You came early today."

"I'm having lunch with a friend," Joan whispered, not at all surprised that he could recognize her without actually seeing her.

Nothing about this man could ever surprise her.

"The lady who is in such great pain?" he murmured in that same gentle tone, opening his eyes and looking quietly at the woman standing in front of him.

Joan nodded and gazed into those eyes, as startling against his darkly tanned skin as sapphires glistening on the parched desert soil. She thought about Abby's pain, about the strange taut stillness of her friend's manner and the troubled look that seemed to haunt her face so often these days.

Joan waited to see if the angel had any message for Abby. But he merely shifted on the sidewalk and nodded with gracious courtesy, spreading out a tattered piece of newspaper on the cement and motioning for Joan to sit next to him.

She stared in alarm, her cheeks flushing painfully. "Oh, no, I really shouldn't . . . I have to . . ." she whispered.

"Just for a moment," he said. "Sit here with me in the sunlight."

Joan lowered herself beside him, mesmerized by his serene manner, and felt the warmth of the sun spill over her face and body. Her embarrassment faded and a sense of peace gradually flooded her mind, driving out all the pain and nervousness, all the long lonely nights, the frustration of dealing with her mother's constant complaints, the prospect of a desolate future all alone.

"I brought you a sandwich from the deli," she murmured at last, coming back to reality with a start and remembering the paper-wrapped parcel in her hands. "And . . . and some coleslaw."

"Thank you," the angel said. "That was very kind of you."

Joan smiled mistily, warmed by his approval. A couple of times she'd tried to put a ten-dollar bill into his cup and had been chilled by his look of gentle reproach as he returned the money without a word. But he got so little money from the people on the street, especially now that the tourist season was over, that Joan worried whether he had enough to eat.

She handed the sandwich over and watched as he unwrapped it and began to eat. His movements were precise, his manner as delicately fastidious as if he were dining off Limoges china using solid gold flatware rather than a sheet of waxed paper and a plastic fork from the corner deli.

Joan relaxed and let the sunshine flow over her, happy just to be in his presence, closer to him than she'd ever ventured before. She gazed across the sparkling waters of the lake at the line of smoky hills on the far horizon, letting her mind drift and wander so that she was startled when he spoke again.

"I beg your pardon?" she asked.

"You look tired today," he repeated patiently. "Very tired."

"I guess I didn't...my mother..." Joan faltered, reluctant to spoil this deep midday peace by telling him the mundane details of her life, of her mother's painful varicose veins and swollen knees and the weary hours Joan had spent applying hot poultices during the night.

"Come here tonight at seven," the man said quietly.

"Come here? Me?" Joan echoed, staring up at him.

"Yes. The sun is low and the evening is so mild at that time. I take bread down to the water's edge and feed the geese and ducks."

Wistfully Joan pictured the scene. She saw the lake lapping tranquilly against the shore and the dying sun gilding the angel's face and shoulders as he moved calmly among the noisy waterfowl, breaking and distributing crusts of bread with his big gentle hands.

An aching hunger assailed her, a kind of fierce yearning that she could scarcely control. But she forced herself to smile politely and shake her head.

"Oh, I'm afraid I can't possibly come. You see, my mother..."

"Your mother needs to discover her own life and let you go. It will be very hard for her. You must help."

Joan gazed blankly at him, wondering if she'd ever told him anything about her mother during one of their brief, stilted conversations.

"It is your duty," he repeated gently. "We all have responsibilities to those we love. Our greatest responsibility is to give them their freedom along with our love."

"But my mother..." Joan began numbly, and paused, feeling tense and out of breath. "My mother doesn't want freedom from me, not at all. She wants me to stay with her forever."

"She clings because she is afraid. And you allow her to cling because you fear her anger. We are all afraid. Part of love is teaching others to have the courage to let go."

More than anything she wanted to say yes, to walk quietly with this man by the water's edge in the soft purple twilight and listen to his voice. But what could she possibly say to her mother?

You see, Mom, there's this man who panhandles on the street corner and I think he's an angel. I've fallen in love with him, Mom. I really want to spend some time with him....

Joan smiled sadly and shook her head, staring down at the dusty swirl of dried autumn leaves in the gutter at her feet.

"Seven o'clock," the man repeated gently, looking at her face. "I will be here."

Joan got to her feet, brushing off the back of her skirt and running an unsteady hand through her hair. She looked down at the man who sat on the curb, his ragged clothes stirring in the noonday breeze as he ate his coleslaw with a plastic fork.

"So will I," she said with sudden recklessness. "I'll be here, too."

Joan squared her shoulders in determination, smiled into those calm blue eyes and then turned to walk away. She was breathless and afraid, stunned at her own daring. Already she wondered what lies she could tell her mother and how she was going to get away with this adventure.

But flowing solid and strong beneath her fear was a shining tide of happiness, warmer and sweeter than anything she'd felt for a long time.

BRAD CARMICHAEL SAT behind the wheel of his gray sports car, watching as Joan Holland said a few final words to the vagabond on the curb and then turned to walk away.

He shook his head, puzzled and amused by the scene he'd just witnessed. Brad had hardly believed his eyes when Abby's prim, inhibited friend had actually sat down on the curb beside the ragged panhandler and entered into a conversation. He'd chanced to be driving by just at that moment and his curiosity had been sufficiently aroused that he'd parked unobtrusively up the street, trying to see what Joan would do next.

Brad remembered Abby's friend as a repressed, mildly unhappy woman who was completely dominated by her tyrant of a mother. He hadn't seen much of her during his time with Abby because Joan apparently wasn't allowed out at night very often. Abby, though, retained a fierce loyalty to her old friend and grew intensely irritated if he ever dared to poke fun at the comic tragedy of a twenty-nine-year-old woman tied so firmly to her mother's apron strings.

Somehow, Joan looked different on this mellow autumn day, Brad mused, watching her trim erect figure as she hurried down the street and around the corner. And she wasn't behaving like the repressed woman he remembered, either. Consorting with vagrants, letting her hair actually drift loose around her head, smiling to herself as she strolled along the sidewalk....

He put his car in gear, still thoughtful, and rolled slowly down the street behind Joan's hurrying figure, parking a few doors up from the restaurant she entered on the following block.

Suddenly, before he had time to contemplate his next move, Abby Malone came striding around the corner. She was walking directly toward him, her dark hair bouncing on her shoulders, glistening with ruddy highlights in the beaming midday sun. Brad caught his breath and stared at her, so overwhelmed by her unexpected appearance that it was all he could do to keep himself from jumping out of the car and wrapping her in his arms.

Lord, but she was beautiful, he thought, gazing hungrily at her slender body, the firm proud lift of her chin, the wide sweet mouth and delicate lines of her face in profile as she passed his car without noticing him.

He found himself drowning in memories, so stunned and shaken by his love for this woman that he could hardly contain himself. He remembered holding her naked body in his arms on a summer night, laughing with her in the mellow darkness while the moonlight shimmered on the surface of the lake and warm water murmured all around them....

"Abby," he whispered aloud, watching as she disappeared through the same door Joan had just entered. "Oh, Abby, I love you so much. I love you...."

He dropped his head onto the steering wheel, resting his forehead on folded hands, his wide shoulders heaving. A uniformed policeman on a bicycle pulled over to knock briskly on the window. Brad lifted a ravaged face and slid the window down, giving the earnest young man a polite smile.

"You okay, sir?" the policeman asked, looking curiously at the handsome dark-haired man in his sleek sports car with his cellular phone and expensive gold wristwatch.

"I'm fine," Brad said, summoning a casual voice. "Just felt a little sick there for a minute, but it's passing now."

"You sure? Better not drive for a while if you feel dizzy or anything."

"I'm fine," Brad repeated. "Thanks for stopping."

He watched as the young man moved off down the street, then pulled his car carefully away from the curb and drove up through the winding hills toward Abby's house.

Outside her rustic little home, he gazed at the veranda, where Wilbur lay in regal solitude on the railing, soaking up the sunlight.

Again he found himself besieged by treacherous mental images. He heard Aaron's high-pitched joyous laughter, smelled the tantalizing morning aroma of coffee and pancakes and bacon, felt the comfy softness of Abby's big feather quilt on a cold winter's night and the melting sweetness of her body in his arms, while the pale moonlight glimmered hazily through frosted windowpanes and her eyes shone like stars in the darkness.

Loneliness washed over him, deep and intense and agonizing. He needed Abby so much. No other woman had ever come close to being all that she was to him, able to ease his restlessness and satisfy him so completely in every way. And he knew that nobody ever would again. If he couldn't somehow find his way back to her, his life would be empty and hollow forever.

But she'd been so furious with him, so coldly withdrawn and remote, that he despaired of ever reaching her. Brad remembered the letters he'd written with such passion, trying to tell her what had happened to him and how he felt about her. She'd returned them all unopened, marked Undeliverable in her firm handwriting.

Abby Malone was not a woman to set the past aside, to forgive and forget just because her man showed up on the doorstep with candy and flowers and a good story. Brad knew how badly he'd hurt her during their time together and how monstrously he'd abandoned her at her time of greatest need. He sometimes wondered if there was anything he could do that would make up for that, anything that Abby would ever accept.

His eyes were dark gray and full of pain as he left her silent house and drove across town to the construction site. He got out of the car, pulled on a battered hard hat and tossed a sport coat over his open-necked shirt while he consulted briefly with the foreman. He managed to set aside his feelings and move around the site for his daily inspection, laughing and joking with the sun-browned laborers in their jeans and heavy boots, thinking a little wistfully about the years he'd spent doing just this sort of work.

There had always been something satisfying to Brad about that life of hard physical labor, where you worked all day and then left the problems behind when evening rolled around. That was why he'd shunned his professional training for so long, refusing to take on the responsibility of planning and direction. Instead, he'd chosen simply to follow the orders of others and keep the rest of his life free to enjoy himself.

But he'd been a different man then. That time seemed like a distant lifetime ago, all those far-off days of wild careless pleasure. Brad left the site and drove back downtown to his office, nodding at his secretary as he strode through the reception area.

"Hi, Gladys. Anything urgent?"

"Everything's urgent," she said, making a face. "Four crises just since lunch. It's mostly the usual, though. I left a pile of messages on your desk."

"Thanks," Brad said with a smile. "I'd better get right to them, since they're urgent."

"Good. Oh, Brad."

"Yes?"

"I left one on top there that sounded... I don't know. Different?"

"Really? Different how?"

"Just different. It was a woman. She called a few minutes ago, wants you to get back to her."

"Did she leave a name?"

"She said her name was Abby. She said you'd know, but it doesn't ring any bells with me."

Brad stared at the matronly woman, his face slowly turning white beneath the tan, his heart beating crazily.

"Do you know her, Brad?"

"Yes," he said briefly, hardly trusting himself to speak. "Yes, I know her. No other calls until I tell you, okay, Gladys?"

"Sure thing."

He hurried into his office, closing the door behind him, and almost ran across the carpet to snatch the pile of telephone messages from his desk.

ABBY FROWNED and scored her pencil through a sentence containing three misspelled words and one grammatical error, then leaned back to brace her knees against the edge of the ancient desk and run a hand restlessly over her hair.

Mitch Flanagan, passing by with a handful of folders and photographs, caught her grim expression.

"Oh, my. Proofing the sports pages, are we?"

Abby shook her head. "Advertising copy. Even the jocks can spell better than these so-called businessmen."

"Entrepreneurs are notorious for that. I guess they spent all their time in school gazing out the windows and dreaming up schemes for making money."

Abby gave her friend a wan smile, then looked at him more closely, a speculative gleam dawning in her eye.

"Say, Mitch . . ." she began slowly.

"Yeah?" The young man paused on his way into his office and glanced back over his shoulder. "What's up?"

"Are you busy tonight?"

"I sure am. I've got a big evening planned."

Abby's face fell. Mitch grinned at her, returning to perch on a corner of her desk.

"Actually," he said, "I just bought a compact disk of Beethoven's Fifth. I was going to listen to it on my new state-of-the-art stereo system. And as if *that* isn't enough excitement, I'm also planning to help my neighbor give his dog a bath."

Abby shook her head, smiling at him. "How can you bear it—all that wild and crazy fun in one evening?" She sobered and gave him another thoughtful glance. "Could those things possibly be postponed?"

"Why? Do you have a better offer?"

"Maybe." Abby paused, then smiled again. "Joan's coming over this evening. I thought you might drop in, just casually, you know, to check with me on some late galleys or something."

Mitch's warm brown eyes crinkled with interest. "I thought she never went out in the evening."

"She hardly ever does. This whole thing is kind of mysterious."

Mitch shifted into a more comfortable position and removed his glasses. "Mysterious? How?"

"Well, we had lunch today and Joan said, just out of the blue, that she wanted to come over to my house tonight around eight o'clock for a visit. She also said that if her mother called earlier, like anytime after seven, I was to say that she was at my place but had just run down to the corner for ice cream, or something like that."

Mitch whistled softly. "Wow," he murmured. "A plot." His pleasant face sobered briefly. "Is there a man involved, d'you think, Abby? Could she be slipping out to meet somebody and using you as cover?"

Abby shook her head firmly. "Oh, goodness, I can't imagine it, Mitch. I don't know what she's up to, but she'd tell me if she was seeing anyone. There's nobody in Joan's life at all except . . ."

"Except?"

Abby chuckled. "Oh, just this angel she's grown kind of fond of." Mitch lifted his eyebrows in surprise, and still grinning, Abby told him about Joan's mysterious street-corner vagrant.

Upon hearing of Joan's stubborn conviction that the harmonica-playing tramp was some kind of celestial traveler, Mitch threw his head back and laughed. "You know, I'm really looking forward to meeting this lady," he said. "I'll drop by your place about eight-thirty, okay?"

"Ever so casually," Abby warned him.

"Ever so casually," he echoed solemnly.

"Hey, Abby? You in there?"

"What is it, Trudy?" Abby called out to the receptionist.

"A guy on the phone. Says he's returning your call."

Abby's fingers tightened on the pencil and her eyes flickered with alarm as she gave Mitch a glance of mute appeal. He nodded in immediate understanding and slid off her desk.

"I was just leaving, kid."

Abby watched until he'd vanished behind the closed door of his office, then picked up the receiver and forced her voice to behave normally.

"Hello?"

"Abby? It's Brad. I'm returning your call."

She felt a surge of panic and took a deep breath, struggling to compose herself. She'd spent several days getting up the nerve to call him, but she still hadn't anticipated the full impact of his voice and the bittersweet memories that flooded her mind.

"Abby?"

"Hello, Brad," she said in a shaky tone, cursing herself for her lack of control. "I'm sorry to bother you at work. I just... I wanted to talk with you about something."

"How did you get my number?"

"From one of the editors here at the paper. He interviewed you about this new performing-arts center that you've apparently designed."

Abby winced at the sarcastic edge to her words, but his voice when he answered was calm and even.

"I didn't really design it, Abby. The plans for the center were pretty well advanced when I joined the firm. I just added a few elements, that's all."

"I see." Abby hesitated, wondering how far to pursue this ridiculous conversation, longing only to hang up and get his disturbing presence out of her life forever. "Funny thing," she said, trying to sound light and casual. "You never mentioned you were an architect."

"Look, Abby, I—"

"Of course," she went on recklessly, "it's one of those little details a person tends to overlook, isn't it? Just a college education and years of professional training, nothing much to speak of. You probably forgot about it yourself, didn't you, Brad? That's why you were out digging ditches all those months, right? It's not as if you were lying to me or anything."

"Abby, I know you're upset with me...."

"Upset?" she said, trying to keep the rising note of hysteria from her voice. "*Upset?* I'm afraid that doesn't quite cover it, Brad."

"All right," he said in that same level tone. "Furious. Outraged. Disgusted. Appalled. You pick the word, Abby, you're the one who's good with words. And I know I deserve all of them. But I'd really like a chance to talk with you. There are so many things I need to tell you."

"How long have you been here?" Abby said abruptly, ignoring his plea for understanding.

"I beg your pardon?"

"Back here. In the valley. How long have you been here?"

"Since early September. I came back because I wanted to—"

"Look, Brad, it's got to stop. That's why I called you today. I don't want to have a relationship with you, or see you again, or even talk to you. I just want you to know that it's got to stop."

There was a moment of tense silence. "I don't know what you mean, Abby," he said finally. "What's got to stop?"

Anger flared within her, steadying her and making her feel suddenly calm and alert. "You know damned well what I mean, Brad Carmichael," she said in low, distinct tones. "You've been sneaking into my house while I'm out, and I want you to know that I won't stand for it. I know what you've been doing and I despise you for it!"

"Abby...I really don't know what you're talking about. Sneaking into your house? What do you mean?"

He sounded so genuinely bewildered that Abby shook her head with a scornful little smile, reminding herself what a consummate actor the man was, especially when caught in any kind of wrongdoing.

"Oh, I think you know what I mean, Brad," she said evenly. "Twice this past month somebody's come into my home and moved Aaron's toys around. I realized almost immediately that it had to be you, because you're the only one who has a key."

"Aaron's toys?" he asked with sudden alertness. "Did you say Aaron's toys were moved?"

Abby gave a tight little nod, remembering how passionately he'd urged her to part with all those toys and clothes after Aaron's death. In fact, they'd been arguing about that very thing the night before Brad had vanished.

"Look," she said, taking a deep breath to steady herself. "I know how you felt about me keeping those things. But this is...don't you think it's a little cruel, what you've been doing? I mean, even by your standards?''

"Abby, I haven't set foot inside your house in almost a year. Not since the night I left.''

His voice rang with such conviction that Abby was briefly shaken, until she recalled once more what he was like. She shook her head, grimly amused at her own weakness.

"Sure, Brad,'' she muttered. "Of course you haven't. And you won't set foot in there again, either, because I've had the locks changed. I just wanted you to know that I'm aware of what you've done, that's all.'' Breathing hard, she slammed the receiver down and sat staring at it for a long time.

Her cheeks were pink with anger and her eyes shone with tears of frustration. But her heart was pounding, and she tingled all the way to her fingertips.

Furious though she was, her body still responded to the sound of Brad Carmichael's voice in her ear and the knowledge that at this very minute he was only a few blocks away from her, living a new phase in his shrouded, enigmatic life.

In the back of her mind was another thought, too, almost imperceptible but nagging and troubling nonetheless. Brad had sounded so sincere in his denial, so completely shocked and surprised— What if the man was telling the truth for once in his life?

What if he *wasn't* the mysterious intruder, the one who slipped invisibly through locks, chains and dead bolts? What if he wasn't the one who'd spread those toys around so carefully and left a whisper of his presence lingering in the silent deserted room?

After all, despite her bitter accusations, Abby knew, deep down, that this sort of mischief really wasn't Brad's style. She couldn't actually visualize him sneaking into her house and tormenting her in such an insidious fashion.

In fact, if she were being brutally honest with herself, she'd have to admit that a lot of the motivation for her call to him had been the need to hear his voice again and make some kind of connection with him.

Still . . . the fact remained that somebody *was* slipping into her house and moving the toys around. And if it wasn't Brad, who the hell was it?

THE PHONE WAS RINGING inside the house as Abby unlocked the front door. She frowned with concentration, wiggling the stiff new key in the lock, then flung the door open, threw her jacket and briefcase onto a chair and hurried to pick up the receiver.

"Hello?" she said, a little breathlessly.

"Abby? Lorna here. How's life up there in the unspoiled wilderness?"

Abby smiled and relaxed. "It's great, Lorna, except for all the bears and moose wandering around in my front yard. Did you read the article?"

"I did, and it's very good. Very, *very* good," Lorna said.

The warm intonation of her voice made Abby's cheeks flush with pleasure. This kind of praise from her hard-edged Los Angeles editor was rare.

Abby allowed herself to bask in the warmth a moment before asking, "Any problems?"

"Well, of course there are problems," Lorna said cheerfully. "You'll have to do a rewrite and tighten up the ending a bit, but the concept is just excellent."

Abby nodded, her pleased expression fading to anxiety.

Lorna's voice was sweet and lisping, a high little-girl voice that made Abby think of a talking mouse. She'd been astounded when she'd finally met the woman and discovered that the she was almost six feet tall, with the shoulders of a linebacker and a commanding air that reduced her timid visiting writers to quivering masses of jelly.

She was good at her job, though, coaxing and intimidating the people who wrote for her into producing the best possible material. And Abby was a dedicated perfectionist, so she'd appreciated the give-and-take relationship with her editor during the three years she'd been working as a free-lancer for the glossy high-profile magazine.

"What kind of rewrite?" she asked, winding the phone cord around her fingers.

"Oh, just bits and pieces," Lorna said airily. "I'll send you a revision letter. Look, Abby, I'm actually calling about your next article. Now, you were originally planning to do this bug thing, right?"

Abby grinned. "Well, that's a little casual, Lorna. Actually it's an article on organic pest-control methods. There's a lot of it going on locally here in the orchards, so the research is easy. There's the use of predator insects to control other harmful types, and the SIR program—"

"What's that?" Lorna interrupted. "SIR, I mean. What's it stand for?"

"Sterile insect release. They develop sterile specimens in the lab and then release them into the environment. The insects mate normally but can't reproduce, so their numbers drop."

"Poor little suckers," Lorna commented. "What a dirty trick."

Abby chuckled. "Actually, it's an excellent program, and very cost-effective. I've already done quite a lot of research on it."

"Well, kid, are you going to be able to set it aside for a couple of months? We really want this near-death thing for the spring issue, so you'd have to get it to us before Christmas."

Abby's fingers tightened on the phone cord. "Lorna, I don't know.... Why do they want me to do it?" she asked. "I mean, that's not a localized topic at all. Anybody could write it. And I have all this research on the—"

"I told you before, somebody up there likes you."

"Okay," Abby conceded reluctantly, "I'll get started on it, I guess. When do you need an outline?"

"Early next month. You'll have to do the general research on your own as always, but I've got those contact numbers I promised you and the place where these people meet. Got a pen handy?"

Abby wrote down the information. "Lorna," she said finally, "who was this mysterious person who recommended me? I don't understand."

"Anonymous tip," Lorna replied. "Have fun, kid. It's a fascinating topic. We're all looking forward to your finished article."

Abby exchanged a few more casual remarks with her editor and then hung up, wondering bitterly who had given Lorna the "anonymous tip."

It had certainly been no friend of Abby's, getting her involved in something so difficult. More and more, she hated the idea of writing this article. In fact, Abby despised the entire concept of people searching frantically for something in the great darkness, some shred of hope that could help them avoid the grim inevitability of death.

The whole thing was so cowardly. Why did people feel such a tremendous need to delude themselves?

It was bad enough that she had to fight it in herself—the feeling that Aaron might be lingering somewhere nearby, still involved in her life in some mysterious way. She was afraid to believe in the survival of the soul because it gave rise to all kinds of hopes and longings that were too painful for her to endure.

She shook her head and paused by the door to Aaron's room, trying not to dwell on her negative feelings.

At least she could relax in the knowledge that her house was once more safe, that the new locks were secure and that nobody could enter in her absence.

Shivering, she remembered Brad's words on the phone, the sincerity in his voice when he'd told her he'd never been inside her house.

Abby held her breath, edged the door open and peered inside. The room was quiet and untouched, with all the toys lined up in neat rows on the shelves and the old stuffed lion in its place against the pillow.

She nodded in satisfaction, then turned and stared, lifting a shaking hand to cover her mouth. The little rocking chair swayed almost imperceptibly, back and forth, back and forth, with a delicate rocking motion that died gradually into stillness under her horrified gaze.

"It's the air," Abby whispered after a long, tense silence. "Just a sudden blast of air from the furnace vent, that's all."

She closed the door with firm deliberation and walked back down the hall to the living room.

CHAPTER FOUR

MITCH FLANAGAN SAT in Abby's kitchen, looking at the mass of blooms adorning the big African violet in the center of the table.

"How do you do it, Abby?" he asked. "When I had this thing I babied it and coddled it and I could never get it to bloom. Now it looks positively vulgar."

"I ignore it," Abby said, giving her friend a brief smile as she crossed the room with the coffeepot. "Healthy neglect. That plant knows it has to perform at its peak or it goes out the door, so it just blooms all the time."

"Scared straight," Mitch said with a cheerful grin, watching as Abby refilled his mug and turned away to get a plate of cookies.

Mitch watched Abby put the coffee tin away and sighed privately. Abby had obviously forgotten that he always drank decaf in the evenings. Usually she was one of the most thoughtful and considerate people he knew, but something was clearly bothering her tonight.

He sipped gloomily at his coffee, knowing he was going to be awake all night but not wanting to upset Abby with his complaints. She already looked so strained and unhappy.

Maybe her present misery had something to do with Brad Carmichael, he thought. Mitch knew she was upset by the man's abrupt return, and no wonder. There'd been no denying the electricity between those two.

In the months after Brad had left, Abby had been so destroyed by pain and loneliness that her friends had wondered if she was going to survive.

And now Brad was back. . . .

Nodding absently, Mitch accepted an oatmeal cookie from the plate Abby offered, watching Wilbur, who sat in the corner regarding him with a malevolent glare. He chewed his cookie and responded automatically to something Abby was saying, still thinking about the intense young architect he'd interviewed recently at the construction site. That man had seemed totally different, worlds away from the brash devil-may-care fellow Abby had first introduced to her friends.

The architect had been quiet and businesslike, knowledgeable and gracious in his responses, showing emotion only when he inquired about Abby. Then his remarkable eyes had suddenly turned a vivid green and his jaw had tightened. . . .

"Beg your pardon, Abby?" Mitch said with a rueful smile. "I was daydreaming." He glanced at the woman across from him and noted with concern that her face was tense.

"About death," she repeated. "I was asking what you think, Mitch."

"About death?" he echoed blankly.

"Actually, about life after death. Harps and heaven, souls and spirits, all that stuff. Do you believe in any of it?'' Abby's tone was casual, but her hands tightened on the handle of her mug until her knuckles were white.

Mitch paused to choose his words carefully.

"I guess, as journalists, we're supposed to be objective about that kind of thing, aren't we? Just observe and report the facts that can be verified, and not speculate."

"Sure, I know that. But we're human, too. We can't help having some kind of opinion. I just wondered what you think."

"About an afterlife, you mean?"

"Yes."

Mitch took another sip of his coffee and looked into Abby's earnest brown eyes. "Why?" he asked gently. "Why is this stuff on your mind lately? Is it because Brad's come back and stirred up all those old memories?"

Abby's face clouded briefly and she turned away, then looked back at her friend as if struggling over whether to confide in him. "Actually," she said at last in a low, choked voice, "some things have been happening that make me..."

Mitch waited tensely while she hesitated, then composed herself with obvious effort. When she spoke again her voice was light and casual.

"The problem is, I have this weird new assignment for the magazine, Mitch. In fact, Lorna just called this afternoon. Wait till you hear what I'm supposed to write about next."

Mitch listened gravely as Abby recounted the details of her conversation with her editor and her despair over having to fashion what she called "a bunch of fairy tales" into a viable scientific article.

She wasn't telling him everything. He sensed the tension in her hands and voice, saw the troubled look in those vivid eyes, and the way she held her slim body rigid as if afraid she might break down.

"Well, it's almost nine o'clock," he observed mildly when the topic of near-death experience had been largely exhausted. "I guess we're being stood up again, Abby."

Abby glanced at her watch in sudden alarm. "Oh, my goodness, look at the time. I can't imagine Joan being so late. I hope nothing's happened to her."

"Is she the kind of girl that things happen to?"

"Never," Abby said with a brief, sad smile. "Poor Joannie, nothing ever happens to her. But there *was* something mysterious going on tonight. I have no idea where she was going before she came over here."

"Do you think we should call her mother and check on her?"

"Oh, no!" Abby said in horror. "I'm her cover, Mitch. Her mother thinks she's been here all evening. There'd really be hell to pay if I were to call over there looking for her."

"I'd like to meet this mother," Mitch said with a small grim smile.

Abby grinned ruefully back at him. "No, you wouldn't. Trust me."

"But if she's—"

They heard a knock, then the sound of the front door opening. "Abby? Abby, are you here?" a woman's voice called. "Sorry I'm so late. You wouldn't believe what happened."

Quick, light steps sounded on the hardwood floor of the living room and Joan appeared in the doorway. She wore a dark plaid scarf and a long navy blue overcoat that fell almost to her ankles. Mitch Flanagan looked up at her and his heart began to do a crazy dance.

The woman in the doorway gazed back at him with wide startled eyes so blue that a man could wander into them and never be found again. Her cheeks were pink with cold and excitement and she was laughing, a breathless happy laughter that sounded girlish and warm in the bright kitchen.

Mitch stared blankly, then looked over at Abby for help. Could this possibly be Abby's plain and miserable friend, the one who was so repressed and beaten down that she didn't even have a life?

This woman looked vivid and joyous, full of laughter and secrets, and so beautiful that Mitch was weak with yearning as he gazed at her.

"Joan!" Abby's tone revealed the depth of her concern. "Where on *earth* have you been? I was getting really worried."

Joan gave her friend a luminous smile and unbuttoned her coat, revealing a sacklike dress of pale tan wool that hung almost as long as her coat, unrelieved by scarves or jewelery.

To Mitch's dazzled eyes this woman didn't need adornment of any kind, not with those dark sapphire eyes and golden highlights in her hair, that glowing skin....

He swallowed hastily and stumbled to his feet, extending his hand as Abby made introductions.

"Joan Holland, Mitch Flanagan. Joannie, remember what I told you about Mitch? He's the—"

"Editor of the fine-arts section," Joan concluded in a low voice, smiling shyly at the stocky young man as she shook his hand. "I really love your work, Mr. Flanagan."

"Mitch," he corrected automatically, still dazzled by her fragile look and the timid sweetness of her voice. Joan met his gaze for an awkward moment, then dropped her head and turned away, coloring slightly at his intensity.

"Abby, I'm really sorry," she began in a breathless rush of words. "I got held up for a little while and then there was an accident on the bridge on the way over here and we had to detour around it."

Abby regarded her friend shrewdly while Mitch looked from one face to the other. Joan sank into a chair opposite him, accepting a mug of coffee and gazing at it with a distant dreamy smile.

"Held up?" Abby was asking. "How exactly did you get held up, Joan? By armed gunmen?"

Joan flushed again and exchanged a nervous glance with Mitch, who grinned at her in sympathy. "You sound just like my mother," she said to Abby.

Abby smiled, and her strained face suddenly lightened and glowed with a little of the old sparkle. "Do I? I'm sorry, Joannie," she said contritely. "I guess I really have been letting things get to me lately, haven't I?"

Both Mitch and Joan watched in concern as she crossed the kitchen to draw the curtain aside and peer out the window into the darkness.

Mitch broke the silence. Turning to Joan with a smile, he said, "I hear you're quite a violinist. Abby keeps telling me about your awesome talents."

Joan smiled back at him, blushing with pleasure and nervousness. "Oh, goodness, no," she protested. "I hardly have time to play at all anymore. But I really love my violin," she added.

"Well, I'd certainly like to hear you sometime," Mitch told her with warm sincerity.

She looked up at him with another of those startled glances that tugged powerfully at his heart.

"I don't know," she murmured finally, with an awkward smile of apology. "It's kind of hard for me to..."

After a moment she dropped her eyes again, but not before Mitch was able to read her look. He sat gazing at her bent head, feeling bruised and stunned with disappointment.

Joan Holland wasn't the slightest bit interested in spending time with him. He'd seen that same expression before. In fact, this was just the way Abby had looked a year or two ago when she was so much in love with Brad Carmichael.

Mitch sat quietly, wrestling with his pain, trying to come up with something light and cheerful to say, but all he could think about was the cruel irony of life. After all the time that Abby had tried so hard to get them together, he'd finally met her friend Joan, and she attracted him more than any woman he could remember.

But that dreamy look, the flush on Joan's cheeks and the glow in her eyes, wasn't for him at all. Joan Holland was already in love, with somebody else.

ABBY STOOD in the vestibule of the church, breathing deeply and trying to calm herself. She glanced ruefully at her blue jeans, sneakers and casual tweed jacket, then gave herself a little shake. After all, she wasn't here to attend a church service. She was doing research on a scientific article, nothing more. Besides, she'd never been particularly concerned about what she wore.

There was definitely something different about this assignment, though, and Abby could feel it in the tension of her hands, the breathless sick feeling in her stomach. She was assailed by a sudden urgent desire to turn and flee, to run wildly out into the autumn night and leave all of this behind her.

Lorna's voice echoed a distant warning in her mind: *"It's not really wise to turn this kind of assignment down."*

Abby drew another deep breath, gripping her leather attaché case as she passed through the wide oak doors that opened onto the church lobby. The carpeted space was deserted, but she could hear the distant sound of music and children's voices shouting with laughter somewhere in the lower recesses of the building.

Main hall, Abby had jotted on her instruction sheet. Eight o'clock.

She glanced nervously at her watch again and slipped through the open doors into the church auditorium, sinking into a pew near the back and looking around nervously.

About a dozen people sat quietly in other pews, reading or talking in low tones. The couple in front turned and smiled at her politely, but made no move to approach her. Abby settled back, still trying to compose herself.

She hadn't been inside a church for years, probably not since her marriage to Jim, and that seemed like a whole lifetime ago. There was a deep settled peace about the surroundings and a stately beauty in the appointments, the gleaming oak and brass, the vivid mass of autumn flowers beneath the pulpit and the tall stained-glass windows.

No wonder people took comfort in this sort of thing, Abby thought. There was something so soothing about the place. Maybe she shouldn't have insisted so firmly on a private, nonreligious service for Aaron. Maybe she should have allowed the traditional church funeral that Jim and her mother had wanted....

Suddenly the old feeling of pain and loss assailed her like a physical blow, striking unexpectedly and leaving her breathless and choking with agony.

Abby stared straight ahead, trying not to cry, her mouth set and grim, her eyes desperate.

I was right, she told herself. *I was right not to look for the hollow, superficial comfort of all this. People just deceive themselves, trying so hard to believe in some kind of supernatural mumbo jumbo. It still hurts just as much, and it always will.*

She tried to distract herself by thinking about all the things that had happened recently, like the strangely awkward meeting last week between Joan and Mitch. There was no doubt in Abby's mind that Mitch had been strongly attracted to her friend. Abby had been so hopeful at first, until she'd realized that Joan had not responded to any of the young editor's advances.

After their first meeting, Mitch had called a couple of times to ask Joan out for a walk in the park or an afternoon gallery opening, but she'd been evasive both to him and to Abby.

"Why won't you go with him, Joannie?" Abby had urged her. "He really likes you, I know he does. And he's so nice."

"I suppose he is," Joan had said absently. "He really does seem nice, Abby. But I just can't go out with him."

"Why not?"

"Well, Mom needs me quite a lot these days, and besides, there are so many other things I have to do."

Abby shifted on the hard wooden bench, thinking about Joan's mysterious behavior. She frowned briefly, recalling her friend's strange preoccupation last month with the vagrant on the street corner. He was still there every morning, playing his harmonica in the crisp autumn air, regarding passersby with that gentle, tranquil smile.

Abby avoided him, feeling uneasy and embarrassed over the conversation she'd had with the man. Joan never spoke about him anymore, either, but there was an odd faraway look in her eyes these days, and a suspiciously guilty expression on her face whenever Abby chanced to mention the street musician.

Abby remembered Joan's earlier insistence that the tall blond man was some kind of angel. She frowned again, her thoughts turning in spite of herself to the eerie unfathomable happenings in her house.

It was strange how something so bizarre could gradually become acceptable if it went on long enough.

There were still days when she sensed a presence in Aaron's room, even though things appeared untouched. And one afternoon the toys had been carefully arranged all over the floor and table again, the way she'd seen them the first time.

But the sight of those stuffed animals and wooden trains, the bright little tea set and the plastic chickens roosting on the fence no longer seemed to cause Abby such intense terror and confusion. In fact, she wondered each day when she came home if there would be anything different in Aaron's room, and found herself rushing through the house to check.

Whenever that breath of presence lingered on the quiet afternoon air, or when the toys had been moved, Abby still felt a chill of fear, but also a curious sort of comfort, a warmth and inexplicable excitement that she knew to be completely irrational.

Sometimes, she seriously wondered if she could be losing her mind, experiencing some kind of nervous breakdown as a delayed reaction to grief and stress. The thought was disturbing, especially because she had always valued logic and common sense, had always been so confident about her efficient, well-ordered thought processes.

After all, the mind was the instrument with which you perceived the world. If your mind started to betray you, how would you even *know?* Abby shivered and tried once more to concentrate on what was happening around her.

"Good evening," a woman's voice interrupted her troubled thoughts. "It's nice to see so many of you out, and we certainly welcome all newcomers."

Abby shifted abruptly on the wooden seat, focusing on the speaker. She was a pleasant-looking woman with graying hair curled around her face, who wore a neat beige pullover and tan slacks. Hardly some kind of mystic or crazy person, Abby thought, unzipping her attaché case to get out a notebook and pen.

"For those of you who are visiting for the first time," the woman continued, "please don't be intimidated by the surroundings. We use this church as a meeting place because it's been donated to us, but we are completely nondenominational. Our membership includes people from all faiths and all walks of life, bound together only by a shared experience."

Abby jotted notes quickly as the woman spoke, recording impressions of the speaker, the atmosphere in the building and the expressions on the faces of the people around her.

Beside her, a heavy middle-aged man sat quietly gripping a newspaper with big work-hardened hands. And in the next pew a young black woman with a shy sweet smile cuddled a plump baby, who regarded Abby over his mother's shoulder with big solemn eyes.

Abby smiled at the baby, feeling a familiar twist of pain. She was distracted briefly from her notes, and looked up as the woman concluded her remarks, then yielded the pulpit to a tall elderly man who walked with a cane.

"Dr. Philip Ashton, our guest speaker for the evening," the woman told the audience as she returned to her seat.

The dignified man smiled at the group assembled below, then reached into his vest pocket for a pair of glasses and settled them on his nose before turning to his notes. Abby scribbled furiously as he spoke, wishing she'd brought along her tape recorder. She'd been reluctant because the meeting was being held in a church sanctuary, but she was sure that none of these people would have minded....

A near-death experience, the man was telling them, was a unique psychological event for adults because it often produced instantaneous and profound personality changes that had lasting effects. No other process, including extended psychiatric intervention, had ever been known to accomplish this type of change.

"But, of course, most of you are well aware of this," Philip Ashton continued. "My particular area of research is in the phenomenon of near-death experiences among children, the majority of whom do not exhibit the same degree of personality shift. However, the research does seem to indicate that most children who have had a near-death experience tend to be somewhat more outgoing and confident than they were prior to the traumatic event."

Abby watched the man intently, trying to assess his level of competence and expertise. He seemed calm and relaxed, and his address was well organized, scholarly and thorough. But how could a man with any kind of valid academic qualifications be spending his time involved in something so ridiculous?

Ashton continued with his talk, citing examples of children who had survived clinical death. He signaled to the woman at the back of the hall and a slide projector was switched on, illuminating the screen behind him.

"We find it helpful to have the children draw pictures of their experiences," Ashton told the group.

"Later, when they interpret their drawings, their observations tend to be very clear and spontaneous."

A picture flashed onto the screen, a series of smiling ghostly blobs with crooked halos, surrounding a grinning stick figure in a striped T-shirt.

"This was drawn by Jason, who was seven when he almost died after open-heart surgery. The white figures are angels who sang beautiful songs and stood all around him, holding their hands out toward him. Jason said he loved them so much, and they loved him."

Abby stopped writing and stared at the screen, her heart racing. Another picture appeared, a group of stick figures colored bright yellow, approaching a larger figure that was blue and a smaller pink one. Green lines filled the background, along with small blotches of color.

"This was done by Lisa, who contracted osteomyelitis after a fall from her tricycle and had a fever so high that her heart stopped for almost five minutes." Philip Ashton went on with a small smile, "Lisa was only four years old at the time, which explains the artwork. But her description was very eloquent."

Abby gripped her notebook in trembling hands, watching the bright images that danced in front of her.

"Lisa said the yellow figures were angels who carried her when she got tired. They came out of the light, she said, and were made of light but looked like people. The figure in blue was Lisa's grandmother, who had died a few months earlier and who came out of the light to meet her. The background is what Lisa described as a 'beautiful, beautiful forest, full of pretty birds and flowers.'"

Abby shuddered with emotion and gazed at the screen with wide haunted eyes. She couldn't hear the man's voice anymore, couldn't make sense of anything he was saying. Images danced and shimmered before her, bright crayon marks and blobs of color, innocent descriptions of angels and shining lights, images of happiness and warmth and safety. She felt an agony of longing for her lost child that surpassed any pain she'd known before.

Had Aaron really passed into some unknown realm where he still existed? Was the moving of the toys an attempt on his part to send her some kind of message? If so, what was he trying to say? That he was unhappy, that he needed her, that he wanted to come back . . . ?

No wonder people were drawn into this fantasy, Abby thought bitterly, forcing her wild thoughts back under control. No wonder they wanted so much to believe. But what a cruel hoax it was, playing on the most tender and painful of human emotions.

She forgot her cool professionalism, forgot that she was supposed to be observing and making notes. The rest of the meeting passed in a blur as she wrestled with her surging tide of hurt and anger.

Philip Ashton concluded his talk and gathered up his notes, smiling gravely at the audience as he took his seat. A brief procession of people followed him at the lectern, but unlike the doctor, none of them were trained or polished speakers.

The young woman beside Abby took the pulpit, still holding her solemn baby, and told the group in a low, halting voice about the medical crisis that had followed her childbirth. She had risen and seen her body lying on the delivery table, heard the doctor say frantically, "We've lost her!" She'd begun moving up through a warm, welcoming tunnel of light. Then, far away, she'd heard her newborn baby crying and understood with terrible reluctance that she had to return to her body.

I should be writing this down, Abby thought. *This is what I came to hear.*

She gripped the pen in numb fingers and struggled to compose herself, to jot down impressions as a very fat woman in a turquoise cotton smock told about a heart attack and about seeing her dead husband and father waiting for her at the edge of a tunnel of light.

While the fat woman took her seat and Abby made a few faltering notes, another person rose from somewhere at the back of the hall and passed close beside her while striding up to the lectern. Abby had a vague impression of tallness and quick, lithe movements, and a scent that was hauntingly familiar.

She looked up quickly, then stared, her eyes wide with shock. A man stood quietly at the front of the church, gazing down at the group in front of him. His hands rested easily on the edge of the lectern and his eyes were smoky gray in the muted light.

It was Brad Carmichael.

CHAPTER FIVE

ABBY'S FIRST horrified impulse was to run or to sink down and hide behind the pew until he was gone. But she forced herself to remain upright and calm, to look at Brad with a face that she hoped was utterly expressionless.

Although she'd spoken to him on the phone and Mitch had interviewed him recently and reported on his appearance, this was the first time Abby had actually seen Brad Carmichael since his return. Her eyes moved over that familiar face and body with a hunger that she couldn't control or understand.

He was casually dressed in jeans, plaid shirt and crewneck pullover, and looked as lean and muscular as ever. His desk job had obviously not affected his physique. Abby glanced at the breadth of his upper body and had a sudden crushing memory of those shoulders naked, gleaming in the moonlight as the two of them had stood in shallow lake water, wrapped in each other's arms, while the crickets sang and the water rippled silvery and warm all around them.

"Oh, dear Lord," she whispered under her breath, looking vaguely toward the stained-glass windows. "Please, please help me survive this. Help me not to feel this way about him."

Brad's eyes roved the group and rested on Abby's face as if her words had been a shout instead of an inaudible murmur. When he saw her his eyes lightened, turning from gray to green as his tanned face took on a suddenly gentle and alert look. He gave her a nod that was almost imperceptible, but no other sign of recognition.

Abby gazed hungrily at his face, so strange and yet so wondrously familiar. She saw the level line of his eyebrows, the flat high cheekbones and broad firm mouth, the crisp black hair and changeable smoky eyes set in a fringe of lashes so dark and long that they were almost girlish, and curiously at odds with the rest of that rugged face.

All the old feelings washed over her—waves of sexual longing and excitement and a yearning so intense that it could scarcely be endured. She gripped the notebook until the hard metal rings dug cruelly into her fingers, forcing her to sit upright and try to calm herself.

What was he doing here, anyhow? she wondered in despairing confusion. What in the world did Brad Carmichael have to do with a group of people meeting to discuss near-death experiences, of all things? But, then, she told herself, the man was completely crazy, so unstable and eccentric that you never knew *where* he might turn up.

Brad was speaking now, addressing the audience in a low, quiet voice, carefully avoiding Abby's eyes. She drew a deep breath and tried to listen.

"It was a very bad time for us," he was saying. "The woman I loved was suffering the worst crisis of her life and I wasn't able to help her. I was terrified of her grief and appalled by the whole concept of death. I was no good to myself and God knows I couldn't help her, so I took the coward's way out and left her. I ran away."

There was a brief shocked silence from the audience, while Brad stood gravely regarding them with a look of quiet sincerity. Abby bit her lip and gazed blindly down at the crumpled paper in her hands.

I was right, I was right all the time, she told herself. *He just couldn't deal with it, any of it, so he escaped the pain by running away.*

"I drifted out to Vancouver for a few weeks, then decided to head on down to California," Brad went on in the same level, unemotional voice. "I had friends there and I thought I'd hang out for while, decide what to do next, try to stop hating myself so much for the way I'd treated her. I was on the I-5 heading south, late at night and driving far too fast, when I saw a deer in my headlights. I swerved to avoid it, caught a patch of ice and hit the ditch at ninety miles an hour. It took them almost an hour to cut me out of the vehicle."

Abby stared up at him, dry mouthed and tense with shock.

Brad's gaze flickered over her briefly, then settled once more on a spot near the back of the church as he went on talking.

"I was unconscious for most of that time. A major artery in my leg was severed and I lost so much blood that I went into deep shock. Sometime just before the paramedics got me out and started working on me, I had a near-death experience."

Abby's head began to spin. She choked and rummaged frantically in her pocket for a tissue, con-

scious of the concerned glances of those around her.
Brad, too, looked at her with brief compassion before
he continued. "My experience was something like Ju-
liet's," he said, smiling down at the young woman
with the baby. "I could see them trying to get my body
out of the car and hear them speculating about
whether or not I was still alive. My head was wrapped
in bandages that were soaking up the blood from scalp
wounds, and my eyes were completely covered with
layers of cloth and towels. But I could still see everything—the flashing lights on emergency vehicles, the
horrified faces of the onlookers, the crumpled mass of
my car. I could hear things, too, sirens and people
shouting and, off in the woods, the sound of owls.

"It all looked so harsh and painful that I just
wanted to get away. I turned and started into the
woods, but I wasn't walking, more like floating just at
treetop level. I remember what a weird sensation it
was, like being thirty feet tall. Suddenly, in the sky in
front of me, a light began to shine. It got brighter and
brighter till it filled the whole sky, but it wasn't like
any light I'd ever seen. It was throbbing and warm,
almost alive. It shimmered and danced and shaped itself into a long tunnel or pathway, but the tunnel was
all light, too. I knew," Brad said simply, "that walking up that tunnel was going to be the most wonderful thing...."

A few people in the audience cleared their throats
and wiped tears from their eyes. Abby continued to
stare at the man at the lectern, her face hard, her eyes
fixed and still.

"The strangest thing," Brad went on in that same
calm voice, "was that I was extremely happy and ex-

cited, but my mental processes were absolutely clear, far more lucid than they'd ever been in my life. I could see how often I'd messed up, how I'd always run from responsibility and let people down. I had a strong feeling that my life wasn't complete because I'd failed so badly. It seemed that someone I couldn't see was carefully putting these thoughts into my head, almost like programming a computer. I was so disappointed, but gradually I began to understand that I wasn't ready to enter the light. I had to go back and do things right.''

Dr. Ashton, sitting near the front, raised his hand. Brad nodded at him politely.

''Did the judgmental presence, the 'computer programmer,' as you describe it, have a religious overtone of any kind?'' the doctor asked. ''Did you feel that it was God?''

Brad shook his head. ''Not at all. At least not in any sense that I've been familiar with. It just seemed supremely logical and intelligent. I wanted to argue and talk my way out of going back, the way I'd always talked my way out of everything in the past,'' he added with a brief ironic twist of his mouth. ''But I knew it wasn't going to work this time. Nobody could argue with that kind of logic.''

''And has your life changed since your experience? Have you managed to right some of the wrongs you spoke of?'' Ashton inquired with deep interest.

Brad glanced at Abby once more, his face suddenly taut, then turned back to his questioner. ''Yes, most of them. I've returned to my profession and made contact with my family. I've worked hard to pay off old debts and stabilize my life. I've apologized to people I hurt in the past with my carelessness and self-indulgence. But I..."

The group waited quietly, watching the tall handsome man at the lectern.

"I still haven't made reparations for my most serious wrongdoing," he said finally, in a husky voice. "I hurt somebody terribly, somebody I love more than anything in the world, and I don't know how I can ever make it up to her."

Abby could endure no more. She stumbled to her feet, muttering broken apologies to people around her as she made her way clumsily out of the pew, then rushed through the lobby and down the church steps.

She paused in the moonlight, trying to remember where she'd left her car. Was it here in the parking lot behind the church, or over in the next block where masses of pale trees arched over the sidewalk, glistening like silvery ghosts...?

While she hesitated, she heard quick footsteps behind her, hollow and echoing on the chill pavement. She drew a ragged, painful breath and looked around to see Brad coming toward her at a run, limping as he approached. She turned blindly and started to flee once more.

"Abby," he said breathlessly, catching up with her easily and grabbing her arm. "Abby, please don't run away. Stay and talk to me for a minute. Sweetheart, there are so many things I have to tell you."

Abby turned to face him, shaking his hand away in contempt. For a long tense moment she gazed at him, at the well-remembered contours of his face, at the gleaming hair, the breadth and strength of his tall body as he stood bathed in moonlight. Bitterness and pain engulfed her. All the old feelings of anger and betrayal were there, sharpened and deepened by his nearness and the powerful physical attraction that he still held for her. And over everything there was this new outrage, this final unbearable hurt.

"Oh, I'm sure you have," she said coldly, wondering how she was able to keep her voice so calm and level, how she could manage to speak at all. "All kinds of beautiful things about lights and angels. Well, I'm afraid I don't want to hear it, Brad. None of it."

"Abby, I tried to tell you this before. I wanted you to know what a profound experience it was. When I was in Vancouver, I wrote letters describing the experience, trying to..."

Abby wasn't even listening to him. "My God, it was you, wasn't it?" she murmured slowly, her eyes widening in shock as she realized the truth of the situation. "*You* were the one who recommended to my magazine that I write this article."

He looked down at her gravely, his face quiet and expressionless in the silver light.

"Weren't you?" she said in a low, furious voice.

Her outrage grew when he didn't deny the charge and she began to understand the enormity of what he'd done.

"It was you, wasn't it, Brad?" she repeated. "You called the editorial department and told them about this fascinating psychological phenomenon and your little support group. You mentioned casually that there was a writer in the area who could probably do a good job of reporting it, didn't you?"

"Yes," he said calmly. "I did."

Abby shuddered, almost frightened by the force of her anger. She'd heard about people "seeing red," but she'd never actually experienced rage that intense.

Now she found herself looking at Brad across shimmering scarlet waves of emotion that made her feel dizzy and nauseated.

"It just wasn't enough for you, was it?" she muttered through clenched teeth. "Leaving me shattered and miserable, vanishing without a trace when I needed you most. All of that wasn't enough for you. You had to come back and mess with my career, as well. How *could* you?"

"I don't understand what you mean," he said quietly. "How am I messing with your career? You write articles for that magazine regularly. And this is an assignment that you can do without even having to travel out of the area to do research."

"I don't want to write this article!" Abby said with a touch of desperation in her voice. "I knew I didn't as soon as Lorna mentioned it, but I was afraid to refuse because I could lose all the credibility I've built with them."

"Why can't you write the article? Even from a purely objective viewpoint, it's a fascinating topic, Abby."

"Well, I'm sorry, but I just can't be purely objective about this," Abby said coldly. "And I certainly don't find it fascinating. I think it's all complete nonsense. It's a lot of fantasy and mumbo jumbo manufactured by people with overactive imaginations and a flair for personal drama."

"Even the children?"

Icy fingers crept along Abby's spine. She stiffened as she gazed up at him with dark haunted eyes. "Look, I'm not going to stand here arguing with you about this, okay? Just leave me alone, Brad. It's not going to work, that's all. Just forget the whole thing."

"What whole thing?" he asked in bewilderment. "What do you want me to forget? You, or my experience, or what?"

"Your *experience*," she said, her voice bitter. "Don't talk to me about your experience, okay?"

"Abby, it really happened—just as I described it tonight. It was the most awesome, wonderful thing I've ever known, and it's genuinely changed my entire life."

"Oh, I'm sure it has. Why don't we talk about *my* experience for a while, Brad? You disappeared less than a month after Aaron died. I was all alone, still completely unglued, and you just dropped off the face of the earth. I was frantic with worry for the first few days. I called the police, the hospitals...."

Brad stared at her in disbelief. "Abby, I left a long message on the machine, telling you what I was doing, apologizing for leaving and trying my best to explain it to you."

Abby met his gaze in silence. "Well, I never got it," she said. "I don't think I believe you, Brad."

"The message must have been erased somehow. Look, Abby, I know I was a rotten guy," he added with a bleak smile, "but not *that* rotten."

Abby looked away, hugging her arms in the evening chill, still struggling with her memory of that awful time. It was entirely possible that he'd left something on the machine and she'd accidentally erased the message without hearing it. That whole part of her life had been so frantic and confusing, anything was possible.

"It doesn't change anything," she said finally, her voice strained. "Whether you left a message or not, it doesn't change the fact that you left me all alone, with nothing but pain and memories and a bunch of unpaid bills."

"I'm sorry about those bills, Abby," he said quickly. "I've been waiting for a chance to pay you back, but you kept returning my letters. I'll come by tomorrow with a check, all right? If you'll—"

"Forget the money," Abby said wearily. "Just leave me alone."

"Abby..."

"I mean it. Leave me alone, Brad. I have to write this stupid article because my profession and my livelihood are at stake. But I don't want to see you or talk to you ever again. And I don't want to hear any more about your own personal 'experience,' either. I don't believe a word of it."

"You think I'm making all this up?" he asked incredulously.

"You bet I do," Abby stated. "It certainly wouldn't be the first time you've lied to me for your own purposes, Brad. You've made a fool of me lots of times. I just never thought—" Her voice broke, then steadied as she looked up at him. "I honestly never thought you could be this cruel. Not even you."

"Cruel?" he echoed. "In what way?"

"Making me listen to all this crap," Abby said. "Little kids seeing angels, people dying in childbirth… Brad, can you even begin to comprehend how painful all this is for me?''

"I thought it would be comforting to you," he said quietly, gazing down at her, his eyes darkly shadowed in the moonlight. "I thought you'd find some solace in coming to one of these meetings and hearing about other children like Aaron who—"

"Don't talk to me about Aaron!" Abby shouted, then shifted awkwardly, embarrassed by the shrill, almost hysterical sound of her voice.

Brad stood watching her in concern. He reached toward her, but she ignored his outstretched hand and stared blindly out at the deserted street.

"It's all been so awful," Abby whispered, almost to herself. "You know, there are times when I think somebody really must be trying to drive me out of my mind. Aaron's toys are moved around all the time, and then this—"

"Aaron's toys?" Brad asked. "What about them, Abby? You mentioned this same thing last time you talked to me. What exactly is happening with Aaron's toys?"

"Nothing," Abby said, suddenly so tired that she felt almost weak with fatigue. "Forget it. Just leave me alone. I mean it, Brad. I'll research and write this article because I have to, but I don't want anything more to do with you. Not ever."

She turned on her heel and plunged off along the darkened street, half-afraid that he might follow and take her arm again, wondering how she would control herself if he did.

But when she reached the corner and glanced back he was standing quietly, watching her, the streetlight behind him casting a long shadow from his body onto the cold moon-washed pavement.

"ARE YOU GOING OUT *again?*"

Joan Holland, wearing only a slip and nylon stockings, glanced over her shoulder at her mother, who stood leaning in the doorway, and marveled that anybody could compress so many emotions into a single brief word like "again."

Anger, self-pity, ridicule, fear, mockery and pleading all vibrated in that strong hoarse voice while Vera Holland stood gripping the front of her bathrobe.

Joan tensed and frowned at the small gold hoop she was inserting carefully into her earlobe. "I've been home the past two evenings, Mom," she said, careful to keep her voice light. "I thought you said you were feeling quite a lot better these days."

"Well, of course how I feel is of *no* importance at all," Vera said.

"Then what's the issue?" Joan smiled at her mother's image reflected in the dresser mirror, then picked up a graceful crystal atomizer and sprayed perfume on her throat and wrists, bending after a moment's hesitation to spray the backs of her knees, as well.

"The issue is *you,*" Vera said, her ruddy face quivering, her plump shoulders tense as she stared angrily at her daughter. "Making a complete fool of yourself—that's what you're doing, just in case you haven't noticed."

Joan drew a deep breath, praying for calm. She gazed at a string of cheap imitation sapphires that lay in the shadowed depths of her jewelery box and tried to visualize the angel's eyes, so utterly tranquil and full of peace.

"I really don't understand what you mean, Mom," she said finally, turning to face the angry woman in the doorway. "In what way am I making a fool of myself?"

Vera needed no further invitation. She limped heavily into the room and lowered herself onto the edge of the bed with a gusty sigh, gathering her bathrobe tightly around her.

"Joannie," she wheedled, trying a new approach. "I just don't want you getting hurt, baby. You know that. All I care about is seeing you happy."

"Well, good," Joan said briskly, pulling on a pale blue cashmere turtleneck, recently purchased, and a gray tweed blazer over a long skirt. "Because I'm really happy, Mom, so you should be glad. And that means there's nothing at all to worry about, right?"

Vera Holland frowned, clearly disconcerted by the direction the conversation had taken. "I just meant..."

"You meant that you're nervous about what I do because somebody might hurt me or take advantage of me," Joan finished for her hastily, rummaging through her handbag for her keys. "And I really love you for that, Mom, but I'm all right—truly I am. You don't need to worry."

"So where are you going tonight?" Vera persisted, heaving herself off the bed and doggedly following Joan down the hallway to the kitchen. "Who are you going to see? Are you going over to Abby's place again?"

Joan hesitated by the door, fighting her guilt. She hated lying to her mother, and part of her felt a real reluctance to leave the older woman alone and miserable.

"My heart's been palpitating quite a lot lately," Vera said. Obviously having seen that flicker of uncertainty, she shrewdly pressed her advantage. "I didn't want to worry you, but the doctor *did* say it could be serious if anything happened while I was alone."

Joan took a couple of faltering steps back into the room, looking at her mother in concern. "Really, Mom? When did he say that? Was it last time you went to see him?"

Vera nodded, leaning against the counter for support. "But," she added bravely, "like I said, my problems aren't the real concern here. It's you I'm worried about, Joannie. Just look at you, darling. All dressed up, bright colors, makeup and perfume and jewelry...people...men...might get the wrong impression about you. You do look like one of those trampy women going off to some singles bar to find a man."

Joan stiffened and her look of concern faded, to be replaced by a new hardness and determination. "There's nothing wrong with a woman fixing herself up a little and trying to look her best," she said. "For that matter, there's nothing wrong with women going out in the evening to meet people and have a little fun."

Vera's mouth twisted with scorn. She seemed about to speak, but Joan cut her off with a nervous, abrupt gesture.

"You may not have noticed it, Mom," Joan went on, flushing somewhat as she warmed to her topic, "but life isn't easy for working girls, especially those of a 'certain age,' as they say. We do most of the drudgery for our employers, take orders from other people and very often our hard work goes unnoticed. Most of us have heavy responsibilities at home, too, like children or...or other family members to care for. And it's not a bit sinful for us to want, just every now and then, to have a little free time for our own enjoyment!"

Breathless with emotion, and not at all anxious to hear her mother's response, Joan hurried through the door and down the walk to the car.

She was a few blocks away before her feelings began to settle again and she could breathe more normally. She gripped the wheel and sighed as she skimmed up the curving highway that wound around the edge of the lake. Why did her mother always have this effect on her?

Even as a child, Joan had been terrorized by Vera, who was by far the strongest presence in her life. Joan's father had been little more than a timid, furtive shadow in their home, terrified of putting a foot wrong for fear of incurring his wife's wrath.

How did she do it? Joan marveled. How did some people seem to have such power that they could control the people around them by their presence alone?

Still, these days, she could sense her mother's control slipping, slowly but relentlessly. And Joan was certain that Vera Holland sensed it, as well. That was why she'd become more tentative, more inconsistent and erratic. These days her behavior toward Joan ranged all the way from blunt viciousness to childish wheedling.

In the past, Joan had to admit, either tactic would have been effective in quashing this small personal rebellion. Until now, Joan had never met a man appealing enough to make her suffer the full weight of her mother's disapproval and panicky fear of abandonment. It had always been so much easier just to say no, to make excuses and avoid confrontations, to stay home and accept her fate.

But that was before an angel had come into her life.

JOAN PAUSED A MOMENT to collect herself, then walked down toward the edge of the lake. "Hello," she called shyly as she approached. "I'm late tonight. I didn't know if you'd still be here."

The tall ragged man turned and smiled at her gently. He removed his old baseball cap and the dying sun gilded his hair with fire. Birds surrounded him, gulls and starlings and even a few chattering jays, their wings beating against the sunset clouds as ducks and geese waddled noisily around at his feet. Joan reached into her jacket pocket and took out a small bag of bread crumbs, then tossed a handful onto the trampled sand.

Still smiling, the tattered man moved nearer, so close that Joan could see the fine ageless planes of his face and the incredible blue of those gentle eyes. He didn't have a jacket yet, she noted with concern, even though the night air was increasingly chilly and there was a risk of frost overnight.

"Don't you have a coat?" she asked, turning to walk with him to a bench placed near the lakeshore.

"There is no need to worry about me," the angel said in his quiet voice. He looked at her. "You didn't have to lie tonight," he added with calm approval.

Joan sank onto the wooden bench and glanced over at his strong aquiline profile. His perception still amazed her, although she'd witnessed it many times.

"How do you know?" she asked curiously. "How can you always tell whether I've lied to my mother or not?"

"Your aura changes," he said simply. "When you lie, it darkens."

Joan was silent, thinking about his words and how cynically most of the people she knew would respond to them. But he was never wrong.

"She seems to be accepting it a little better these days," Joan said.

"Your freedom, you mean?"

Joan nodded.

"Is she accepting it better," he asked, smiling at a fat duck who was squatting nearby, pecking energetically at his torn boot, "or are you insisting and giving her no choice?"

Joan grinned faintly. "Well, a little of both, I guess. I should have done this long ago."

"It would have been the loving thing to do," the angel agreed gently. "Allowing her to possess you was an imprisoning thing for both of you."

Again Joan felt that little breath of unreality, warm and mysterious in the autumn sunset. All the rules and logic that governed her life seemed to be suspended when this man looked at her. There were no secrets from him, no closed areas or misunderstandings. His perception of her was complete, even though she'd told him almost nothing about her life.

More surprising still, their intimacy was purely mental. She'd never gone anywhere with him, never been closer to him than a seat on a park bench, never even touched his hand.

"Is it too late?" Joan asked, turning to face him directly. "She was just nineteen when I was born, you know. She's only fifty-one now. She could still have a meaningful life, if she'd only..."

"You must stand aside and allow her to grow," the man said gently. "Your continued presence has been crippling to her."

"I never meant to hurt her!" Joan protested, stung by his words. "But she always got so angry if I tried to go away or do things with...with other people. And sometimes when I..."

"I must go," the man said, standing with the same fluid grace that characterized all his movements. He picked up the tattered khaki sack holding his meager belongings.

"So soon?" Joan said, disappointed.

"I must go," he repeated gently, giving no further explanation. "Stay and watch the sunset for a little while."

Joan nodded, her face bleak, knowing that the splendor of tinted clouds and shimmering water, the darkness of moonrise and the brilliance of stars would be lessened without him. "May I drop you somewhere?" she asked, suddenly consumed with a need to see where he lived, where he went when he strolled out of the park at sunset. "It's no problem, really. I have my car and I can—"

"You must stay a little while and watch the sunset," he insisted in that same gentle tone. "Watch until the colors fade and the moon comes out."

He sounded as if he were giving instructions to a small child. Joan nodded obediently. She folded her hands in her lap and gazed after him until his tall ragged form grew hazy and was finally swallowed up in the dusky twilight.

When he was gone the world seemed darker and melancholy. Joan bit her lip, trying not to cry, feeling like an abandoned child. It was always the same when he went away. He never allowed her to follow, and he usually left her with some kind of assignment, something to look at or think about until he disappeared from sight.

Joan gazed up at the sky, where the tinted clouds were fading gradually to silver. The water shifted and murmured at her feet, a deep whispering sound that she could hear clearly because all the chattering birds seemed to have vanished along with the angel.

She blinked back tears of pain and loneliness, forcing herself to concentrate on the scene in front of her as he'd instructed, waiting for the pale crescent moon to rise above a shallow bank of gleaming clouds.

Suddenly she became aware of a rhythmic thumping sound, distant at first but growing nearer all the time. She turned and peered into the gathering darkness, recognizing the form of a solitary jogger, a man who was approaching rapidly along the deserted beach.

Even from a distance there was something familiar about him. Joan leaned forward intently, finally recognizing the jogger as Abby's friend, the editor from the newspaper.

Mitch Flanagan, she thought, pleased with herself for being able to remember the name. The jogger reached her bench and stopped abruptly, gazing down at her in surprise, his chest heaving from the effort of his run.

"It's Joan, isn't it?" he asked with obvious pleasure. "Joan Holland?"

Joan nodded shyly, a little overwhelmed by his sudden appearance and the nearness of his warm stocky body in shorts and T-shirt.

He was a bit soft at the waistline, she thought, peeping up at him and smiling politely, but his physique wasn't all that bad, really. He had well-shaped muscular legs, and his chest was . . .

She blushed, shocked by her thoughts, and got hastily to her feet to accept his outstretched hand.

His face was really nice, Joan told herself, looking shyly up at him again. He wasn't wearing the heavy horn-rimmed glasses tonight and his features had a pleasant, open look as he smiled at her.

She realized in surprise that he was probably even more nervous than she, and took pity on him by falling into step beside him as they moved slowly up the curved walk that wound along the beach. "How far do you run?" she asked, knowing that joggers always took great pleasure in recounting their exploits of endurance and personal stamina.

But this man was clearly different. He looked down at her with a rueful grin. "Oh, hardly far at all," he confessed. "Mostly I walk and enjoy the scenery, and just break into a run if I notice somebody watching me. But they're great shorts, aren't they?''

Joan laughed aloud, forgetting how miserable and lonely she'd been feeling just a few minutes earlier. "Great shorts," she agreed solemnly. "Very athletic looking. I was really impressed."

"It's not important to *be* athletic," Mitch observed with satisfaction. "It's only important to *appear* athletic."

"Image is everything," Joan echoed, sending them both off into cheerful laughter.

An awkward silence fell as the laughter faded and died on the mellow evening air.

"It's getting really cool," Joan observed finally, looking with concern at his hairy bare legs and arms. "Do you have a jacket or something?"

What a woman, she thought, smiling at her ineptitude. Abby would really tease her about this compulsion of hers to ask men if they had jackets. She sounded more like somebody's mother than an irresistible sex object....

Mitch surprised her by unzipping the little black nylon pack at his waist and shaking out a square of pink fabric that turned into quite a substantial jacket when he pulled it over his shoulders.

"Oh, my," Joan observed, glancing at him dryly and trying not to smile. *"Pink.* You really are into this running thing, aren't you?"

"I'm very serious about it," Mitch said with a solemn twinkle. "Serious, in fact, to the point of fluorescence. Would you like an ice-cream cone?"

Joan looked dubiously at the little ice-cream stand that cast a cheery glow into the darkening evening.

Moths circled and bumped softly together in the bright lights over the stand, while fifty-seven varieties of ice cream vied for the customer's attention.

"Isn't that pretty high calorie?" Joan ventured. "I mean, it'll undo everything you've accomplished by running so hard, won't it?"

"That's why I run down here," Mitch said placidly. "This is my reward. I figure if I run the last half mile along the beach, then have an ice-cream cone, I'm probably just about maintaining the status quo. I can live with that."

"Well, why not? I think the status quo is pretty good," Joan said, surprising herself with her sincerity as she glanced at his stocky body and cheerful smiling face.

His eyes kindled with warmth and he looked at her, clearly about to say something further.

But Joan had a sudden overwhelming image of another pair of eyes, tranquil blue eyes full of understanding. She turned away hastily and pretended to study the tubs of ice cream, conscious of the quick flare of disappointment on Mitch's face. "I think maple walnut sounds good, don't you?" she asked, trying to recapture the bantering tone of their earlier conversation. "As long as the walnuts aren't all dark and sour. I hate them when they get like that."

"Me, too," Mitch agreed. "Are the walnuts plump and juicy? Very, *very* fresh?" he asked the bored teenager who presided over the ice-cream bins.

She gazed at them impassively from mascara-darkened eyes and shrugged, snapping her gum loudly. "They're walnuts," she said at last. "That's all I know."

Mitch and Joan exchanged a glance. "Better not risk it," they both said at once, then laughed again.

"I'll have rocky road," he told the attendant. "A double," he added with satisfaction. "And the lady will have...?" He turned to Joan with an inquiring arch of his eyebrow.

"Pistachio," Joan said firmly. "A small one. I haven't had a pistachio ice-cream cone for..." She frowned. "I can't even remember," she confessed.

"Then it's high time you had another one," Mitch told her comfortably, taking her cone from the young attendant and wrapping it in a napkin before handing it over.

Joan watched as he extracted a couple of bills from his little pack, knowing instinctively that he would be insulted if she offered to pay for her cone. She fell into step beside him and they wandered along the path in the mellow dusk.

"Do you live far from here?" Joan asked, looking at the lights shimmering across the water.

"Walking distance," Mitch told her briefly, pursuing a wayward trickle of ice cream with his tongue. "I hate to admit it, but I actually live in one of those waterfront condos over there."

"Why do you hate to admit it?"

"Because it's a cowardly compromise. It's not what I really want. Actually, I dream of being a home-owner." Mitch turned to glance at her. "My idea of heaven would be having a lawn to mow on the weekend."

"You can come over anytime and do mine," Joan said dryly.

"Anytime," Mitch echoed with a quiet sincerity that made her cheeks feel suddenly warm. "Just say the word, Joan."

They walked on, the silence lengthening awkwardly between them again until Mitch made an effort to resume conversation. "How about you? Where do you live?"

"Across town," she said. "Up on the hillside over there." She waved her hand vaguely at a bank of lights glimmering off to the east.

"Lovely view from there," Mitch said politely.

Joan was silent, thinking about the big comfortable house that had grown to feel more like a prison with every passing year. And these days, she brooded, it was starting to feel like a grave.... She shuddered and turned to the man beside her with a bright forced smile. "Have you seen Abby lately?" she asked. "I haven't talked to her since Tuesday."

"Just in passing. She was in and out of the office all day. I think she's doing research on her new article."

Joan nodded, reluctant to discuss the subject matter of Abby's article. Her friend was so upset by the topic, and so strangely distracted and unhappy these days.

"Brad was in the office this afternoon, too," Mitch went on.

Joan stopped abruptly and gazed up at him in alarm. "*Brad?* In the newspaper office? What did he want? Did Abby see him?"

Mitch shook his head, answering only the last of this barrage of questions. "She was out. He left an envelope with some money he owed her and told me to have her check her tires."

"Her *tires?*" Joan gazed blankly at the young man beside her, ice-cream cone forgotten for the moment.

Mitch nodded. "I guess she'd left her car in the lot and run out somewhere on foot when Brad stopped by. He was looking at her car, he said, and felt some concern about the wear on the tires. He thought she probably needed a wheel alignment."

"A *wheel alignment?*" Joan echoed in disbelief, conscious that she was beginning to sound like a parrot, repeating everything he said.

"When your tires wear unevenly," Mitch explained, "it usually means that your wheels are out of alignment. It can be pretty dangerous, especially on an older car like Abby's. Brad was just concerned, that's all."

"I know. I mean, I know what a wheel alignment is. But that's . . . that's not like Brad at all," Joan said, frowning. "I can't imagine Brad Carmichael even *noticing* that Abby's tires were worn, let alone bothering to express concern over it."

"People change," Mitch said. "Brad seems like a different man these days."

"Abby doesn't think so."

"I know," Mitch said with a wan smile. "Women can be awfully hard to convince sometimes, can't they? I guess that's your car parked over there," he added in a more businesslike tone before Joan could respond.

She shifted awkwardly on her feet, suddenly wanting to be away from him before something happened to embarrass both of them.

But Mitch just nodded with that same distant look, gave her a courteous smile and strolled over to wait as she unlocked her car. He held the door for her, bending to look in.

"Thanks for the walk and the talk, Joan," he said with quiet sincerity. "It was really nice."

Joan nodded abruptly, unable to meet his eyes. She started the motor, then watched as he turned and strode off along the path in the opposite direction from the one the angel had taken.

Joan waited until Mitch Flanagan was just a distant flash of pink against the darkening sky. Finally she shifted into gear and pulled out of the lot, her face quiet and sad as she turned toward home.

CHAPTER SIX

LITTLE JAGGED BITS of color, mostly browns, ranging from palest tan to rich velvety chocolate, spilled across the work table in Brad's office.

He took his gold-framed glasses off and squinted at them, giving them a cursory polish with a tissue that he'd lifted from a desk surface nearby. Then he returned his attention to the bewildering array of shapes in front of him, sipping absently from a coffee mug and frowning in concentration.

Gladys bustled into the room with an armful of file folders, stopping abruptly next to the drafting table when she saw what her employer was doing.

"Oh, dear," she said mildly. "Not another one."

Brad removed his glasses once more and turned to smile at her a little sheepishly. "It's an addiction, Gladys. I can't help myself."

Gladys moved across the thick carpet to peer over his shoulder. "What's this one? It looks like—"

"Chocolate," Brad finished for her. "All different kinds of chocolate. Fudge, truffles, brownies, that kind of stuff."

"Better you than me," Gladys observed. "If I had to do a jigsaw puzzle like that, I think I'd die. Just *looking* at the thing, I'm gaining weight."

"I like the challenge," Brad told her. "It helps me to concentrate when I'm working something out in my mind. But," he added, fitting his glasses back in position and staring at the table, "I just can't find this piece. See? It needs to have a bit of tan on it, and a bump like that, and I don't see it anywhere."

"Maybe it's missing."

"It can't be. I just bought the thing and unwrapped it this morning."

"Well, leave it for a while," Gladys suggested. "Go on to another part. Sooner or later it'll pop up at you."

"I can't leave it," Brad said, staring at the mass of puzzle pieces. "I need to finish the edge before I start on the rest, and I can't until I find that piece."

"Who says?"

"Who says what?"

"Who says you need to finish the edge before you can go on?"

"*I* say so," he said mildly. "I never allow myself to plunge into the main part without finishing the edge. That would be undisciplined."

"Not really. Just sensibly noncompulsive," Gladys remarked dryly.

Brad grinned at her over his shoulder, his face creasing with humor. "Never forget that I could fire you for that kind of insubordination."

Gladys chuckled. "Yeah, right," she scoffed. "I could just see you trying to run this office without me. You don't even know where the computer key is."

"I do so," Brad said. "It's in your top desk drawer."

"Not anymore," Gladys told him mysteriously, turning to leave.

Brad's face shadowed briefly as he watched her plump matronly form. "Gladys?"

"Hmm?" Gladys paused by the door and grinned at her employer. Then, seeing the seriousness of his expression, she turned and came slowly back across the room, displacing a pile of blueprints and sinking into one of the leather chairs by the desk. "What is it, Brad?"

Brad leaned back and removed his glasses again, setting them down beside his mug of rapidly cooling coffee.

"Gladys," he began, "you're a woman, right?"

"It's been extensively rumored," Gladys agreed solemnly.

"You know what I mean."

"Of course I do. Ask your question."

"Well, is it possible to generalize about women at all? Are there really things that all women feel the same about?"

"I *hate* generalizations about women. It's taken me almost thirty years to train my husband not to make them."

"But," Brad persisted, "in some areas, aren't there certain common factors?"

"If there's any human emotion that all women agree about," Gladys said firmly, "then it's likely something that *everybody* agrees about. Men and women, the population in general. Not just women."

Brad was silent, pondering her words.

Gladys looked at him shrewdly. "Why, Brad?" she asked, in a more gentle voice than she usually used with him. "What are you thinking about specifically?"

"I'm thinking about relationships," Brad said, feeling another wave of pain as he remembered Abby's face earlier in the week, when she'd stood before him on that cold moonlit pavement outside the church.

"Well, *that* certainly narrows it down."

Brad grinned, then sobered. "I mean, if a man loves a woman but treats her badly...."

"How badly?"

"Really badly. I mean, if he does something that's terrible and cowardly, betrays her and lets her down completely...will she ever be able to forgive him and love him again?"

"Could you?" Gladys said bluntly. "If somebody you loved treated *you* that way, could you love her again? Could you trust her?"

Brad glanced up, startled by her words. He sat for a moment, thinking deeply, then shook his head. "Only if I was convinced that she'd really, truly changed," he said finally. "That she was a completely different person."

"And how would she convince you of that?"

Brad looked into his secretary's shrewd, kindly eyes and shook his head again. "I don't know," he said, getting to his feet and reaching for a pen. "I'll just sign these papers, okay? Then I'll be out of the office for an hour or so. If Mclean calls..."

"Tell him the landscape designs have been holding things up for a day or two," Gladys finished.

"Stall like crazy," Brad agreed. "Don't let him know we're having problems with suppliers. He's upset enough already."

"Poor man," Gladys said cheerfully. "No wonder he has ulcers. He should just relax and do a jigsaw puzzle or something."

Brad smiled at her with warm fondness. "Everybody should adopt your philosophies, Gladys, and there'd be no more problems in the world."

"Absolutely," she said, smiling back at him as she left the office.

Brad continued to gaze at the closed door after she'd gone, his face still lit with affection. Then, abruptly, the shadow of unhappiness returned. He finished signing the papers she'd left on his desk and crossed the room, shrugging into his leather jacket and reaching for his keys.

ABBY'S HOME HAD a cautious, shuttered look in the late fall afternoon. The little house, nestled in its screen of trees as if bracing for winter, seemed to be gathering a warm cloak around its eaves to shield itself from the gusty wind and drifts of snow that were sure to come.

Brad sat in his car, tapping his fingers absently on the wheel as he gazed at the front door. It was painted a rich dark green.

He could still remember the arguments he'd had with Abby over what color to use on the door, and their mutual delight when they'd visited the hardware store and both fallen in love with the identical shade of forest green.

He could remember, too, painting the door on a hot summer day, while Aaron played on the lawn with his wooden trains and Wilbur lay on the sun-warmed veranda floor. Abby had been weeding the flower bed in cutoffs and a halter top.

Her voice echoed in his mind as he pictured her holding a weed aloft and waving it triumphantly, her face sparkling with happiness. *"I swear, Brad, this root went halfway to China, and I got the whole thing out! Just look!"*

He swallowed painfully and got out of the car. Glancing up and down the quiet street while he approached the house, he wondered why he felt as if he were doing something sneaky. After all, there was nothing wrong with strolling up the walk in the middle of the afternoon and ringing the doorbell. Anybody could do the same thing.

But, Brad admitted, anybody else approaching this door certainly wouldn't feel the same emotions he did. They wouldn't be buffeted by waves of pain and loss, of wistful yearning to be inside the little house again and a fierce aching desire for the slim dark-haired woman whose spirit was all around the place.

"I love you, Abby," Brad whispered to the warm breath of her presence. "If I have to, I'll spend the rest of my life trying to show you that I—"

Just then, Wilbur padded into view and gave him a brief contemptuous glance before settling near the steps and licking in a desultory fashion at one of his front paws.

"Hi, Wilbur," Brad said, smiling. "Just as bright and cheery as ever, I see. And even fatter! You know, when you came walking around the corner I thought you were a human being. I actually thought—"

Brad paused suddenly, listening to something as ephemeral as a passing gust of autumn warmth.

Did it come from around the back of the house? Was it another breath of Abby's presence, or was it just the wind, after all?

Brad stood thoughtfully gazing at the big cat's glossy multicolored fur and thinking about Abby's strange accusations regarding Aaron's toys. She'd made the same disjointed comment both times they'd spoken together—something about her house being invaded and Aaron's toys being moved around.

Brad frowned, remembering the conversations and worrying over the implications. If someone really was trespassing in her house, the intruder had to be coming in through the doors, leaving no evidence of arrival or departure.

Even after she'd had the locks changed, Brad realized with a strange little shiver of apprehension.

He stood by the door of the empty house, still looking down at the heavy calico tomcat, who returned his gaze with cold detachment. Brad bent automatically to gather up the tumbled newspaper from the step and fold it carefully before fitting it into the mailbox by the door. As he tucked the newspaper down in the metal box he thought about Aaron's room. Brad had argued right from the start that Abby should part with the toys and clothes immediately. Her grief was so terrible and all-consuming, and having constant reminders of the little boy's presence had, in his opinion, prevented her from healing. What if he'd been right? Had Abby slipped into some twilight world of unreality? Perhaps the displaced toys and other signs of trespassing were being manufactured somewhere inside her mind, some kind of bizarre manifestation arising from her anguish and loneliness.

This thought, which would at one time have appalled and frightened him, now only served to deepen his feelings of protectiveness and loving sympathy. He yearned to comfort Abby with his new faith and understanding, to take her gently in his arms and hold her, to make her feel the same hope and joy that he'd found in the simple fact of being alive.

While he was brooding over her unhappiness, another sound reached Brad's ears. He tensed, listening carefully. It was more a feeling than a noise, he decided, a slight vibration on the still autumn air, a sense of someone nearby.

Brad's hair prickled at his nape as he looked down at the big tomcat. Wilbur had also tensed and lifted his head alertly.

The sound came from inside the empty house.

Without taking time to think, concerned only with the safety and well-being of the woman he loved, Brad took a deep breath, eased his way down the front steps and crept around the side of the house until he was directly beneath Aaron's window.

He edged his way into the dried mass of honeysuckle vines, trying hard not to make a sound as he neared the window. Still holding his breath, he lifted his body gradually upward until his eyes just cleared the sill and he could see, beyond the jutting outline of the bed, a small portion of the child's room.

Brad blinked in the slanting rays of sunlight and waited until his vision adjusted to the relative dimness within the room. Then he gazed at the braided rag rug on the floor and felt his blood slowly chill in his veins. He could see the edge of the little farm set, arranged carefully on the rug just the way Aaron had always set it up.

"This end of the rug is the field, see?" the child had once explained earnestly to Brad. *"So the tractor has to be on the field like this because the farmer is working, and the barn is at the edge of it because the animals like to go out in the field, too."*

And they were there, just as usual, the cow and the horse and the two fat woolly sheep, grazing contentedly on the nap of the rug.

Abby must be doing it, Brad thought in confusion. Maybe she arranged the toys and couldn't remember doing it afterward. Otherwise, how would the animals all be in exactly the same positions as—

Suddenly his eyes widened in horror. He stared, numb and stiff with fear, as the little tractor began gradually to move. Something, some force just beyond Brad's field of vision, was pulling the string attached to the front of the plump red machine. It rolled slowly along the rippled surface of the carpet, rocking and swaying in a cheerful jolly fashion as it vanished from his sight.

Brad dropped back into the tangle of honeysuckle vines, sweating and panting as if he'd just run a marathon. He moved silently out of the vines, flattened himself against the house and edged around to the back. He checked the door, which was locked, the dead bolt in place, just as it was on the front door.

All the windows were locked and secure, and the house was utterly still and silent in the golden afternoon.

Again Brad thought about that little red tractor, rocking and swaying over the braided oval carpet. He swallowed hard and looked around wildly, wondering what to do.

Maybe he should smash one of the windows, leap through it, rush into Aaron's room and confront whoever . . . whatever was in there.

While he was wrestling with this possibility, willing himself to action, he heard the sound of a vehicle stopping outside. He peeped around the rose trellis at the rear corner of the house and saw Abby's old car pull up to the curb.

She got out, looked curiously for a moment at the low-slung sports car parked near her driveway, then shrugged and started up the walk toward the front door while Brad stood flattened against the back of the house, wondering what to do next.

ABBY SMILED AT WILBUR who waited for her at the top of the steps. She glanced briefly around once more at the smoke gray sports car by the curb, wondering who it belonged to.

Probably the college student across the street, she decided. Or, more accurately, one of his friends, since her young neighbor was an earnest scholarship student who studied all day when he wasn't in class. At night he washed dishes at a downtown pizza restaurant.

Abby grinned at the irony of a student being able to afford a car that probably cost more than her annual income. She put the vehicle out of her mind and moved over next to Wilbur on the veranda, rummaging for her keys.

"Everything's in order here, Wilbur?" she asked. "You've been looking after things with your usual cheerful efficiency, I assume?"

Wilbur flicked her an inscrutable glance and then returned to his bored study of a flock of starlings perched in the bare poplar branches.

"Well, guess what I did today," Abby told him, feeling the need for someone to talk to, some living being to express interest in her day and pleasure over her accomplishments.

By now she was deep into her research on near-death experiences, and the project wasn't half as upsetting as she'd thought it would be. In fact, she found herself getting more relaxed all the time, amused by humanity's endless fascination with the search for the meaning of life.

"Do you know what, Wilbur? This afternoon I went to the library and found—" Abby paused abruptly, staring at the folded newspaper in the mailbox, her heart pounding.

The newspaper boy *never* put her paper neatly in the box. Often when she came home, she had to retrieve the paper from a mass of rosebushes or from the flower bed where it lay in a sodden mass.

She touched the soft edge of the paper, checked the lock on the door, then turned and crept down the steps again, edging around the house toward the back.

Holding her breath, she slipped past the mass of honeysuckle beneath Aaron's window, flattened her body against the rough cedar exterior and crept around the corner, looking at the quiet garden, the deserted backyard, the locked door and sturdy shuttered windows.

She shook her head and moved toward the border of the rose trellis, then screamed aloud.

A man crouched there, huge and menacing, startling her so badly that she almost fainted with shock.

Strong hands gripped her shoulders. "Don't, Abby," she heard a voice saying earnestly through her haze of terror. "Please, darling, don't be frightened. I'm so sorry. I just didn't know what to..."

Something penetrated Abby's terrified brain, a dawning understanding, accompanied by a bracing surge of indignation.

"Brad Carmichael!" she said in a shaking voice, glaring up at the handsome concerned face that hovered above her. "What in God's name are you *doing?*"

"Abby," he said sheepishly, "look, I was just...I came over here to..."

The poor man seemed even more startled and taken aback than she was, Abby realized with a sudden wayward touch of amusement. And no wonder, being caught in the act like this.

She studied him with a cool level gaze, moved in spite of herself by his tall lithe body in dress slacks and leather jacket, his crisp white shirt and well-polished shoes and the clean hard planes of his tanned face.

"What are you doing here, Brad?"

"I was really concerned," he said in a low voice. "The more I thought about it, the more worried I got about...about what you told me, that somebody was coming into your house."

"It hasn't happened for quite a while," Abby said calmly. "Or have you just not had time to come around lately?"

She couldn't resist the small stab of accusation, but even as she said the words, Abby knew there was no truth to them at all. In fact, she understood that she'd never really believed it was Brad who was breaking into her house. She'd only fixed on him as the likely perpetrator, Abby realized with a little shiver, because all the other explanations were simply unthinkable.

He was still looking down at her with anxious concern, his eyes a dark smoky gray in the slanting afternoon light.

"It hasn't happened lately? Not for how long, Abby?"

"Oh, I don't know," she said vaguely. "A couple of weeks, I guess. I think maybe it was just..."

She paused, horrified by a soft brush of warmth that touched her ankles.

"Wilbur," Brad told her when she looked down a little wildly. "If I recall correctly, just giving you a gentle reminder that it's almost dinnertime."

"He really doesn't like to wait for his meals," Abby agreed, looking up again with a small shaky grin. She forgot her anger with Brad for a moment and felt only a warm flood of gratitude because he was a living, breathing human being, something she could see and understand.

Brad gazed down at her, his eyes shading to green as he returned her smile. "I haven't seen your face sparkle like that for such a long time, Abby," he whispered. "God, how I've missed that smile."

"My smile?" she asked in surprise. "What do you mean?"

"Nobody smiles like you, girl. Nobody in all the world," he told her huskily. "Your mouth tucks in and lifts at the corners like that and then your whole face lights up, like the sun coming through clouds." He paused as if searching for words, his face pale with emotion.

Abby stared at him, mesmerized. At last she forced herself to turn away and began rummaging blindly in her handbag for her key.

"Look, Brad," she said abruptly, "it was nice of you to be concerned, but I'm okay. Really I am. You can leave now."

He hesitated, still gazing down at her, then waved his hand at the empty house with a small abrupt motion. "Aren't you afraid to go in there alone?"

Abby shook her head. "Of course not," she said firmly. "Why would I be afraid?"

"Abby...if somebody's been coming into your house..."

"I don't know that for sure, Brad." Abby looked up directly, meeting his gaze with steady eyes. "Maybe I just imagined it. Maybe I move the things around myself and then forget about it. Grief can make the mind do all kinds of strange things."

"Is that what you really believe? You think your imagination manufactured those incidents?"

Abby grinned again. "My goodness, you seem awfully intense about this," she said, unable to resist a little teasing. "Has your near-death experience given you some kind of passionate interest in paranormal phenomena, Brad?"

He shook his head without smiling back. "Not really," he said abruptly. "But I've always had a passionate interest in you and your welfare. Nothing's changed that."

Abby began to feel tired, wearied by the stress of his presence and the need to fight against a physical attraction so powerful that it kept threatening to sweep her away on a wild sweet tide of yearning.

What a mystery, she thought, this whole business of sex and physical appeal. She was completely finished with the man, had been for almost a year, but still it was all she could do to keep from flinging herself into his arms and covering his face with kisses.

"Well, I guess I shouldn't be so surprised. You've always had a strange way of showing concern for my welfare." She forced her voice to sound cold and level, though her heart was pounding erratically. "Now, if you'll excuse me, Brad, I really have to..."

"I can't let you do it," he said suddenly. "I can't let you go in there alone."

Abby stared at him, caught by the intensity of his voice.

"Why not?"

Brad shifted uncertainly and looked down at his feet, then cleared his throat and met her gaze again. "Abby, I saw something in there a few minutes ago. Through Aaron's window."

"You saw something? What do you mean?" Abby stared at the man in front of her, feeling another touch of inexplicable dread.

"I came here, as I said, to see if there was anything obvious that might explain these...incidents," Brad began. "I was really worried about the idea of somebody having access to your house. Especially some-body unkind enough to... to do what you said they were doing.''

Abby waited tensely, her eyes fixed on his mouth as he spoke. She'd kissed that mouth a thousand times, delighted in its sculpted contours, in the hardness of his face and the surprisingly rich softness of those lips as they moved against hers.

But did she really know him? Was this the same man she'd lain with, caressed and loved, laughed and talked and dreamed with through a whole year of loving? Or was he truly an enigma, an unfathomable stranger?

"I edged up and peeked over the sill," Brad was saying, "and the farm set was all carefully arranged on the rug, just the way... just the way Aaron used to do it."

Abby pushed aside her memories and concentrated on his words. "With the chickens on the fence?" she asked tensely.

Brad nodded. "And the cows and sheep out in the field. You know how he always used to say they liked to be in the field where the farmer was working on his tractor?"

Abby stared at him. "You... you saw that? Just now?"

Brad nodded.

Abby shivered again and glanced at the deserted yard, the bare shrubs and quiet sunny lawn. "Maybe I... maybe I did it this morning," she suggested in a whisper. "Brad, maybe I really am going crazy. Could it be possible for me to go in there in the morning, put all those toys out and then forget completely about having done it?"

She gazed up at him in an agony of appeal. Brad met her gaze for a moment, then looked away and cleared his throat awkwardly.

"Abby," he said, "I saw..."

"Saw what?"

"I saw the tractor move."

"What?" Abby stared at him, aghast. "What did you say?"

"While I was watching," Brad said unhappily, "the tractor moved. It bounced across the rug as if..." He paused and licked his lips, then gave her another stricken look. "As if somebody were sitting behind the bed and... and pulling on the string."

CHAPTER SEVEN

INSIDE THE HOUSE Abby gave Brad a long measuring glance, then turned and started off down the hall toward Aaron's room. Brad followed her so closely that she could sense the growing tension in his body as they reached the door.

"Don't open it!" Brad whispered suddenly. "Let me do it."

Abby shrugged and stood aside to watch as he edged the door open, flicked the light on and stood gazing, wide-eyed with shock.

The room was in perfect order. All the toys were neatly arranged on the shelves, not even a woolly lamb or a teacup out of place. The room was silent, deserted and utterly still in the thin glow of late-afternoon sunshine. The shabby lion on the pillow looked as if he'd been sleeping for all eternity.

Abby peered up at Brad, who stood regarding this scene with an incredulous frown.

He made it up, she thought. He made up the whole thing about the tractor and the toys. Why would he do such a thing?

"Abby," Brad said in confusion, "I swear to God, I saw the toys spread all over. I saw the tractor move."

"Sure you did," Abby said, trying to sound cold. But she was badly shaken by the events of the past few minutes and her growing suspicions about Brad's part in all of this.

Earlier in the week she'd arranged for a wheel alignment because he'd been concerned about her physical safety. Was it possible that he'd actually lied to protect her emotional well-being, too? Did he have some kind of irrational idea that it would comfort her to think that other people sometimes saw things that weren't there?

"What do you think, Abby?" he murmured in her ear, dropping an arm around her shoulders and drawing her close to him in a gesture of comfort. "Do you really believe I imagined seeing that stuff? Just a few minutes ago?"

Abby drew her breath in sharply, overwhelmed by the feeling of being in his arms again, of standing so close to the long hard body that she recalled with such vividness. She could feel the warmth of him against her, smell the pleasant fragrance of fabric and aftershave and clean skin that was so uniquely Brad's, even feel the beating of his heart in his powerful chest.

"I think..." she faltered, "that you did it on purpose."

"Did what? Made up a story about Aaron's toys?"

Abby nodded, unable to look at him. "I think," she went on, still speaking so softly that he had to bend his head to make out the words, "that you want me to think I'm not going crazy, that other perfectly normal people can sometimes see things that aren't there. It's...it was very sweet of you, Brad. I don't know if I understand you," she added, trying to smile, "but it's still very sweet."

He was silent, gazing down at her thoughtfully. "You really believe I'm that nice a guy?" he asked finally. "That I'd make up a fantasy just so you wouldn't be the only one doing it? That would have to be a pretty considerate kind of man, Abby."

She smiled wanly again. "Well, you noticed my tires," she pointed out. "You told Mitch I should get a wheel alignment."

"And you did," Brad agreed. "I stopped by this morning on my way to the construction site to make sure you'd had it attended to. It's pretty dangerous, having your wheels out of alignment."

"See?" Abby said. "You really must be changing, Brad. The man I knew before would never...he wouldn't even have thought of things like that. Most of the time you were completely self-absorbed."

"Well, I'd like to take credit for being a changed man, but I didn't make it up, Abby. I really saw the tractor move. Someone was in that room just a few minutes ago. Don't you think we should call the police or something, get to the bottom of this?"

"No!" Abby said, desperately pushing aside the bizarre, improbable image of the little tractor bouncing slowly across the rug. "It never happened. You saw a shadow or something, then used it to comfort me. Let's just drop it, okay? It's never been the kind of thing you enjoyed, anyhow, all this metaphysical stuff."

"Abby...look, you don't even know me anymore. We haven't talked much since I got back, and there's a lot that you don't understand. I wish you'd let me tell you a bit about what's happened to me."

"Like what? What do you want me to know?"

Brad was silent a moment, a withdrawn and sober look on his face while he considered her question. "I'm not afraid of death anymore," he said at last. "I was always so afraid, Abby. I was terrified of death because it cheated people out of life. I felt this awful restlessness all the time, like my life was going to come crashing to an end someday and I had lived it to the absolute fullest before it was snatched away. That's why I did a lot of those crazy things."

"What happened to make you so afraid?"

"I watched my brother die of leukemia. It took months and months for him to go."

Abby stared up at him, wide-eyed. "Oh, Brad," she whispered. "You never told me that."

"I never told anybody. I couldn't bear to talk about it."

"How old was he?"

"Twenty when he died. I was eighteen. I went kind of crazy for a while, Abby. I made a sort of pact with Jerry that I'd live life for both of us and keep moving so fast that death would never come close to me again."

"And when Aaron died . . ."

"It just reinforced my worst fears," Brad said. "When the reality of death came so close to me a second time, I couldn't stand my life anymore. I went almost wild with anxiety over what I was missing and the feeling that I was just wasting my life in some kind of aimless trap."

"But now you feel different?"

"I'm not afraid anymore," Brad repeated quietly. "I know that nobody's life is ever wasted and there's a purpose to everything. Now I'm able to be contented, to live from day to day without a lot of anguish or restlessness.''

Abby gave him a calm measuring glance. She noticed for the first time the look of deep settled peace in his eyes. She recalled the quiet sincerity of his voice when he addressed the group in the church hall, and her amazement when Mitch had passed on Brad's concern over her worn tires. That kind of caring and consideration were so completely unlike the man she'd known.

Again she fought a treacherous flood of desire, and forced her voice to sound casual and teasing. ''You say you're not frightened anymore, but when you told me about that tractor moving, you seemed pretty scared,'' she observed.

Brad looked sheepish. ''Well, that's different. Near-death experiences have nothing to do with the supernatural or the occult, no matter what anybody tells you. They're supremely real and human.''

''But that tractor...''

''That didn't seem human. Whatever was moving that tractor, it had a...spooky feeling.'' Brad drew another deep breath and then smiled again, looking even more abashed. ''Do you think I really imagined the whole thing? Are we both having strange fantasies, Abby?''

Abby considered. ''I'm as rational a person as you are, and I've certainly been having them. It doesn't seem so terribly odd that you might, too.''

They walked back down the hall and into the cozy living room, smiling as Wilbur pushed rudely past their ankles and headed for the kitchen with his tail high and twitching.

Brad and Abby exchanged a glance.

"Is there food in his dish?" Brad whispered.

Abby shook her head, still grinning. "Not a scrap," she whispered back.

Brad spread his hands in eloquent sympathy. "Poor girl," he murmured. "Heaven help you."

Then he sobered, took a deep breath and gazed around the room, while Abby watched him quietly. Finally he turned back to her, his eyes warm with happiness. "It's all just the same," he said. "Every bit of it. Abby, you don't know how I've missed all this, how many times I've dreamed about it. No other place in the world has ever felt so much like home to me."

Abby tensed, increasingly troubled by the depths and undercurrents to their conversation. After their first bitter encounters had left her cold and miserable, she'd decided to be civil to Brad when their paths crossed. But she had no intention of trusting this dangerous, unstable man ever again, with her heart or her love.

And he *certainly* wasn't ever going to share her house again.

Still, there was something perilously satisfying about seeing him standing here again in the midst of the things they'd chosen and arranged together, and the furniture that he'd built with his own hands down in the tidy little basement workshop.

"Brad..." she murmured awkwardly, still feeling tense and uncertain.

He was studying a cabinet door that sagged a little on its hinges, his long capable fingers moving lightly over the wood and the faulty hinge mechanism.

"What is it, Abby?" he asked. But when he turned and caught her expression he understood instantly. "Don't worry. No pressure, now or ever. You'd be crazy to get involved with me after what I did to you, and both of us know it. For now I'm happy just to be friends. This hinge needs to be replaced, you know. Are all my tools still downstairs?"

Abby nodded in confusion, absurdly deflated by his words. *She* should be the one, Abby told herself with vague indignation, to decide what course their relationship would take in the future. And instead here was Brad, marching back into her life and laying down the law as calmly as ever.

"I just think..." she began nervously, then paused.

Wilbur stalked down the hall and sat in the doorway, glaring at her in bitter accusation.

Abby and Brad both chuckled, their tension subsiding.

"If looks could kill," Abby said cheerfully, "I'd be having a near-death experience right now."

Brad's jaw tightened. "Don't joke about it, Abby," he said gently. "Believe me, that experience isn't something that anybody should joke about."

"Well, it does seem to have changed you, all right," Abby said, trying to make a joke out of their earlier tension. "Right to the point where you'll pretend to see things that aren't there."

Brad put his other hand on her shoulder and drew her closer to him, gazing down at her with burning intensity. "Have I changed enough for you to kiss me, Abby? Just once, for old time's sake?"

As if transfixed, Abby stared at the well-remembered planes of that handsome face, the lips and cheekbones and eyelashes, the broad forehead with its errant lock of crisp dark hair, his white teeth and the warm creases around his smoky green eyes.

"You said...you said there'd be no pressure," she whispered at last.

"I know I did. And I meant it. But, Abby, sometimes I just want you so much. Oh, God, so much...."

He gathered her closer in his arms with a husky moan of anguish and longing and bent to kiss her forehead, her earlobes, her cheeks and chin and throat. Abby stood silent in his embrace, fighting a wild tide of emotions, of fear and uncertainty and doubt.

But when his lips finally found hers, all the tension was gone. She yielded and folded warmly into him, melded against him, tasting the richness of kisses that she'd expected never to feel again, experiencing a new soaring joy and excitement that carried her far out of herself, far beyond any realm of rational thought and caution.

At last, gasping and stunned with the force of her emotions, Abby pulled away and stood facing him, her hand over her mouth.

"I need...I need to feed Wilbur," she whispered urgently. "He's so hungry."

Brad was breathing hard, his face flushed with passion, his eyes so green they sparkled with emerald fire.

"Okay," he agreed after a moment's silence in which their ragged breathing was clearly audible. "Let's feed Wilbur."

Abby touched her hair, straightened her clothes self-consciously and stumbled off toward the kitchen. She was still a little a shaky, and felt that some terrible danger had been narrowly averted.

But the future had to be negotiated somehow. Despite his marvelous attractiveness and the wild uncontrollable yearnings of her body, Abby didn't want to resume any kind of intimacy with this man. She still didn't trust him and knew that, fragile as she was, it would be fatal for her to risk more hurt.

"Brad," she murmured over her shoulder as she reached into the pantry, "Brad, I don't really think we should—"

He came up behind her, draped one arm casually around her shoulders, while the other hand removed her scarf to lift the silky hair at her nape.

"You don't think we should move so fast," he agreed, bending to kiss her neck, "and you're absolutely right. Let's just feed Wilbur and then I'll go. May I call you?"

Abby paused by the electric can opener and brushed Wilbur aside. The big cat always jumped onto the counter at this point and tried to supervise, just to speed things up.

"Look at that animal," Brad said sadly. "Completely untrainable. Give him a clout."

"Yeah, sure," Abby said in a shaking voice, trying to smile. "Look who's talking about giving him a clout. You couldn't even stand to take him to the vet for his shot, you were so afraid it might hurt him."

"You know, women never forget anything," Brad said soulfully to Wilbur. "They get some little thing against you and they never forget it."

Wilbur ignored him, his fierce attention on the nasty pinkish mass that Abby was spooning into his dish.

"Abby?" Brad asked, pausing by the kitchen door.

"Hmm?" Abby watched the big calico tomcat, intrigued despite herself by the dainty greed with which Wilbur attacked his meal.

"May I call you?"

Abby hesitated, her vivid imagination supplying her with rapid opposing scenarios. She saw herself falling in love with Brad again, being drawn back into that warm, laughing, sweet intimacy that once filled her whole life, then losing him as abruptly and brutally as she had before.

On the other hand she saw herself turning him away, living a lonely colorless life with her cat and her books, fading and turning gray and brittle while life went on all around her, while Brad found someone else to love and spring blossomed in the world. . . .

"Abby?"

She turned to face him, her body tense. "Were you lying about the toys, Brad? I need the absolute truth from you."

Brad met her gaze steadily. "No, Abby," he said at last. "I wasn't lying. I saw the tractor move. And God knows what I think was doing it. The whole thing just scares the hell out of me."

"I see." Abby turned away and looked out the window with a remote, brooding expression.

"Abby?"

"Yes, Brad," she said finally. "All right. You can call me."

"A DRINK while you're waiting, sir? A glass of the house white, perhaps?"

Mitch looked thoughtfully at the waiter who hovered by his elbow. The man was past middle age, slim and erect, with one of those long flaps of hair that grew from a low side part and was swept carefully across a bald pate.

"Do you have beer on tap?" Mitch asked.

"I'm afraid we just have bottled beer," the waiter murmured, looking anguished. "But," he added uncertainly, "I could probably get you some draft beer from the bar, if you'd like to..."

"White wine will be just great," Mitch said at last, watching as the waiter smiled in relief and hurried toward the kitchen.

Alone at the table, Mitch relaxed and looked around. Suddenly his eyes fixed on the entrance. His breathing halted and even his blood seemed to stop pumping, and the whole room was frozen in space and time.

Joan Holland had appeared in the doorway, wearing a soft pink suit of expensive tailored wool with a creamy silk blouse. The muted lights behind the reception desk shone on her light brown hair, giving her a gentle halo that matched her delicate face, her wide blue eyes and tender mouth.

She spoke shyly to the headwaiter and then stood next to him, gazing uncertainly around the room. Her glance fell on Mitch and she looked startled, relieved and finally embarrassed as the waiter escorted her to Mitch's table.

"Hi, Joan," Mitch said warmly, just as if he were a normal person in full command of his heart and mind.

"Hello," she murmured.

She seated herself across the table and gave him another of those shy, luminous smiles that made his throat tighten with longing.

"I didn't expect you to be here alone. I mean, I thought Abby would..."

"Abby won't be here for a while," Mitch said, trying frantically to remember the words he'd rehearsed, hoping she wouldn't be upset with him.

"She won't?" Joan glanced at him uncertainly, then smiled up at the waiter and ordered a glass of wine.

"No." Mitch cleared his throat and plunged ahead. "You see, I deceived you a little about this evening."

Joan's eyes widened and she began to look a bit panicky. "But... but Abby *is* coming, isn't she?" she asked in confusion. "I mean, it's not... I called and invited her, and she said..."

"Abby's coming," Mitch assured her. "But," he added after a brief pause, "so is Brad."

"Brad!" Joan looked quickly up from her study of the leather-bound menu.

"Yes." Mitch shifted uncomfortably in his chair.

"But you said... you said we were having a surprise birthday dinner for Abby. You said I should call her and pretend that just she and I were going to meet for dinner, then you'd turn up with a cake and some gifts."

"I know. But I didn't mention that the whole thing was Brad's idea and that he was going to be here, too."

Joan's cheeks turned a delicate pink and her blue eyes darkened. "Why?" she asked bluntly. "Why didn't you tell me Brad was involved?"

"Because I was afraid you wouldn't come if you knew," Mitch told her. "And I was sure that Abby would want you here."

"I don't like Brad Carmichael," Joan said in a low voice, nervously fingering the cutlery on her linen place mat. "He was terrible to Abby. He hurt her so much."

"I know," Mitch said uncomfortably.

"I don't think you do. I don't think anybody really knows what Abby went through last year." Joan choked briefly, then continued. "He just vanished without a trace. I really thought she'd go out of her mind."

"I know," Mitch repeated gently, feeling like a complete idiot.

Four years of journalism, an entire life devoted to communication and all he could do was keep saying those same two words.

Joan glanced up at him, her cheeks still pink. She looked so shy and pretty that he wanted to sweep all the glass and silverware from the table, seize her in his arms and kiss her with thunderous passion. But he realized sadly that those romantic gestures were not for overweight editors with horn-rimmed glasses.

He decided to change the subject, instead. "You look beautiful, Joan," he told her sincerely. "That's a terrific suit. The color is perfect on you."

Joan's flush deepened and she glanced away, clearly both pleased and embarrassed by his compliment. "I just bought it yesterday," she murmured. "I feel a little . . . I feel silly wearing it."

"Why?"

"I haven't worn anything pink for years. My mother said I looked like I was trying to be a high school girl again."

"Well, your mother's wrong," Mitch said firmly. "Besides, that's a very sophisticated color. I saw one of the network news anchors wearing it the other night on television, and she certainly wasn't trying to look like a high school girl."

Joan smiled at him gratefully. "Shoes, too," she murmured after a brief awkward silence.

"I beg your pardon?"

"I have pink shoes," Joan said with the air of someone making a reckless confession. "I bought them with the suit."

Mitch pulled the tablecloth aside and bent to examine the slim foot she extended, shod in a soft leather pump that was undeniably pink, with a graceful creamy inset on the vamp.

"*Great* shoes!" Mitch said fervently. "Absolutely top drawer. If I'd known you were going to be such a fashion plate," he added with a cheerful grin, "I'd have worn my tux."

Joan smiled at him across the rim of her wineglass, responding gratefully to his lighter mood. "Do you have a cummerbund and everything?"

"Red paisley," he told her solemnly. "With a matching bow tie."

She laughed aloud, and he laughed with her.

Inside, though, his resolve was growing stronger than ever. Mitch Flanagan had never met a woman he wanted as much as he wanted this quiet gentle friend of Abby's. But he was sure that Joan was in love with another man. He could see it in her cautious reserve, in the way she allowed herself to go so far and then reined in her feelings and settled back into a kind of cool friendliness.

But the man she loved wasn't very much in evidence, Mitch decided. Maybe he was married or otherwise involved and she could only see him on rare occasions. Whoever he was, he certainly didn't monopolize Joan's life. And that left an opening for someone else, some other man who was enterprising and determined enough to win the lady's favors. Mitch Flanagan wanted to be that man.

"Well, look at this," Abby's cheerful voice interrupted his thoughts. "Isn't *this* cozy! What's going on, Joannie? I thought you were proposing a girls' night out."

"I was," Joan said, meeting Mitch's eyes for a moment as she obediently recited the lines he'd told her when he'd called to arrange the dinner. "I thought it would be nice for us to have an evening meal in a restaurant for a change, Abby. I was just sitting here waiting for you, when Mitch happened to come along, so I invited him to join us."

"I see." Abby's clear gaze moved slowly from one face to the other. "So it was just an accident that Mitch happened along. There's no sinister plot here or anything? I mean, you two wouldn't be ganging up on me by any chance?"

"Of course not," Mitch said firmly, seeing that Joan was uncomfortable with lies, even tiny white ones. "Some wine, Abby? We're both drinking the house white."

"Is it good?" Abby asked, smiling up at the waiter. "Would you recommend it?"

The balding man beamed at her, obviously captivated by her sparkle and her warm animated face.

Mitch, too, found himself a little surprised by the way Abby looked. She and Joan had clearly agreed to dress up for their "girls' night out."

Abby wore a tailored silk dress of deep gold. With her dark glossy hair and vivid brown eyes, she looked like some kind of lovely autumn flower. And her face was glowing with the pleasure of finding her two friends together.

"You look just beautiful, Abby," Joan said, voicing what Mitch was thinking. "Is that a new dress?"

"I got an advance on the article," Abby explained with a brief grin. "'For expenses,' the invoice said. I thought a new dress was a completely valid expense."

"Absolutely," Mitch agreed, toasting the ladies gallantly.

"Speaking of beautiful," Abby said, after sipping her wine, "look at you, Joannie. Where did all these pastels and patterns come from? I thought you never wore anything but basic beige."

Joan smiled. "I know. Mitch and I were just discussing that. I always looked at all the pretty colors and then passed them by and chose something drab."

"Why?" Abby asked.

"Because I thought the drab things suited me better, I guess," Joan said after a moment's thought.

"What would give you that idea? You look wonderful in those delicate pale colors." Abby gazed at her friend. "Whatever made you think drab things suited you, Joan?"

"My mother said so," Joan told them, trying to smile. "She always said I looked ridiculous in colors and patterns, and I believed her."

Mitch watched Joan's diffident smile, her shy blue eyes, and his heart ached for the years she had spent believing all the negative things that had been said to her. But why had she suddenly stopped believing them?

"What happened to make you change?" Abby asked, once more voicing Mitch's unspoken thoughts. "I keep wondering, Joan, why all of a sudden you have the courage to defy Vera. I know what a dragon she can be."

"You shouldn't talk that way about her, Abby," Joan said automatically. "She isn't as awful as you think. She's just...frightened, I guess."

"Sorry," Abby said with an unrepentant grin. "I've never believed that she has the right to smother you with her fears, that's all."

"You're right," Joan said. "But it's still my fault if I allow it. I just decided not to allow it anymore, that's all."

"Why?" Abby repeated, gazing intently at her friend. "Why now, Joan?"

Joan shrugged and eyed Mitch nervously. "I just...a lot of things have happened in my life lately," she murmured. "I've started thinking about...who I am, and where I'm going, and how I want my life to be. I've started feeling better about myself."

"Bravo!" Mitch applauded, then reached out with his wineglass to touch Joan's. "That's great! And you look beautiful. And Abby should quit bullying you."

"I'm not bullying," Abby said, joining their toast. "I love her. I always have."

"Who do you love?" A deep teasing voice inquired behind them. "I missed that."

Abby glanced up quickly. Mitch was a little shaken by the flare of joy on her face when she saw Brad standing near her chair, appearing relaxed in brown dress slacks, tweed jacket and a soft tan shirt. So that's how it is, Mitch mused, looking at Abby's vivid glowing eyes, her flushed cheeks and parted lips and sparkling face.

He met Joan's glance briefly and caught an expression that exactly mirrored his feelings...a look of surprise, caution and deep concern.

"What's this?" Abby was saying, laughing a little breathlessly. "More coincidence? Or do I sense a real conspiracy?"

"Well...maybe a bit of conspiracy," Brad admitted, seating himself in the empty chair and smiling up at the waiter.

Abby gazed at the other two. "I'm not surprised at *you*," she said, giving Mitch a severe glance. "But Joannie...I never expected deceit from you."

Joan turned pink and shifted uncomfortably in her chair, while Abby laughed and reached out to squeeze the other woman's hand.

"Don't worry, Joan," she said with a smile. "I know you were probably led astray by experts. Why all the secrecy, though?" she asked, looking at Brad. "Why not just arrange for us all to have dinner together?"

"I wasn't sure you'd come," Brad said, smiling at her, his green eyes glowing. "You've never been big on parties or celebrations."

"Party?" Abby asked blankly, glancing from one smiling face to the other. "What party? What's the occasion?"

"It's your birthday, dummy," Brad said gently. "Happy birthday, Abby."

"My *birthday?*" Abby stared at all of them, her eyes wide with shock. "My God, it is," she muttered finally. "I completely forgot."

"I thought you might have," Brad said in that same gently teasing voice. "You've never kept very close track of those little milestones."

"I remembered Aaron's birthday," Abby said with a faraway look of pain. "It was in March. He would have been four. I made a little cake and put four candles on it...."

Her voice broke, and Brad leaned closer to her, resting an arm around her shoulders. "I was thinking about him on his birthday, too, sweetheart," he murmured.

So where were you? Mitch thought, exchanging another troubled glance with Joan. *Where were you while she was there all alone, making a little cake and drowning in sorrow?*

But neither of them spoke, just waited while Abby composed herself enough to smile at them. "Thanks, guys," she said finally. "It was sweet of you to do this. I honestly forgot all about it."

"Happy birthday, Abby," Mitch said, breaking the awkward silence by taking a small wrapped package from his pocket and handing it across the table.

"Presents!" Abby exclaimed, as delighted as a child. She pulled the wrapping aside to reveal a small device that resembled a pocket calculator.

"It's for addresses and appointments," Mitch explained. "And it has an alarm that beeps. Guaranteed to keep you completely efficient and organized."

"Oh, my," Abby murmured, entranced, gazing at the sleek little instrument. "It must have been expensive."

"I got a deal," Mitch said comfortably. "The supplier advertises with us."

"My gift isn't nearly as grand," Joan said, taking a package from her big handbag. "But I think it's something you'll like."

"This is incredible," Abby protested as she opened the bright flaps of paper. "Really, I never imagined... Oh, *Joan!*" Smiling with pleasure, she held up a glossy book of quilt patterns.

"I hope it's the one you wanted," Joan said modestly, pleased by her friend's response.

"It's the very newest one. I've yearned over it in the bookstore for weeks. You know, I'm just about ready to start a new quilt, too. I've been thinking about colors since summer."

"It's obvious that these people know you pretty well," Brad said with a smile, taking a slim wrapped box from his pocket.

Abby smiled back at him, then opened his gift to find a dainty gold pen nestled in velvet.

"The only girl I know who still uses a fountain pen," Brad told the others.

There was a brief pause while the waiter arrived to take their orders and Abby tidied away the masses of paper and ribbon.

"Oh, yes," Brad said with the air of a man recalling some insignificant detail. "There's this, too." He took a bulky rectangular gift from his briefcase and handed it across the table, looking almost shy.

Abby drew back the silver paper to reveal a leather-bound album. She opened it and looked slowly up at Brad, her eyes filling with tears.

"Oh, Brad..." she whispered. "Oh, I can't believe...where on earth did you...?"

"The pictures were in my camera when I...when I left last year," Brad said, shifting awkwardly in his chair. "I'd finished almost the whole roll, but then we..."

"Abby?" Joan asked. "What is it?"

Abby held the book out, her hands shaking, and gave her friend a trembling smile. "It's pictures of Aaron. Eight-by-tens, all candid shots that I've never seen before. Look, he's playing with Wilbur, and here he's in his little cowboy suit."

"Is it all right, Abby?" Brad asked anxiously.

Mitch understood what the man was saying. Brad wanted to be certain that he'd done the right thing, that the pictures didn't still have power to hurt her, even after all this time.

"It's wonderful," Abby told him with a misty smile. "Brad, this is the most wonderful thing anyone's ever given me. I'll treasure it forever."

"They're beautiful pictures," Joan said quietly, leafing through the book. "You're an excellent photographer, Brad. And it's really a lovely gift."

"Last year," Abby said with a shaky smile, "he gave me a laser printer for my birthday. Lots of expense, but not much imagination, right?"

Brad grinned, visibly relaxed by the favorable reception of his gift. "Anybody who heard you swearing over that old printer of yours would consider a laser printer a *very* romantic gift," he said, smiling at the others around the table.

Mitch gave the tall man a quiet appraising glance, conscious of Joan's troubled gaze resting on his face again as he did so. Both of them, Mitch knew, were wondering the same thing.

Was this new Brad Carmichael the genuine article?

Or was Abby, with her shining eyes and glowing face, just heading for another heartache, for deeper anguish and more loneliness?

CHAPTER EIGHT

ABBY SAT QUIETLY in Dr. Ashton's waiting room gazing at a big oil painting on the wall in front of her, an autumn scene in vivid shades of russet and gold and bronze. She studied the painted background, thinking about quilting fabrics to distract herself from the tense feeling she always had before an interview.

An autumn quilt would be a nice change. Maybe some kind of bright sunburst pattern in dark gold, offset with little printed triangles in rust and earth tones. But should the background be dark or light?

She shifted restlessly on the soft upholstered chair, suddenly feeling a fierce wave of homesickness. She yearned to be back in her cozy house, sitting by her quilt frame with a drift of bright fabric scraps all around her.

Actually, Abby admitted to herself with a brief wintry smile, she wanted to be anywhere but where she was right now. Although she was trying to be detached and professional, part of her still dreaded the upcoming interview....

She shook herself a little and turned her attention to the window, where a cold autumn rain hissed and splattered on the glass. Sodden trees outside the window bowed low in the wind, waving and dripping, and the rain flowed in a dirty trickle down the gutter.

Every time she came to Vancouver it seemed to be raining, she thought gloomily. Especially late in the fall, when the sky closed over the beautiful city, gray and brooding.

Abby shivered, thinking about the long drive home in sopping darkness over the Coquihalla, one of the highest and most isolated wilderness freeways in the world.

At least her wheels were properly aligned now, and not nearly so treacherous on the slippery pavement. She smiled again, thinking about Brad's worry over her safety.

It was still hard to believe that he'd been so concerned and observant. And there were other things happening lately that were even more difficult to fathom...his new gentleness and consideration, the strange tenderness over Aaron's toys, his thoughtfulness and generosity last week on the night of her birthday.

Abby shook her head, once more almost overwhelmed by the frightening unreality of this new situation. There was no doubt that pampering could be pleasant, but she often felt that she was teetering on the very brink of a long slippery incline. One false move and she'd be sliding and tumbling, head over heels, back into the pit of unfathomable dangers below.

She knew that Joan and Mitch felt the same way. They'd expressed warm interest in the album of photographs, and had been cordial and pleasant with Brad. But both of her friends had a cautious, shuttered look when they spoke about these recent developments in Abby's life. She sensed a kind of unspoken warning that rang louder than words.

It was a warning she ought to heed, Abby thought gloomily. She remembered the night in her house when Brad had held her and kissed her. After that first time, he hadn't attempted any further intimacy, even when he was puttering cozily around the house fixing hinges, repairing the toaster, studying a faulty catch on Abby's quilt frame.

But Abby could never quite free her mind of the memory of that one kiss, the wonderful homecoming feeling of being in his arms, the flame of desire that had briefly consumed her and left her weak and shaky with longing.

I wish he hadn't come back, she thought suddenly. *I was doing so well. I was starting to recover and feel better about life, and now I'm just so—*

"Miss Malone?" the receptionist asked, interrupting her troubled thoughts. "The doctor will see you now."

Abby smiled politely and followed the young woman down a wide carpeted hallway. She entered a comfortable office paneled in oak and decorated with shades of dark green and cream, an effect that she noted with approval before smiling at the trim silver-haired man behind the desk. "Dr. Ashton," she said as the doctor stood and shook her hand. "It's very good of you to see me."

"Not at all, Miss Malone," the doctor said pleasantly. "This is a topic I always enjoy discussing."

"Even with the media?" Abby asked, sitting in the leather chair opposite his desk and getting out her notebook.

"Especially with the media," Dr. Ashton said with a courteous smile. "The media have been very fair with us, Miss Malone. Generally, reports of near-death experiences don't seem to be overly sensationalized or trivialized."

"Why do you think that is?" Abby asked.

Dr. Ashton leaned back and frowned thoughtfully as he considered the question. "I think perhaps it's the nature of the phenomenon," he said at last. "I think this is something that everybody wants to believe in, at some level of consciousness. It can arouse skepticism in the general public, but not the kind of anger that tends to produce a really negative reaction."

Abby nodded, considering his answer, then jotted down a few notes. "There certainly is skepticism, though," she said, looking up at the doctor's quiet face. "In my research I've found all kinds of dismissive explanations for this experience."

"I'm sure you have," Dr. Ashton said with a brief smile. "Oxygen deprivation resulting in hallucinations, a surge of hormones caused by the failure of vital organs at the time of death, a spasm of the temporal lobes producing brief electrical charges within the brain...."

He paused and looked at her with polite inquiry.

Abby nodded. "I've been researching all those rational explanations. There are a lot of scientists who dismiss the near-death experience completely."

"There certainly are." The doctor was silent a moment. "But," he said quietly, "you know, I'm not aware of any nonbelievers among those who have sat at the bedside of a dying child and seen that child recover."

Abby shivered suddenly and gripped the notebook tighter, hoping her discomfort wasn't obvious. "I believe that's your area of specialty," she observed, fighting to keep her voice calm. "Near-death experiences in children."

"Yes, it is. Children tend to have somewhat purer and more vivid experiences than adults. And they describe their experiences with great eloquence because they aren't inhibited by their own skepticism or embarrassment."

"I attended one of your lectures recently. I saw the slide presentation and the pictures the children drew for you."

"They're very inspiring, aren't they?" the doctor asked, his austere face softening with emotion.

"Yes, they are." Abby was quiet a moment, remembering those bright stick people and the "beautiful, beautiful forest, full of pretty birds and flowers."

She flipped nervously to a fresh page in her notebook, while Ashton watched her with sudden interest. "If near-death experience is a genuine phenomenon," Abby said, "why does it seem so recent? The first documented instances were recorded in Moody's book in 1975. Wouldn't you think something so truly universal would have been a widespread, well-known occurrence in the human population long before that?"

"Near-death experiences have always been widespread and well-known," the doctor said mildly. "They just weren't discussed or reported until recently. Major statistical firms estimate that over eight million Americans who are alive today have had some form of near-death experience.''

Abby looked at him in surprise, then nodded and wrote the figure down.

"And that number is growing with amazing speed," the doctor added.

"Why?" Abby asked quickly. "Why would there be more of these experiences now? Don't you think a lot of people are just 'jumping on the bandwagon,' so to speak, and imagining something they've been programmed to see?"

"Not at all. Especially not the children. Most of the children I've interviewed had never heard of the phenomenon prior to their own experience. They were just overwhelmed by the sheer impact of what they'd seen and felt."

"But," Abby persisted, "it still seems questionable that..."

"That there are so many more NDEs being reported now," the doctor concluded with a smile. "Actually, Miss Malone, it's not questionable at all if you think about the facts for a moment. Far more people are having these experiences now simply because we have the medical technology to bring people back from the brink of death with a much higher success rate. And many of those people have the same story to tell us when they return."

Abby sat gazing at the doctor's quiet, intelligent face. "I suppose that makes sense," she admitted finally. "But still, there is no real proof that the experience is genuine. I mean, it could be easily explained by one of those scientific theories you mentioned, like oxygen deprivation or hormone surges."

"It could," the doctor agreed. "Except for one thing."

"What's that?"

"The fact that this experience often produces lasting personality change. No other single human experience has been known to have such a powerful effect. A near-death experience sometimes takes no more than a minute or so in real time, but it can cause more profound and lasting changes to the personality than years and years of psychotherapy."

Abby thought about Brad, the new depth and peacefulness of his manner. There had always been such a terrible restlessness at his core, a kind of frustrated energy that had been evident even while he slept. Now that agitation seemed to be gone, replaced by a calm acceptance of life and confidence in the future.

"You still look rather skeptical," the doctor commented, interrupting her wandering thoughts.

Abby stirred and nodded, annoyed with herself for being unable to separate her personal and professional lives. "It doesn't really matter whether or not I'm skeptical, Dr. Ashton," she said. "I'm doing research, and I want to present a balanced view of the phenomenon, that's all. I know from other articles I've researched that it's very difficult to alter the personality in any substantial way. What causes you to make this claim about near-death experience?"

"Simple observation," the silver-haired man told her calmly. "I've heard firsthand accounts from many, many people who tell me about the personality change in themselves."

"But how exactly do they change?" Abby persisted. "What are the most common features of this transformation?"

The doctor frowned, considering. "I suppose," he said at last, "it's a kind of contentment, a new willingness to accept the reality of life. An absence of restlessness, you might say."

Abby glanced up at him sharply, her eyes wide. Again he met her gaze with that expression of calm professional interest.

"So, if that's the common experience," Abby said at last, "then somebody who heard about this could probably do a fairly realistic job of faking a similar change if... if there was some personal advantage for him. Couldn't he?"

"I suppose he could," the doctor said. "Why do you ask, Miss Malone? That's a rather odd question."

Abby's cheeks warmed and she murmured something noncommittal, then forced herself to return to her list of research points. She wrote down the responses to her queries with deliberate composure. Finally she closed the notebook and smiled politely at the doctor as she folded her papers away in her briefcase. "Thank you very much," she said, getting up and extending her hand. "You've been most helpful, Dr. Ashton. I'm grateful for your time."

He waved off her thanks. "It was a pleasure. But if possible, I'd like you to send me a copy of your article," he added with a smile. "I want to include it in my collection."

"I certainly will." Again Abby nodded politely, then turned to leave.

"Miss Malone," the doctor said from behind his desk.

"Yes?" Abby paused with her hand on the door-knob and looked back at him.

"If you don't mind my observation, I sense a certain reluctance in you to deal with this topic. Now that your professional task is finished, would you like to take just a moment for a discussion on a more personal basis?"

"No!" Abby said, feeling exposed and frightened under his clear-eyed gaze. "I'm sorry," she added awkwardly, her cheeks burning. "It's just that I—I'm afraid I don't really believe in any of this, Dr. Ashton. I honestly think it's something like those people who claim to have been abducted and taken away in spaceships for observation. It's simply some kind of hysterical desire to gain attention. Nothing more."

"I see." The doctor watched her thoughtfully, forming a steeple with his slender hands on the desk top. "What leads you to believe this with such conviction?"

Abby returned his gaze steadily, the color fading from her cheeks. "I sat by the bedside of a dying child, Dr. Ashton," she said. "I was there every single minute, for hours and hours, while he was fighting to breathe. And he didn't see angels or beautiful lights or anything. He just died."

She turned on her heel before the doctor could answer and hurried from the room. Gripping the big leather briefcase in her shaking hands, Abby rushed down the corridor and through the building. She wanted only to escape, to get outside onto the street and into the sheltering rain before her tears began to fall.

BRAD PARKED by the curb and sat once again gazing thoughtfully at Abby's empty house. Although he knew that she was in Vancouver doing research on her article, and wouldn't be back until late at night, he still felt furtive and nervous.

She was softening toward him...actually beginning, ever so slowly, to show a little warmth and trust. But if she should happen to return unexpectedly and catch him hanging around her house, all that could change in a second.

He knew just how tenuous his position was in this fragile new relationship with Abby. Her cautious trust and friendship were so precious to him that he couldn't bear the thought of losing her again. He hated to take this kind of risk, but he still couldn't keep himself away from her house, simply because he could never forget the image of that little red tractor bouncing along the braided surface of the rug.

Abby thought he'd invented the whole thing as a comfort to her, a strange kind of assurance that other rational people could also sometimes imagine things. She'd been so insistent about that explanation that Brad hadn't pressed the issue.

Deep in his heart, though, he knew he hadn't imagined what he'd seen. He frowned and tapped his fingers on the wheel, considering.

There was no logical explanation for the moving tractor. The house had been locked tight and had remained so. If somebody had slipped out while he'd been talking to Abby by the rose trellis, that person would have had to pause to unlock the door, then lock it again on the outside, since every bolt had been in place when they'd checked. That, of course, would have had to be done with a key, because Abby had bought the most expensive and difficult-to-burglarize locks on the market. And how would anybody get their hands on a key?

Questions circled and collided in his mind, but he kept coming back to only one explanation. Some agent other than a human being, something that could cause things to move and yet remain invisible, had entered the house.

Brad shifted his body on the soft leather seat of his car, still brooding over the problem.

A year ago, Abby would have been the first to scoff at such a suggestion. But now he suspected that despite her protests, she really believed, at some deep level of her consciousness, in a supernatural explanation for the occurrences in her house. Maybe she didn't even fully realize it herself, but she believed that Aaron was somehow returning to his room, playing with his toys just as he had before he died.

Brad, though, didn't believe this at all.

He examined himself, wondering why he was so sure, and understood that it stemmed from his shining moments at the brink of death.

It was because of the light, he realized, his body flooding with familiar warmth and joy as he remembered. When he'd truly *felt* that light, looked into the glow and understood that it was drawing him, he'd been filled with a sense of peace and homecoming unlike anything in the world. He'd wanted passionately to continue on toward the light, to let it gather him in and enfold him in safety and teach him all the wonders of the universe.

Nobody who had been given all of that profound experience, Brad thought simply, could possibly want to return to earth and hang around being mischievous, moving objects and frightening people. And he wasn't alone in that belief. He knew that others who had survived near-death experiences tended not to believe in ghosts and restless souls or in the idea of the dead coming back to haunt those who were still living.

Yet he'd seen the tractor move, watched with his own eyes while some power that clearly wasn't human had drawn it slowly and relentlessly across his line of vision.

Finally he shook himself, opened the door abruptly and got out, hunching his shoulders against the damp autumn chill.

He cast an eye at the clouds brooding above the horizon, so livid and ominous that it was difficult to see where the mountains ended and the stormy sky began. The wind was blowing fresh and chill, hinting of early snows.

Brad frowned, thinking about Abby driving home late tonight over that high, remote freeway. He felt an almost physical ache, a yearning to be with her, taking care of her. What if she ran out of gas up there, or had a flat on one of those worn tires and had forgotten to take a spare? What if somebody came along while she was stranded....

Brad tensed and shook his big shoulders, recognizing the futility of such thoughts. After all, Abby had been looking after herself for a good many years. And the painful fact was that even during the year they'd lived together, she'd often been forced to look after herself because Brad had been unavailable, off somewhere driven by his restless urge for freedom and adventure.

But he was different now. It was a hard irony to endure, knowing that just when he'd come to recognize her as the ultimate prize of his life, the woman he wanted to be with through time and eternity, it was perhaps too late. He didn't know if he could ever truly win back her love and trust.

Brad couldn't bear to lose her. Not to accident or harm or simply to her final rejection of him.

He thought about the happy times they'd had during that bright summer while Aaron was still alive and the three of them were a little family. He remembered Abby's glowing eyes, her warm laughter, her slim body alight with joy as they ran and played on the beach while the gulls circled overhead and the fat ducks and geese waddled along by their feet.

Brad's face took on a hard intent look. Bending swiftly, he picked up a golf club from the back seat and hefted it lightly in his hand, then locked the car and strolled toward the house, trying to look casual and unobtrusive, in case any of the neighbors might be watching.

The front door was locked, as usual. Wilbur wasn't around to serve as a welcoming committee, and Brad figured it was probably getting too cold for him. He recalled with a wistful grin how on days like this, Wilbur preferred to sprawl full-length on one of the furnace vents, absorbing the entire flood of warmth into his fat body and blocking it from the rest of the room.

Walking silently on sneakered feet, Brad crept back down the front stairs, glanced up at the windows and then moved around to check the back door, which was also locked and bolted. He hunched his shoulders into the wind and zipped his ski jacket a little higher, feeling another deep chill of reluctance. At last, he slipped around the other side of the house and edged into the space beneath Aaron's window, lifting himself by degrees until he could see into the room.

He shuddered and caught his breath to keep from swearing aloud. The toys, which he'd seen tidied away just before Abby had left on her trip, were now spread all over the place. The lion was in the rocking chair, cuddling a small stuffed turtle. The same crew of dolls and animals dined sociably at the tea table; he could see liquid in their little cups. The bright windup train was running merrily, and so was the music box.

Brad drew another deep shuddering breath and dropped below the window, listening to the faint tinkle of the music box through the wall. It was a few moments before he could control his powerful emotions and emerge from the sheltering nest of honeysuckle vines. He crept once more toward the front of the house.

He had to get into the house. *Think Brad,* he admonished himself. *If you were Abby and wanted to hide the house key outside, where would you put it?*

Not the mailbox—that was too obvious. Same for the doormat and the top of the doorsill. Ever practical, Abby would most likely hang a key out of sight at the edge of one of the veranda railings, where it would be handy but anyone searching for it would have to look a long time. *Good strategy,* Brad thought ruefully. By the time he found it, whatever was in there would surely have heard him and fled.

He continued to gaze with narrowed eyes at the silent veranda, forcing himself to concentrate on Abby's probable state of mind.

She would be likely to hang the key on the section of railing closest to Aaron's room, Brad decided, simply because Aaron was still, even after all these lonely months, the most important part of her life. And, he realized with growing certainty, she'd probably put it inside the *third* railing, because that was Aaron's age when he died. Acting on his hunch, he held his breath and edged back around toward the child's room, searching each railing as he went.

Sure enough, there it was, cleverly tucked up inside the third railing where the top rail met the upright. With shaking hands, he wiggled the key from its hiding place and moved silently back up to the front door.

When he put the key in the lock he was assailed by a sudden paralyzing wave of pure terror, a craven urge to turn and run as fast as he could, away from this house, this place, this woman and all the strange problems that surrounded her.

"Damn it," he muttered, clenching his jaw. "No more running. I've done enough running for a lifetime. She needs me, and it's time to stand my ground like a man."

There was a faint comfort to hearing his own voice, even in the most subdued of whispers. It gave the bizarre scene a welcome bit of reality, a small sense of normalcy.

Brad bent swiftly to remove his shoes, then gripped the golf club in his shaking hands. He edged the door open soundlessly and crept into the foyer in his stocking feet, holding his breath and listening.

He could hear the music box tinkling, the soft creaking of the rocking chair and another, quieter, sound that made his skin prickle and turn icy cold all along his neck.

A child's voice came drifting down the hall, somewhat muffled, singing a little toneless song about teddy bears and picnics.

Brad drew a deep, ragged breath that almost turned into a sob. He glanced wildly around the empty house, then edged across the living room toward the hallway.

Though he was being painfully careful, one of the hardwood floorboards creaked. The child's ghostly singing stopped abruptly. Brad stood frozen, as well, looking around, wondering if he was battling some invisible adversary who could watch him while remaining unseen. If so, then at this moment he could be in terrible danger.

He continued to edge toward the closed hallway door, directly across from which was Aaron's room.

For a long shaking moment Brad stood looking at the door, then flung it wide and stepped into the hallway.

There was no sign of life in the narrow passage, just a distant view of the kitchen table with its potted African violets, looking so cozy and homey that it seemed an eerie touch in the midst of this terror.

Brad stood in front of Aaron's closed, silent room. He willed his heart to stop pounding so fiercely, then opened the door. The room was empty, too, at least of visible presences. The toys were still in the same cheerful disarray that Brad had witnessed through the window, and the rocking chair continued to sway back and forth with its two cuddly occupants.

"Aaron?" Brad whispered, his voice husky with fear. "Aaron, are you here? What do you want?"

Suddenly a new sound penetrated his fog of dread, a distant, muffled noise that seemed to be coming from the kitchen. Brad turned, still shuddering at the sight of that swaying little chair, and crept down the hall, brandishing his golf club in menacing fashion.

At the entrance to the kitchen he stood in numb disbelief, staring in horror at the bizarre and improbable sight before him.

CHAPTER NINE

BRAD STARED for a long time, then found himself shouting with laughter and relief, hardly able to control his reaction.

A child, or what he could see of a child, lay writhing on the linoleum tiles near the door. Only the lower half, clad in tiny blue jeans and ragged sneakers, was visible; the rest was on the other side of the swinging pet flap on the bottom of the kitchen door.

Adding to the absurdity of the scene, Wilbur was attacking the small flailing legs and feet that hammered against the tiled floor. The big cat kept leaping on them with hissing, stiff-legged intensity, as if this wasn't a child at all but a mouse in blue jeans, trying to escape through a hole in the wall.

Brad had a brief powerful flash of memory, recalling how he'd impressed Abby by installing that flap after they'd bought the puppy for Aaron. He'd cut the opening so carefully, fitted the little hinges flush with the door and tacked weather stripping all around the edges so the flap was completely airtight.

But the whole opening wasn't more than eight or ten inches square, even smaller than a piece of writing paper. Brad watched in amazement at the little body that was apparently able to wriggle through that diminutive space. Probably the kid had to lead with one shoulder, he decided, and pull the other arm through afterward. But the belt of a ragged cotton jacket was now stuck on one of the hinges.

Brad wiped tears of laughter from his eyes and bent to grasp Wilbur, who was continuing his furious attack on the little denim-clad legs.

"Wilbur," Brad scolded, scooping the big tomcat into his arms and grinning at the baleful slitted eyes. "You quit picking on a guy while he's down. Is that fair, you big bully?"

Wilbur hissed and squirmed in Brad's grasp. Still chuckling, almost light-headed with relief, Brad hurried to toss Wilbur without ceremony onto the basement landing. He closed the door on the indignant cat and hurried back into the kitchen, then knelt to study the small body, which continued to struggle in furious silence.

"Can you hear me?" Brad shouted through the door, placing his hands gently on the tiny wriggling hips.

There was no answer, but the child's movements stopped abruptly and the small body went tense and rigid beneath Brad's hands.

"That's good," Brad called in a voice he hoped was reassuring. "Just lie still like that while I..." As he spoke he tugged at the belt, working it carefully out from the teeth of the metal hinge. As soon as the child felt some slack he began to snake forward. Brad caught hold of the legs just in time, tugging the child's body gently back through the opening.

"*Ow!*" with an outraged shout the child tumbled into the room.

Brad found himself looking into a small dirty face contorted with fear. The child glared silently back at him. Brad caught an impression of round cheeks reddened with cold and huge blue eyes swimming in tears that trickled down, making blurred tracks through dirt and grime.

Though far from expert in such matters, Brad estimated the child's age at about three or four years. The little body smelled stale and unwashed, and tangy with the cold leafy freshness of the autumn day. Brad hesitated, wondering what to do. As he leaned back on his heels and relaxed his hold the child bolted for the door again, diving toward the opening with quicksilver swiftness.

"Hold it!" Brad shouted, grabbing the little body and scooping it up in his arms. He carried the kicking squirming child into the living room. "Not so fast, kid. You and I have a few things to talk about, don't you think?"

He sat in the rocking chair with the child firmly in place on his knee, looking helplessly down at the tangled cap of brown hair that was cut in a ragged bowl shape framing the dirty face. "Are you a boy or a girl?" he asked.

The child sat in stubborn silence, rigid and tense in his grasp.

"What's your name?" Brad asked, trying to sound gentle. He was beginning to realize that the small person in his arms was deeply frightened, but fighting hard not to show it.

"I know you're scared. But I have to tell you," Brad said in a cheerful conversational tone, trying to ease the child's tension, "you sure scared me, kid. I didn't know *what* you were."

He peered into the silent face with slowly dawning recognition. "I've seen you before, haven't I? You used to play with Aaron sometimes. You live somewhere up the street, right?"

No reaction from the child, though the eyelashes flickered briefly. Brad looked at those long dense eyelashes and realized that this would no doubt be a very attractive child if it was cleaned up and dressed properly.

But the little person on his knee was in truly wretched condition. The grubby hands looked as if they hadn't been thoroughly washed for months, and a few nasty cuts were healing unevenly on the wrists and ankles. The little feet, Brad noticed in concern, were without socks and the jacket and T-shirt were worn ragged, far too light for the day. The shivering body felt thin and ill-nourished in his hands, as bony and fragile as a captive bird.

"Are you cold?" Brad asked, reaching for a knitted afghan that Abby kept over the back of the rocking chair. "Here, let's wrap up a bit, shall we?"

He held the child firmly with one hand while he wrapped the afghan around both of them, then took a fresh grip and leaned back to rock the chair slowly. The child was still watchful and silent, but Brad sensed with a flood of protective concern how the little body relaxed somewhat and huddled gratefully into the warmth of his body.

"You know it's not right to sneak into somebody else's house like that, don't you?" Brad murmured, looking down at the tangled dirty head by his shoulder. "Didn't you know it was wrong?"

"I put the stuff away," the child said in a low, husky voice, startling him. "I put Aaron's toys back on the shelves and stuff, *every* time."

Brad grinned, thinking how adept the child had become at doing that very thing. He remembered the afternoon when he'd gazed in at the red tractor moving across the rug, then stood at the doorway with Abby minutes later and found the room in eerie, perfect order, apparently untouched.

"Not every time," he said gently, recalling, as well, the times that Abby had found the toys scattered around the room. "Sometimes you left them all over the place."

"Only if somebody was coming and I had to run away." The child twisted and glared up at him with some belligerence. "Are you going to whip me?"

Brad looked down at those watchful blue eyes and the shivering little body wrapped in the folds of the afghan. He was still searching his memory to recall just who this child was and which of the neighborhood families he belonged to.

"What's your name?" he asked finally.

"Tony," the child muttered after a brief hesitation. "I'm Tony. I live in the pink house."

Brad nodded, remembering dimly a silent, unkempt little person who had sometimes come over to play with Aaron. The pink house was a shabby dwelling near the corner, with an old mattress spilling its stuffing on the front lawn and a couple of rusted automobiles abandoned in the back. One of Abby's neighbors, as he recalled, had tried to organize a petition to get the place cleaned up, but apparently nothing much had ever come of the project.

"Don't you have any toys to play with, Tony?"

"Not like Aaron," the child said matter-of-factly. "Aaron's toys are neat."

Brad hesitated again. "Do you know that . . . that Aaron doesn't live here anymore?" he ventured.

Tony nodded vigorously. "Aaron's dead, just like my mom."

Brad felt himself drifting into deeper water all the time. He rocked and frowned uncertainly. "Your mother's dead, Tony?"

"Yes," the child said without emotion.

"So who do you live with now? Who's in the pink house?"

"Clara. And Walt. But he's not home anymore. They had a fight and he left."

"Is Clara . . . is she a relative?"

The child twisted to look up at him with bright curiosity. Brad caught a flash of lively intelligence in the wide blue eyes. "What's a reltiff?"

Brad tried to recall his time spent with Aaron and how much small children like this understood of abstract concepts. "It's like . . . it's somebody who's part of your family. Like an aunt or a grandma or something."

Tony screwed up his dirty face in concentration. "I don't think I have any reltiffs," he announced after thoughtful consideration.

"Well, we'd better go see Clara, anyhow," Brad said helplessly. "Come on, Tony."

"Okay." The ragged child slid from Brad's knees and marched toward the kitchen door in a businesslike manner. "Wilbur's still in the basement," he said over his shoulder. "He gets real mad if you leave him in the basement."

Brad grinned, thinking about the big ill-tempered cat. "Yeah, I know he does."

He went into the kitchen and watched as Tony opened the door to release a slit-eyed Wilbur, who stalked past both of them, his tail high and stiff as he vanished into Abby's bedroom. Brad and Tony left the house together, and Tony waited on the veranda while Brad put the key back in its hiding place.

As they neared the pink house, Brad noticed that his diminutive companion began to lose some of his composure. The child's steps lagged and he glanced fearfully into the cluttered overgrown yard.

"Clara's gonna be really mad if you tell her what I did," Tony muttered, in a strained voice. "She'll hit me."

"Why?" Brad asked.

Tony shrugged. "She always hits me," the child said in the fatalistic manner of one announcing some immutable law of nature.

Brad frowned and followed the child through a torn screen door, catching his breath as he entered the shabby stucco house.

The smell was appalling, a stale gust of human misery, of garbage and ancient grime. Junk and clutter lay everywhere—stacks of old newspapers, soiled clothes, rotting food, dirty dishes and empty liquor bottles.

The only evidence of Tony's presence in the house was a tiny pair of torn rubber boots by the door and some crayons neatly boxed on the kitchen table, lying next to a coloring book that was open to a bright picture of flowers and baby chicks. Brad picked his way across the messy kitchen and glanced at the picture, impressed by the neatness of the coloring and the vivid hues that Tony had chosen.

"That's a nice picture," he said, smiling down at the silent boy. "You really do good work, Tony."

Tony's dirty face relaxed suddenly into a smile of shining gratitude that startled Brad and brought a lump to his throat. "So where's Clara?" he asked, his voice deliberately brisk.

Tony looked hopeful. "Maybe she's out. She goes out lots of times."

"And leaves you all alone?"

The child nodded cheerfully. "I like it when she goes out. I make cereal and do my coloring."

"Or go over to Aaron's house," Brad suggested dryly.

Tony nodded agreement, unaware of the gentle irony in Brad's voice. "It smells good in Aaron's house. It's nice there."

Again Brad felt that treacherous tightening in his throat. He paused helplessly beside a teetering stack of soiled cups and dishes, wondering what to do.

"Who else lives here? Does Clara have any other children?" he asked.

Tony looked up from a thoughtful examination of the coloring book. "No, just me. Clara says she doesn't like kids."

As the child spoke a young woman appeared from the other room, her face puffy with sleep. She was very thin, and wore a dirty pair of black jogging pants and a sagging pink sweatshirt, also badly soiled. Her long reddish hair was matted and lank, and her face was smeared with makeup.

Brad looked at her with distaste. Even from a considerable distance he could smell her rank unwashed body and the reek of stale liquor.

The woman gaped at Brad in sullen surprise, then shifted her cold glance to the child. "Oh, for God's sake," she muttered with a gusty sigh. "What's she gone and done *now?*"

Astonished, Brad gazed blankly at the woman, then down at Tony who had instinctively pressed against him, in the shelter of his leg. He studied the child's matted head, hastily amending his first impression of Tony.

"Are you Clara?" he asked finally.

"Yeah, I am," the woman said with growing belligerence. "What the hell do you think you're doing, coming into my house like this?"

Brad ignored her question. "What's your relationship to this child?"

"I'm her guardian," the woman said, moving to the sink to run herself a glass of water. "Take off, okay? Whatever she did, I'll see that she gets punished for it."

Again Brad was aware of Tony pressing against his leg. He realized that the child was shivering, and wondered just what form Clara's punishments took.

"How did you come to be her guardian?" Brad persisted. "By whose authority?"

"Look, who are you, anyhow?" Clara asked. "Are you from Social Services, or what?"

"I'm a neighbor," Brad said briefly.

"A *neighbor*," the woman echoed with vast contempt. "Yeah, sure, some neighbours I got. Never lift a finger to help, do they? Not even when I'm all alone and got this damn kid to look after. Costs a fortune for clothes and stuff...."

Brad raised a hand to cut off this rambling litany of self-pity. "How did you come to be Tony's guardian?" he repeated.

"Her mother was a friend of mine, okay?" Clara said, glaring at him. "She died a couple of years ago, overdosed one night with some people I knew, and I took the kid."

"Why? You don't seem to be enjoying her very much."

The woman shrugged again. "There was nobody else to take her. Shelley had no family at all. And they pay me," she added. "I get an allowance from Social Services for looking after her, and more money from Welfare, too. Otherwise I just couldn't make ends meet."

"I can see that it's been hard for you. But..."

"Get out," the woman said wearily, waving her hand in dismissal, then advancing on Tony in a threatening manner. "And as for *you*, missy, you know what I told you about talking to strangers. *Don't* you?"

Again the child cowered behind the tall man, gripping his pant leg with a frantic hand and whimpering in terror. Brad remembered her courage when she was trapped in the door. She'd struggled frantically but in absolute silence, then faced him after her capture without even blinking.

He knelt suddenly and removed the little girl's cotton jacket, examining Tony's thin arms, pulling up the sagging T-shirt to look at her skinny torso, which, as he had suspected, was covered with bruises. Some were fresh and livid, others faded to yellow and green on the tiny jutting ribs.

Anger flooded him, so powerful that the squalid room blurred around him. He gathered Tony's thin body into his arms and stood up, looking coldly at the young woman.

"I'm taking her with me," he announced recklessly.

Tony shifted in his arms and stared at him in amazement, her eyes wide.

"Like hell you are," Clara said. "Get out of my house, or I'll call the cops."

"Go right ahead," Brad told her coldly. "Here's my card." He gripped Tony in one hand and rummaged in his shirt pocket with the other, extracting a business card. "You call the police and when they get here, you give them my card so they'll know where to find me. I'd certainly like to talk with them about Tony and her welfare."

The woman looked at the card, then up at Brad, her eyes shifting uneasily away from his.

"Maybe I'll just do that," she said without conviction.

Brad turned toward the door with the little girl tight in his arms.

"Look," he said quietly, pausing by the ragged screen and looking at Clara's filthy littered kitchen, "it was a generous thing for you to take this little girl when her mother died. Is there anything we can do to...to help you now? A friend of mine lives just down the street, and we could help if you'd let us."

The woman glared at him sullenly, her face blank and vicious. Brad hesitated a moment longer, then shrugged in defeat and carried the child out into the welcome freshness of the cool November afternoon.

AN HOUR LATER, Tony marched at his heels into a department store, shoulders back, arms swinging jauntily at her sides.

Brad marveled at her resilience. Safely away from Clara's threatening presence, Tony had completely recovered her self-assurance and was now studying her surroundings with lively interest. She seemed not to be concerned in the least that she was in the company of a stranger apparently bent on taking her to some unknown destination.

Of course, Brad thought, she probably didn't look on him as a stranger. It was more likely that she still remembered him as Aaron's "father," a safe neighborhood figure.

Brad watched as she paused and looked with pleasure at a small Christmas tree set up next to a display of perfumes and cosmetics.

"Will it be Christmas pretty soon?" she asked.

"It sure will. This is the last week in November, so Christmas is less than a month away." Brad looked at the child, wondering if she had any concept of weeks and months. "How old are you, Tony?"

She held out a grubby hand with her thumb folded against the palm, examined the fingers for a moment, spread the thumb out as well, then tucked it out of sight again.

"I'm four," she announced finally. "Not five."

Brad had a sudden mental image—so vivid that it caused him intense pain—of Abby sitting in the rocker with Aaron on her knee while they recited numbers together from a big storybook. He tried to picture Clara doing the same thing with Tony, but imagination failed him.

"Where did you learn your numbers, Tony?"

"From *Sesame Street*," she replied cheerfully, still absorbed in her fascinated study of the shining Christmas tree. "And Aaron's number board."

"I see." Brad turned and moved off down the aisle with Tony trotting at his side.

They stopped in the children's section to gaze at the vast and colorful array of miniature shirts, pants, coats and shoes.

"There's so much *stuff*," Tony breathed, echoing Brad's first bewildered impression.

"Well," he said briskly, taking a fleece-lined sweatshirt off a hanger, "we have to start somewhere. Do you like this?"

Tony's eyes widened. "For me?" she whispered, looking up at him in awe.

Brad grinned. "Well, it sure won't fit me. I guess you'll have to wear it. Look, there're pants that match. They look nice and warm, don't they?"

The child put a finger in her mouth and stared at the bright little suit, her composure temporarily shattered. She looked up at Brad again, then finally collected herself with a visible effort and turned away, trying hard to appear casual and offhand.

"I guess it's okay," she said gruffly. "Can I have socks, too?"

Brad chuckled and followed her as she marched, brisk with purpose, among the racks of clothes. They selected a couple of the fleece-lined suits, some jeans and corduroy trousers, several long-sleeved shirts and a winter coat with matching ski pants.

Throwing caution to the winds, Brad also picked out panties, woolly socks, diminutive sneakers and slippers and a package of little undershirts. Finally he paused beside a rack of frilly dresses and gazed down at the child beside him.

"Want one of these, Tony?"

She looked at the dresses, then up at him. "A *dress?*" she asked in disbelief.

"Why not? You're a girl, aren't you?"

"Yes, but I don't wear *dresses.*"

"I just thought..."

Tony's face turned scarlet with anger. She kicked Brad's ankle with her ragged sneaker and began to shout. "I don't *want* a dress! I *hate* dresses! You can't make me wear a stupid dress!"

Brad clutched at her flailing arms and tried to hold her still, feeling foolish and awkward. A salesclerk appeared in the aisle and looked at them with suspicion.

"Sir?" the woman asked. "Is there some kind of problem?"

Tony stopped shouting and turned, still panting with emotion, to look up at the woman in the aisle. She shrank against Brad's leg and put her thumb in her mouth.

Brad could see the thoughts clicking through the woman's well-trained mind. Ragged child, obviously ill-kempt and agitated. Well-dressed man trying to silence her by buying huge amounts of children's supplies. Evidence of recent bruises....

"Look," he began awkwardly, "this isn't what—"

"I think you should come with me and wash your face, little girl," the clerk said, ignoring Brad and holding her hand out to Tony. "You can wait here," she added with a frosty glance in Brad's direction.

She hadn't reckoned on Tony, though, who had forgotten her anger over the dresses and was now screaming even louder. She wrapped herself around Brad's leg in a frenzy of weeping, clinging like a kitten, and wouldn't allow the woman to touch her.

"All right," the clerk muttered grimly. "If she wants that badly to stay with you, there's certainly not much I can do, is there? The checkout's over to your left."

Brad gave the woman a courteous smile and handed her his card. "Really, this isn't what it looks like," he murmured, bending gently to peel a teary, red-faced Tony away from his pant leg.

He carried their mountain of purchases to the checkout, prepared to face yet another hawk-eyed female. He needn't have worried. The cashier was a blank-faced girl in her teens with a huge topknot of frizzy hair and an expression of terminal boredom. She probably wouldn't have noticed, Brad thought, if he'd been wearing a ski mask and carrying a machine gun.

"This here's a coupon for the toy department," she announced tonelessly, handing over a piece of paper along with the receipt. "For a purchase this big you get a ten-dollar credit."

Brad shouldered the packages and led the child among the massed shelves of toys. After much discussion they selected a coloring book and crayons, some building blocks and an assortment of picture books.

"Anything else?" Brad asked.

For the first time, Tony was beginning to look a little overwhelmed by the whole experience. She put her finger in her mouth again and shook her head, setting her dirty hair swinging around her face.

"That's enough," she whispered, so low that Brad had to bend over to make out the words.

She remained subdued until they were in the elevator riding up to his apartment, where she stared with renewed interest at the bank of lit buttons.

"What's this thing? Why do the numbers light up?"

Brad explained the workings of an elevator, amused by her delighted reaction. He wondered if the child had ever been taken anywhere or taught anything at all about the world around her.

Inside his apartment he set the mass of parcels on the floor with considerable relief, then turned to look at Tony, who stood in his tidy living room, gazing around in awe at the soft tweedy furniture, the books and plants and framed watercolors.

"It's just like Aaron's house," she whispered. "It's all nice and clean."

"I like things nice and clean," Brad said cheerfully. "Which reminds me, kiddo, that *you* need a bath."

He hesitated, struck once more by the frightening implausibility of the situation he'd somehow gotten himself into. This child was no relation to him at all, a person to whom he had no valid claim. Worse still, she was a little girl. How could he possibly keep her in his home, bathe her and dress her and look after her physical needs?

But Tony solved one of his most pressing concerns by marching briskly past him in the direction of the bathroom. "I need to go," she told him.

"Can you...can you manage by yourself?" Brad asked hopefully.

Tony gave him another of the scornful glances to which he was becoming accustomed. "'*Course* I can. I can bath and dress myself and everything."

Brad relaxed visibly at this welcome news. "That's good. Tell me when you're done, Tony. I'll come in there to run the bathwater for you," he called as the door closed.

Alone for the moment, he stood helplessly in his comfortable gleaming apartment, unwrapping parcels and thinking rapidly.

There was a second bedroom that he used as a den and workroom, but it had a pullout couch. She could sleep there and keep her things on the bookshelves. His major problem was going to be finding someone to care for her while he was at work, and when he...

Brad paused, shaking his head in disbelief, wondering just what he was doing. He was actually envisioning keeping this child with him on some kind of permanent basis. In a legal sense, he'd kidnapped her. He might even be liable for criminal charges. But taking Tony back to the vicious young woman in that squalid house was unthinkable.

And, he decided, so was turning her over to some faceless official. He knew he had to report the situation to someone in authority and take some kind of legal steps, but how could he—

"I'm ready," Tony announced, standing in the doorway. "Can I have lots of water in the tub?"

Brad turned and followed her into the bathroom, his mind still whirling.

ABBY SMILED across the flickering candlelight as Brad walked through the restaurant, returning to their table. "Any problems?" she asked.

He shook his head and reached for his wineglass. "Nothing at all," he said. "Just a . . . a little business matter I had to check on."

Abby looked at him curiously. Brad seemed different this evening, distracted and worried about something, though he definitely looked more relieved now that he'd finally gone and made his phone call. Still, it certainly wasn't like him to be concerned over business when he was enjoying a night out.

But, then, Abby mused, Brad wasn't like himself at all anymore. Apparently she'd have to get to know him all over again, even though she'd lived with the man for almost a year. She savored a mouthful of strawberry cheesecake, thinking about her interview earlier in the week with Dr. Ashton and his claim that a near-death experience could cause definite and irreversible personality changes.

Part of Abby, the professional scientific researcher, longed to question Brad about his experience. After all, she had this article to write and here was a prime subject for analysis right in front of her. She'd even known him prior to his experience.

But whenever she considered Brad as a source of research material, she felt a deep instinctive recoil. Their relationship had already been complicated enough by past resentments and unanswered questions. She just couldn't bear the thought of talking with him about all this "mumbo jumbo," as she'd described it to Dr. Ashton during those final disastrous moments of their interview.

In fact, Abby's distaste for the entire project was beginning to interfere seriously with the objectivity of her reporting, so much so that she often had a helpless despairing feeling about the assignment. She knew that the magazine expected a cool, professional, well-edited package, hopefully with some fresh twists and insights, but Abby was approaching her topic with gloves and mask, so to speak, as if to avoid personal contamination.

"I had lunch with Mitch the other day," Brad said, interrupting her thoughts. "He's a real nice guy, isn't he? I never really got to know him when you and I were together."

"Mitch?" Abby echoed blankly, forcing herself to concentrate on what Brad was saying. "You had lunch with Mitch?"

Brad nodded. "I ran into him at city hall yesterday morning when I was down there to see about—" He broke off abruptly, looking awkward and evasive. Abby glanced at him curiously, but he tensed his shoulders and continued. "I had to see about some...some business I'm involved in, and he was there checking on the budget for culture and recreation. We went for lunch over in the Parrot Cage."

Abby grinned faintly. "Mitch hates the Parrot Cage. He says it's just too yuppie pretentious for words."

Brad smiled back at her, his eyes crinkling with humor. "I agree with him. I think both of us were hanging out there because we knew you and Joan go there sometimes for lunch. Two middle-aged lovesick guys, just acting like school kids."

Abby's cheeks turned pink under his warm gaze. She stared at her empty plate and scrambled frantically for safer conversational ground. "Mitch?" she asked finally. "Do you really think Mitch feels that way about Joan?"

"Oh, he can't hide it, poor guy. He's deeply, deeply smitten. He thinks this is it."

"My goodness." Abby looked at Brad across the table, her eyes wide and troubled. "I don't think Joannie feels that way about him at all."

Brad nodded grimly. "Mitch knows she doesn't. He says he can't get to first base, and he doesn't know why. He suspects there's another man in her life."

Abby shook her head. "People keep saying that, but it's ridiculous. If Joan had a man in her life, don't you think I'd know about it? We've been best friends for twenty-five years."

"So why doesn't she like Mitch? He seems like a great guy. And he's perfect for Joan, especially now that she's actually starting to break away from Mama. They like the same music, they read the same books, they even share the same independent politics. A marriage made in heaven."

"Marriages may be made in heaven," Abby said with a sad note to her voice. "It's when they have to survive down here on earth that they run into trouble. Are you ready to go, Brad?''

He helped her into her coat and followed her out to the car, keeping a protective hand on her arm as they crossed the street.

Abby shivered at his touch, so warm and firm even through the heavy fabric of her coat. This whole situation was increasingly difficult for her to deal with, especially seeing Brad socially after all they'd been through.

It was strange to be sitting politely across the table from him, discussing municipal politics, when both of them were thinking about nights filled with passion and glistening with stardust. There wasn't a place on Brad Carmichael's body that Abby didn't know, no caresses so intimate they hadn't exchanged and savored them. What's more, she knew what kind of toast he liked for breakfast, how much salt he put on his poached eggs, what kind of socks he wore with jeans and which of his knees hurt when the weather was damp.

But, she thought, glancing up at his profile, this man was still a mystery to her in so many ways. He'd either been through an amazing, life-changing experience or he was telling her the most blatant and colossal lie for his own purposes. And now there was something else he was hiding, something more recent that had to do with his awkward evasive behavior tonight and the phone calls he'd made to some unidentified person.

No, Brad Carmichael couldn't be trusted.

But he was still irresistible, Abby thought in agony, glancing over at him again as they settled themselves in his car. More and more, she longed to forget all her concerns and simply nestle against him, cuddle warmly into him and let their bodies flow together.

They'd always fitted together so perfectly. She could remember the wonder of lying in his arms after lovemaking, touching him with her whole body, melding with him in such a wondrous joining of two separate people that they seemed to fuse and became a single, breathing, loving unit.

Nothing in Abby's life had ever felt more sweetly comfortable than that easy union of bodies. . . .

"What are you thinking?" Brad asked, gliding effortlessly through the busy evening traffic.

Abby's cheeks warmed and she looked out the side window, grateful for the darkness. "I was thinking," she began rashly, startling herself, "that I should get rid of Aaron's toys. I think I'm just going to burn all of them."

His head turned sharply and she found his eyes resting on her in alarm. "*Burn* them? Why would you do that?"

Abby shrugged. "You always said it was morbid to hang on to them. Maybe you're right. Maybe I should just dispose of them altogether, repaint the room, make it into a nice little guest room."

"I think that's probably a good idea," Brad began with an unusual note of caution in his voice. "But why burn the toys, Abby? They're really great toys. Why not just give them away so some other little kid can enjoy them?"

"*No,*" Abby said, her voice sounding sharp and loud in her own ears. She bit her lip and smiled awkwardly. "Sorry, Brad. I know it's really awful of me, but I just can't bear the idea of any other child touching Aaron's things. They were *his* toys. I think that's probably why I've held on to them all this time. When I think of somebody else using them, breaking them, throwing them around... It just...I just couldn't stand it. I want the toys to be gone."

Brad stared ahead at the oncoming traffic. Abby glanced over at him, surprised by his reaction.

"Maybe you should wait a while," he said at last. "No need to rush. See how you feel about it in a few weeks."

Abby nodded slowly, still gazing at him. This was such a different attitude from the one he'd expressed last year before he'd left. At that time Brad had wanted so much to get the toys out of the house that he'd offered to haul them away himself, just so Abby wouldn't have to see them anymore.

Regardless of his motives, she was still relieved to have the decision postponed. She didn't really want to get rid of Aaron's toys. There was always the possibility that he might want to come back and play with them again....

She caught herself before she could pursue this seductive line of thought any further. Abby knew that it was dangerous to think that way, irrational and threatening to her emotional well-being. But every time she recalled the plastic chickens perched on the fence posts or the stuffed lion rocking happily in the little chair, she felt a flood of hope and breathless excitement that almost choked her with its intensity.

"How was the trip to Vancouver?" Brad asked, apparently worried by her silence.

"It was fine," Abby said briefly. "I interviewed Dr. Ashton. The one who—"

"I know who he is," Brad said. "He counseled me in Vancouver after I'd recovered from my accident. I wanted so badly to talk to a professional about the near-death experience, and I had no idea who I could turn to. I saw his name in a medical journal."

Abby nodded without speaking, watching as the blurred images of stores and cars and neon lights flashed past their windows in the darkness.

"Abby," Brad said gently, "do you want to talk with me about it? My experience, I mean. Is there anything you want to know?"

Abby shivered and gripped her handbag tight in her lap. "Oh, I don't think so, Brad," she said, fighting to keep her voice casual. "I think I've got lots of research material. Besides, it's best for a journalist not to get too personal with her subject, you know?"

"Damn it!" he exploded, pounding his hand briefly on the wheel, then turning to her with an apologetic smile. "Sorry, Abby. I wasn't talking about your research article. I was talking about us, and my life, and how much it's changed. Why are you so reluctant to talk about this with me?"

Abby turned away, feeling chilled and defensive. "I just don't believe in it," she said finally. "I truly don't, Brad. Even after all the books and articles I've read, and all the subjects I've interviewed, I honestly don't believe that people go through some magic tunnel when they die and encounter lights and angels. I think death is the end, and all of this is some kind of mass hysteria designed to make a difficult truth more acceptable."

"So you think I'm just lying about what happened to me?"

Abby frowned, choosing her words carefully. "I don't know. You used to lie to me fairly often, Brad, so I can't say there isn't a precedent. But some of the other people I've interviewed don't strike me as liars. They seem very earnest and sincere. I think it's most likely that one of the scientific explanations is accurate. Probably at the moment of clinical death the brain is deprived of oxygen and these hallucinations are the result."

"So why does everyone have the same experience?"

"Because everyone has essentially the same brain-wave patterns. We're all constructed in a similar manner."

Brad parked by Abby's house and turned to look at her. "If you honestly believe death is the end of everything," he asked her quietly, "then what do you think has been going on with Aaron's toys?"

She stared at him, then looked quickly away.

"Haven't you been half believing in ghosts, Abby? Hoping, somewhere in the irrational depths of your soul, that maybe Aaron is still around somewhere? Isn't that really why you resist all this, because you know how irrational your feelings are and you're fighting them as hard as you can?"

"What are you doing?" she asked in despair. "Trying to torture me?"

"No, sweetheart. I'm trying to comfort you."

"It's almost a year," Abby whispered. "Next week it'll be a year since he died. There are Christmas decorations everywhere, and Christmas music playing in all the stores. Brad, sometimes I wonder if I can stand it. He feels so close—'' Her voice broke.

Brad took her gently in his arms and bent to kiss her cheek. He hesitated, and Abby felt a vague stirring of uneasiness. But when he finally spoke his words were so shockingly unexpected that she gaped at him in confusion.

"Abby, I know what was happening with Aaron's toys. I solved the mystery."

"Aaron's toys?" Abby echoed blankly, pulling away from him. "Brad, what on earth are you talking about?"

"His toys haven't been moved around lately, right? Not for the past week or so?"

"No, but . . ."

"That's because I found out what was causing them to move. Abby, relax. Here, let me hold you. You're shivering, darling."

She nodded in a stiff jerky fashion and submitted to his embrace again, hardly aware of his arms around her.

"What . . . what was causing it?"

Brad paused again, obviously choosing his words with care. "Abby," he said finally, "do you remember Tony? The little girl from up the street?"

Abby frowned, her head still spinning crazily. "She was a little girl about Aaron's age? She used to live in that pink house on the corner, but they moved away just recently, I think. The house is up for rent again."

"That's right. And she used to play with Aaron sometimes, remember?"

Abby nodded numbly.

"Well, she never forgot his toys, and her life at home was pretty awful. I'll tell you about that later. Anyway, she started slipping into your house to play with Aaron's toys. She was careful, but sometimes you'd come home and catch her before she had the chance to put things away and tidy up."

"How...how did she get in?" Abby whispered.

"Through the pet flap," Brad said, grinning briefly in the darkness.

"The *pet flap?* Brad, that's just...that's ridiculous."

"You'd think so, wouldn't you? But I saw it with my own eyes, Abby. I came over one day while you were away because I was really worried about the idea of somebody getting into your house. I caught her in the act, and I mean literally. Halfway through the opening."

Abby felt another wave of shock, and a slow-growing, burning outrage that surprised and frightened her.

"She...she actually came into my house and...and played with Aaron's toys while I wasn't home? She touched all his things?"

"Abby," Brad said gently, "she's just a little girl. She's only four years old."

"I don't care! Those are *Aaron's* toys. She had no right to..."

Abby fell silent, biting her lip awkwardly, conscious of Brad's eyes resting on her in the muted light.

"Anyway," she said finally, struggling to get her emotions back under control, "it's over now, right? They've moved away. I know she's just a little girl, Brad, and it's wrong for me to be so possessive about

Aaron's things. But I can't bear to think of another child touching them. I'm glad I won't have to see her. It upsets me so much.''

Brad gave her a strange troubled look, as if he were on the verge of confiding something. Then he got out of the car, walked around to open her door and followed her up the sidewalk.

"Let's not worry about it now, Abby, okay?'' he murmured, his voice husky. "I don't ever want you to be upset again. We wasted so many precious hours fighting when we could have been loving, and now I'll never get them back.''

Abby stood by the door and gazed at him, stunned by the depths of remorse and unhappiness in his voice. For the first time she found herself looking at the situation from his point of view. She thought of his loneliness and obvious regret over his behavior, and the hungry yearning in his eyes whenever he looked at her or talked with her about their shared past.

Whatever else she believed about the man's behavior and his motivations, Abby knew that Brad Carmichael loved her, and she also suspected that for whatever reason, he had undergone some kind of fundamental personality change.

She hesitated at the door, brutally torn by conflicting emotions. Fear and longing, anxiety and terror and raging sexual desire all warred within her mind and body as she and Brad stood with their eyes locked.

"Oh, Brad,'' she whispered finally, moving toward him and wrapping her arms around him, sighing in bliss at the familiar strength and sweetness of his embrace. "Brad, stay with me tonight. I don't want to be alone in this house.''

CHAPTER TEN

BRAD LOCKED THE DOOR carefully and switched on a lamp in the living room. He turned to look at the woman beside him.

"Abby..." he whispered.

She smiled up at him with the touch of shy awkwardness that he'd always found endearing.

"I'll just...I'll just run and change, okay?" she murmured. "I spilled a little coffee on my skirt. It needs to be..." As she spoke she edged toward the door, her dark eyes wide and anxious.

Brad smiled at her, feeling so full of love that he wondered if she could see his heart swelling within him.

"That's my girl," he whispered, his voice husky with tenderness. "In the movies, when women go and slip into something more comfortable, it's a transparent negligee. With Abby, it's going to be jeans and a sweatshirt."

She relaxed somewhat and paused in the doorway to smile back at him. "Brad Carmichael, if I came back here in a transparent negligee you'd die of shock, and you know it."

"Yeah? Try me," he said with a wicked grin.

Abby chuckled and vanished down the hallway. Brad stood quietly for a moment, hardly able to believe the wonder of what was happening to him. He looked around at the cozy little house, at the furniture and bookshelves that he'd made with his own hands and the quiet rooms where he'd felt more at home than anywhere else in his restless wandering life.

All through the long dark months since his accident, Brad's primary desire had been to make his way back to this place. For a hundred lonely nights he'd pictured the bright living room with its woven rugs and hardwood floor, the warm knitted afghans and walls of books, and had ached with helpless yearning for Abby and the life he'd thrown away so carelessly.

And now he was here, inside the house, with the door closed against the frosty winter evening. The woman he adored had invited him in and told him she didn't want to be alone.

Brad frowned, wondering just what had caused Abby to issue that impulsive invitation. Did she really want to resume their relationship, or was she just frightened of the mysterious "presence" that haunted her home?

He grinned briefly, thinking about the little girl trapped in the pet door.

Abruptly his smile faded. He moved across the room to take a few logs from the copper basket and began to lay a fire in the hearth, still thinking about Tony.

The child was staying with Gladys tonight, the first time she'd been away from Brad since he'd removed her from Clara's home. When he'd called from the restaurant, Brad had been assured that Tony was already sound asleep in the guest room after an exhausting evening of play with Gladys's husband, Stan, who was an accomplished grandfather.

"She's so sweet, Brad," Gladys had told him on the telephone. "She's just such a neat, well-behaved little darling, isn't she?"

Brad grinned again, thinking about the feisty independent, bright-eyed waif who had shared his home these past few days. She was certainly neat and well behaved when she wanted to be, but he didn't know if he'd actually describe Tony as "sweet." Obviously the child had been on her very best behavior for Gladys and her husband.

He wadded some newspaper and tucked it between the rough cedar logs, then lit a match and held it to the curled edge of the paper, frowning again as he thought about Tony and the awkward situation the child's unexpected presence had created in his life.

Brad had spent the past few days at home, working on a set of blueprints at the drafting table in his spare room and running his business by telephone, while Tony played and bustled cheerfully around the apartment. But he couldn't keep doing that indefinitely, a fact that Gladys had strongly reinforced when he'd confided the whole situation to his secretary. Brad agreed that he had to formalize things somehow, decide where Tony was going to live and how she was going to be cared for on a daily basis.

The child-welfare authorities, whom he'd visited the day after stealing Tony from her "guardian," had not been particularly helpful. They'd interviewed Tony, examined her bruises and tried to get in touch with Clara, who had apparently disappeared. Attempts were then made to remove the child from Brad and place her in temporary foster care, but Tony had re-acted to this suggestion with such unaccustomed and convincing hysteria that even the world-weary social workers were concerned.

"Maybe we'll leave her with you just for a little while," they'd told Brad with obvious reluctance. *"Fill out these forms and submit them immediately. The last three documents need to be completed in triplicate, with extra copies to the authorities listed on the back, and the yellow one is..."*

He'd done the paperwork, and he was learning quickly how to care for a bright energetic four-year-old. In just a few days, with some proper care, a hair-cut, regular baths and healthy meals, Tony had bloomed noticeably. Her cheeks were growing round and plump, the angry bruises were fading from her body and her huge blue eyes sparkled with happiness.

When Brad thought about the little girl he felt an-other surge of protective love, somewhat different in nature but almost as overwhelming as his feelings for Abby.

Since his accident Brad had truly come to under-stand the profound importance of love. He knew now that nothing else really mattered in human existence except loving those around him. And since that night, even his soul seemed to have expanded, turned aside from its selfish preoccupation and learned to em-brace others with deep, surging tenderness.

He watched the small blue flames licking at the wood and thought about Abby, about her wide dark eyes and slim graceful body, about the love they'd shared and the suffering she'd endured over this past year. More than anything, Brad yearned to tell her about the ragged little girl he'd found in this house, about the child's wretched past and the bleak prospects for her future. He wanted to throw himself and Tony on Abby's mercy and let her decide what should happen next. But some form of instinctive caution was holding him back.

Brad adjusted the screen carefully across the glowing fire and arranged a cozy nest of cushions and blankets on the rug in front of the fireplace, then moved over to the stereo to select some music. As he leafed through the disks he remembered Abby's abrupt decision to get rid of Aaron's toys and her insistence that she couldn't bear the thought of another child playing with them.

He decided finally that tonight was their night, his and Abby's. Tomorrow would be time enough to discuss Tony and her future.

Abby came back into the room at that moment, wearing navy jogging pants and a baggy red plaid shirt, driving all the worried thoughts from his mind as she smiled at him and moved over to look into the fire.

Brad gazed at her hungrily, longing to take her and crush her in his arms, to wrap her in warm folds of love and never let her go.

"Hey, that's my shirt," he said, fighting to keep his voice calm and steady.

"I know. You left it behind. I've always liked to wear it, because it made you feel closer somehow, I guess."

"Oh, Abby..."

She turned to him and Brad gathered her into his arms, unable to contain his feelings any longer. He kissed her forehead, her shining dark hair and dainty earlobes, her eyelids and cheeks and lips.

"Darling," he murmured with his mouth on hers. "My sweet darling, I've dreamed about this so many times...."

She clung to him while he opened the top button on the shirt and bent to kiss the hollow of her throat, thrilling to the sweet remembered fragrance of her, the texture of her skin, the lissome slenderness of her body in his arms.

"Is it all right, Abby?" he whispered, reaching under the billowing shirt to cup her breast gently in his hand. "Is this what you want?"

She shivered at his touch and drew closer to him, her head lowered so he could only see the curve of her cheek and her shining hair.

"Brad...I don't know what I want. I've missed you so much, but I'm still scared that you'll..."

"Don't be scared of me, Abby. Please don't be scared. I know how I treated you before, but I'm a different man now."

Abby turned in his arms and gazed up at him with searching eyes. "How can I be sure of that, Brad? And how can I bear the pain if you hurt me again?"

Brad met her eyes, momentarily at a loss for words. He remembered the night of the accident when the events of his life had flashed before his mind in lightning sequence, all the selfish unkind things he'd done in his restless pursuit of happiness and fulfillment. A lot of those memories had involved Abby, who was the only woman he'd ever truly loved.

Still, his love for her had never stopped him from lying to her, disappointing and letting her down on countless occasions. And, ultimately, abandoning her when she'd needed him most.

"I don't know, Abby," he told her honestly. "I don't know how to make you understand the way my life has changed. I guess all you can do is give me a chance and let me prove it to you. Are you willing to take that chance?"

She met his eyes in silence for a long breathless moment, an eternity of waiting. Then, almost imperceptibly, she nodded and reached out toward the buttons on his shirt.

Brad laughed softly with joy, switched off the lamp and drew her down onto the nest of pillows and blankets in front of the hearth. Moving in silence, gazing intently into each other's eyes, they unfastened their clothes and slid them over bare shoulders that glimmered orange and blue in the wintry darkness.

Brad stood, unzipped his trousers and tossed them aside, then pulled Abby up beside him, loosening the tie on her jogging pants and letting them slip to the floor. He fondled the soft fabric covering her hips, luxuriating as he did so in the feeling of her firm rounded body, her narrow waist and long graceful thighs.

"My Abby still wears sensible underclothes," he whispered against her cheek, smiling down at her white cotton panties.

"Abby's always been a sensible girl," she whispered back, running a delicate finger around the waistband of his shorts. "Until now," she added ruefully, noting how his body was beginning to react to her caress. "Oh, Brad . . . what am I *doing?*"

"You're having a good time," he murmured, drawing her down beside him on the blankets, "with a very good friend. Quit asking so many questions, because I don't have all the answers."

"I hope you have some of them," Abby said in a soft voice as his big hands gripped the elastic of her panties once more and gently peeled them away. "Because I really need some answers, Brad."

He stripped off his shorts and stood in front of her again, shamelessly naked and erect, his fine male arrogance beautiful in the firelight. "Look at me," he whispered with a teasing grin. "This is the answer to everything, darling."

Abby lay gazing up at him in awe, clearly almost overcome by the sight of him. But she was still sufficiently self-possessed to shake her head. "Brad, that's not usually the answer to anything. It's more often the cause of the problem."

Brad chuckled and swooped down upon her, gathering her in his arms and rocking her fiercely. "Quit all this negative talk, you beautiful woman. I'm about to make you the happiest girl in the world, and you're being a pessimist."

Abby laughed in his arms and glanced up at him with a sparkling grin. "To tell the truth," she whispered, "I'm *very* optimistic about what's going to happen next."

"Yeah? Why?"

"Because I remember how it used to feel."

"This? You remember how *this* used to feel?"

"Oh, God, yes. Oh, Brad, don't ever stop...."

He held her and whispered to her, broken words of love and desire as he caressed her yielding body with long, slow, gentle strokes, remembering just what kind of touch had always pleased her. But for Brad, there was more to it this time, much more than simply being a successful lover.

This was the first time he'd made love since his life-changing experience. Like so many other things in his life, the act of sex seemed profoundly different to him now. He found that his own pleasure, though powerfully intense, was secondary to Abby's needs. The love that surged within him required an outlet, and the only way to express that love was to make Abby understand, with his mouth and hands and body, just how deeply and tenderly he cherished her, how much he adored her.

By the time she was ready for him and they moved together, the union felt like a sacrament to him, a loving commitment so rich and transcendently lovely, so wondrously satisfying, that his soul was lost in beauty. He felt Abby's body moving beneath him, straining and soaring toward her release, and he held her close, treasuring her, adoring her with every fiber of his being, until they disappeared into the sun together and fell back gasping with joy.

For a long time they lay wrapped in silence while the firelight glowed and flickered softly on their entwined naked bodies. Brad was the first to move, easing away so she wouldn't have to bear the full weight of his spent body on hers. She moaned softly and pulled him back into her arms, clearly reluctant to let him go.

"All right, darling?" Brad murmured, lifting a tumbled strand of her dark hair and whispering into her ear.

"Just wonderful," Abby breathed, lost in some faraway place of her own. "Just wonderful. Oh, Brad, I've missed you so much...."

He withdrew his body from hers gently and turned to gather her into his arms, pulling a soft blanket up over her bare shoulders.

"Brad..." Abby frowned and stretched drowsily against him, her face pink with contentment.

"Mmm?"

"I've thought about this a million times while you were gone. I lay in bed missing you and aching for you, remembering how it used to feel. But tonight it was...this was different."

He glanced at her in concern. "How? Are you disappointed?"

"Oh, no! It was wonderful. You were so...sweet. And so intense somehow. I don't remember you being like that."

"I just love you so much, Abby. I've never loved anyone else the way I love you, and I never will. And my...my experience taught me about the overwhelming importance of love. Sometimes," Brad told her earnestly, "I just want to go around like some prophet in a three-piece suit, telling everybody that nothing matters except love."

Abby glanced up at him quickly and he grinned. "Don't worry, darling. I'll still keep being an architect, and confine my preaching to my immediate household."

She frowned and rolled her head on the pillow, clearly uncomfortable with the topic. "Do you like it?" she asked finally. "Being an architect, I mean."

"Yeah, I do. I've always enjoyed the tidiness and the special challenge of it, you know, designing the perfect space and then trying to make it cost efficient and functional."

"So why did you quit? During all that time we were together, why were you pretending to be a construction worker?"

Brad shrugged and drew her into his arms again, toying idly with a strand of her hair as he gazed at the fire.

"It was both an escape and a quest, I guess. You see, all through my life..." He shifted in the nest of blankets, leaning up on one elbow so he could look down at her earnestly. "All my life, whenever I made a decision and accepted a job somewhere, I'd immediately start to feel trapped. I'd think about all the other things I might have chosen and I'd start getting crazy, thinking I was missing out on life. After a few years, I just dumped the profession altogether and headed out with a pickup truck to work at a succession of blue-collar jobs and have some life experiences."

Abby frowned thoughtfully. "Were you the same way with relationships, Brad? Did you start to feel hemmed in and trapped as soon as a relationship got serious?"

He nodded. "All the time. I just hated the feeling of being tied down and without options. Until I met you," he added. "Right from the beginning, I loved you so much that I was content to stay with you, because I honestly didn't believe the world could hold anything better for me."

"Then why did you leave?"

Brad frowned and gazed into the fire again, his sculpted lips and cheeks burnished with the ruddy glow of the flames.

"It was because of Aaron. Death had come that close to me once before, Abby. I couldn't bear your grief, and I was terrified by the need to confront my own mortality again. I just panicked, thinking that someday I was going to die and I'd never even had the chance to live. I was overwhelmed by this terrible restlessness, the worst it had ever been, and so ashamed of myself for giving in to my weakness because I knew how badly I was letting you down. Finally I just sneaked off like a coward, knowing that if I stayed any longer I'd go off the rails and cause terrible pain to both of us."

"So you ran away," Abby said calmly, "and left me with the pain."

"Please forgive me, Abby," he murmured, gathering her into his arms and burying his face in her hair. "I'm so sorry."

"I'm sorry, too, Brad," she whispered, drawing away and looking at him earnestly. "That's really not fair of me. I know I'm not the only one who suffered. You loved Aaron, too, and you loved me. It must have hurt a lot to leave. I just…I missed you both so much. I was so terribly alone."

"Well, you won't be alone anymore unless you choose to be, darling. I promise."

Her face suddenly took on a guardedly cautious look. "I'm not ready for any kind of commitment, Brad," she warned him. "I enjoy spending time with you, but I don't want you moving in again or anything."

"I know. You can take your time over decisions like that, Abby. I'm prepared to wait a lifetime for you to invite me back into your life."

"We were so happy together, the three of us," she said in a dreamy faraway voice. "Then suddenly Aaron was gone and it was just the two of us. And then you disappeared, too, and I was all alone, more alone than I'd ever been in my life. It's going to take me a while to get over that, Brad. I have to learn to share my life again, even with you."

"I know," he repeated, relieved that he'd followed his earlier instincts and not mentioned Tony's presence in his life. Still, listening to Abby's halting explanations about her feelings, Brad was beginning to feel increasingly uncertain over the matter of Tony's future.

"Anything wrong?" Abby asked, leaning up on one elbow and looking at his worried face.

"Not a thing. I was just trying to make a tough decision."

"What's that?"

"Whether to make love again or make a big bowl of popcorn."

Abby chuckled. "Why not do both?"

"What a completely intemperate woman."

"In that order," Abby added firmly. "Lovemaking, then popcorn," she explained, bringing a startled grin to Brad's face as she reached for him again.

JOAN WEARILY ARCHED her back in the padded secretarial chair and ran a distracted hand through her hair.

"Maybe it's been misfiled," she said to her employer.

Lenny Wolzer looked up at her and grinned, the fluorescent lights overhead gleaming warmly on his bald head and the lenses of his glasses.

"Remember that little girl—what was her name?—Lisa? The one who kept recipes in the filing cabinet? Remember how she kept filing 'claims' under 'clams'?"

Joan smiled back at him, then bent forward to peer at the files again.

Lenny leaned back with his arms behind his head, ample paunch straining at the waistband of his bright checked slacks. "Or the time she filed every boat we covered under the 'floater policy' section. Remember that, Joannie?"

Joan sighed. "That was a mess, all right. Took me months to straighten it out." She glanced up with a sudden sparkle in her blue eyes. "You know what was Lisa's funniest stunt, though? I never told a soul about this, Lenny."

"Yeah?" the plump little insurance man let his chair drop forward and looked at his secretary with interest. "What's the scoop, Joannie? Why are you getting all red in the face?"

Joan chuckled. "It's just so... Lenny, about three months after Lisa quit working here, I found a pamphlet on bust enlargement that she'd left behind. Guess where she filed it?"

Lenny grinned expectantly, waiting.

"Endowment policies!" Joan said, and they both roared with laughter.

"Well, this place sounds indecently happy," Abby said, coming in through the corrugated glass door and smiling at them. "Lenny, shouldn't you be out there protecting people from disaster?"

"Can't an employer have a pleasant discussion with his secretary about breast enhancement?" Lenny inquired with dignity.

Abby grinned. "Breast enhancement? Which of you is considering it?"

"Insults and abuse, that's all I get," Lenny muttered sadly, hoisting himself out of the chair and reaching for his shiny topcoat. "You're a hard-bitten newspaperwoman, Abby Malone."

"No, I'm not. I'm a gentle, absentminded writer. How's your dog, Lenny?"

"She's pregnant, that's how she is."

"Oh, my."

"Yeah. Oh, my—that's what I said, too. Eighty bucks to have her fixed and a month later she's pregnant. I should sue. Joannie, how much insurance does my vet carry?"

"Come on, Lenny," Abby said, smiling at the little man. "Your kids will love the puppies. Cute furry Saint Bernards bouncing all over the house. Won't they be just too sweet for words?"

Lenny glared furiously, but his eyes sparkled behind his thick glasses. In fact, Joan suspected that Lenny was more excited about the future puppies than his children were, and would probably suffer terribly when he had to sell them.

"Well, I'm off," he announced. "I'm having a health lunch."

"What kind?" Abby asked.

"A sandwich with alfalfa sprouts and carrot curls. No fat, no cholesterol, no calories and no flavor. Guaranteed."

"Then he has a chocolate fudge sundae with whipped cream and cashews," Joan said with a reproving glance at her employer.

He shrugged defensively. "A man's gotta keep his strength up. Hey, dieting is a strenuous business. If you don't keep your strength up, how you gonna make it all the way to the end of the damn diet? I ain't no *quitter,* you know."

Abby and Joan smiled at each other as the little man bustled out, his coattails streaming behind him.

Suddenly Joan leaned forward and looked more closely at her friend. "Abby!" she breathed. "Just *look* at you."

Abby reached a nervous hand to her face. "What about me? Do I have lipstick on my teeth or something?"

"You're gorgeous. Positively glowing. What's happened to you?"

Abby shifted nervously, avoiding her friend's gaze for a moment, then turning to her with sparkling dark eyes. "I was... Brad and I went out for dinner last night and then we..."

"Abby!" Joan gazed at her friend, not knowing whether to congratulate Abby or to warn her sternly about the possible consequences.

Abby helped by moving closer and placing a gentle hand on her shoulder. "I know what you're thinking, Joannie. I know you don't trust him, and I'm still not sure if I do, either. I'm going to be very, very careful this time. But, oh, Joanie, it was just so wonderful last night...."

Joan gazed up at Abby's glowing face and felt a sudden deep wistfulness. Would it matter if things between Brad and Abby didn't work out? At least Abby was getting to experience this kind of sweet fulfillment. Even one day of perfect love, Joan thought with unusual bitterness, would be worth a whole lifetime of loneliness....

"Joan?" Abby asked in quick concern, seeing the bleak expression on her friend's face. "Is there anything wrong?"

"I'm fine. Just really busy, Abby. I don't think I'll have time to go for lunch today."

"Oh, that's too bad. I really wanted to talk." Abby chuckled. "Actually, I just wanted to bore you by talking for an hour about Brad and how wonderful he is. It can wait for another day."

"If he's still wonderful by then," Joan said dryly, softening her words with a smile as she stood up and reached for her coat.

"Where are you going? I thought you were planning to work through the lunch hour."

Joan hesitated, shifting uncomfortably under her friend's curious glance. "I have to... to run some errands. I need to pick up filing labels and some dealer estimates from the auto-body shop. I'll just grab something later to eat at my desk. See you, Abby. Call me tonight, okay?"

Joan ran down the hall toward the elevators, conscious of Abby's eyes on her back.

Out on the street, she paused to look around, then hurried off toward the corner, turning her coat collar

up and plunging her hands deep in her pockets against
the winter chill. A skiff of snow had fallen overnight
and was melting slowly in the pale noonday sun.

Before she'd even reached the next street, Joan
somehow knew what she was going to see. With a
sickening feeling of despair, she stood and gazed at the
empty curb where the angel had sat every morning to
play his sweet music.

There was no sign of him. Bits of paper and dried
leaves skittered past on a bleak winter wind, swirling
down into the gutters where the dirty slush melted in
trickles around the storm drains.

For a long time Joan stood looking at the deserted
street, her mind conjuring up images of his wondrous
gentle smile, his tranquil air of tolerance and understanding, the perfect contentment in his tall spare body
as he lounged on the curb. Even more vividly, Joan
remembered the feelings in her heart when he'd looked
at her with those eyes of pure transcendent wisdom,
when he'd spoken to her about her life and the things
she needed to do.

She felt sick and empty with loss, almost dizzy as
she stared at the empty curb.

"I'm not ready," she whispered. "I'm not ready for
you to go away. Please, please don't go away. I need
to talk to you about so many things...."

But she needed more than to talk. Despising herself, scornful of her weakness, Joan nevertheless realized that she was in love with the mysterious
stranger. She ached for him in a physical sense. She
wanted to feel his arms around her and his gentle
mouth on hers, and she wanted to look the way Abby

had looked today, glowing and rich with fulfilled womanhood.

But he was gone. As loudly as a proclamation, the dreadful emptiness of the curb told her what had happened. He'd moved on, drifted away to a warmer climate or to some realm even more far removed, and Joan would never see him again.

She just couldn't accept it.

I'll go back to the park tonight, she thought feverishly. *I'll come by here every day and I'll keep going to the park every night until he comes to see me. He'll know that I'm doing it. He always knows everything I do. I'll force him to come back and talk to me, and when he does I'll tell him—*

"Joan? Is something the matter?"

Joan turned, badly startled, her eyes wide and frightened. "Mitch!" she exclaimed, sagging with relief when she recognized the cheerful young journalist. "You scared me."

"Sorry. I was coming over from the stationer's and I saw you standing here. You look a little... distressed, Joan. Is something wrong?"

Joan's face flamed and she shifted nervously under his calm inquiring gaze. "Nothing at all, Mitch," she said lightly. "It's the pressure, you know."

"What pressure?" he asked, falling in step beside her.

Joan found herself grateful for his presence and instinctively drew closer to his comfortable bulk. "Oh," she said in answer to his question, "just the usual. Jobs, deadlines, annoying people who don't send things out on time, that sort of thing."

"The story of my life," Mitch agreed dryly. "Hey, how'd you like to go out for a really decadent three-martini lunch and forget the whole thing?"

Joan hesitated, looking up at his pleasant face and warm intelligent eyes.

"Two pink ladies? Okay, one fast cappuccino, and that's my final offer," Mitch went on, trying bravely to bring a smile to her troubled face.

"I'm sorry, Mitch," Joan said, anxious to get away from him before she buried her face in his warm woolen lapel and burst into tears. "I already turned Abby down for lunch. I have so many errands to do."

"Then how about dinner?" Mitch asked comfortably. "Dinner's more fun, anyway. Let's dress up and do the town, get rid of all the winter blahs. We can take in a show, have a nice dinner, go dancing.... Come on, Joan. Let's have some fun together."

Joan gazed at him wistfully, picturing the evening he was offering, a prospect that was hers to enjoy if she just said yes. A few months ago, such an evening would have been no more than a wonderful impossibility for Joan Holland. Now, she thought with grim irony, she'd achieved her independence, freed herself at last from her mother's iron-forged emotional bonds, but the freedom was useless to her.

There was only one man she wanted to be with, and he had vanished from her life like a cold autumn wind. Joan Holland didn't want to dine and dance. She wanted to go rushing out into the darkness and search for her angel.

"I'm sorry, Mitch," she murmured finally. "I really don't think so."

His face barely flickered, and his smile remained calm and polite. But Joan saw the disappointment in his eyes and knew that Mitch Flanagan would not ask her out again.

He nodded politely and strode off down the street, the wind whipping his heavy topcoat around his legs. Joan watched him go, feeling as if everything wonderful and warm in her life were being torn from her, piece by piece, until she'd be left with nothing but a handful of ice and faded leaves.

CHAPTER ELEVEN

BRAD PUSHED his glasses back on his forehead and rubbed his eyes briefly, then cocked his head in the direction of the kitchen, where an ominous silence had fallen.

"Tony?" he called. "What are you doing?"

The silence lengthened.

"Tony?" Brad's face creased with concern. "I asked what you're doing out there."

"Nothing," she called.

"You can't just be sitting and doing nothing. What's happening?"

"It's a s'prise."

Brad's concern deepened. Like anyone who lived with a four-year-old, he was rapidly growing wary of surprises.

"What kind of surprise?"

"If I *tell* you," Tony said, clearly impatient with his stupidity, "it won't be a s'prise."

Brad grinned. "Yeah. Actually, that's the general idea."

He took his glasses off, straightened the pile of papers on his desk and started to get up. Tony appeared in the doorway at that moment, her round face bright with anticipation, her hands hidden behind her back.

"S'prise!" she shouted, extending her hands in triumph. Brad looked dubiously at the offering in front of him. A couple of frozen waffles rested on a plate, imperfectly heated and swimming liberally in butter and syrup. Beside the waffles was a dollop of cottage cheese, along with a fork, a rather wizened carrot and a massive dill pickle, still dripping with juice.

"I made lunch," Tony announced with beaming pride.

"Tony, that's so nice of you, but I . . ."

"Eat it," the child ordered, seating herself on the edge of the couch and folding her hands expectantly in her lap.

Brad looked at the little girl helplessly. Not only was he not hungry, he really disliked frozen waffles. This box had been purchased expressly for Tony, who considered them one of the world's ideal foods and ate them whenever she was allowed.

He wavered, trying to decide what to do. The book on child care he'd purchased—and read several times from cover to cover—instructed that you should never, ever lie to children. You were supposed to be sincere at all times about your feelings, as well as theirs. But, like almost every other rule in the book, Brad had already broken this one a number of times in the ten days that Tony had been living with him.

What's more, he suspected that every other parent in the world broke the rules, too. How could you be completely honest when a child was sitting there watching you in breathless excitement, eyes sparkling, small body tense with anxiety, waiting for your reaction?

"This looks delicious, Tony," he said weakly, setting the plate on his desk. He picked up the fork and realized too late that the handle was covered with syrup. "Really delicious." Brad forced himself to swallow a hearty mouthful of partially thawed waffle, then looked at the pickle with deep reluctance.

By now he was sufficiently familiar with Tony's personality to understand that he would be required to eat every bite on his plate. This small child's determination and persistence were truly formidable.

Brad took a bite of the pickle, then a swallow of syrupy cottage cheese, wondering if he was causing the little girl some kind of permanent psychological damage by giving in to her all the time. He knew that he shouldn't allow himself to be pushed around and manipulated like this. But Tony was so passionate about everything she did, so intensely concentrated on the small perimeters of her life.

Besides, he thought with a feeble grin, she was just so damn cute.

Tony sat on the couch watching him, wearing a stiff new pair of blue jeans and a bright red sweatshirt with a cartoon dog on the front. Her chin was resting on folded hands and her blue eyes regarded him steadily beneath a shiny fringe of freshly trimmed brown hair.

"Eat the pickle," she ordered when she saw him faltering. "I picked the very biggest one out of the bottle."

Brad made a tenuous effort to regain authority. "Tony, I really don't think you should be using the toaster when I'm not in the room with you."

"I didn't stick the knife in. I remembered what you told me. If you stick the knife in, 'lectricity comes up the handle and kills you. Zap! Just like that," Tony said with relish, slapping her small hands together.

"That's true. It's very dangerous. Lots of children have been badly hurt by electricity from toasters."

"Sometimes," Tony told him cheerfully, swinging her small sneakered feet, "Clara used to stay away for a long time and I looked after myself and made toast and everything."

"How long?" Brad asked, girding himself to attack the soggy waffles again.

Tony shrugged and looked with interest at the control knob on the tilted drafting table. "This makes it go up and down, right?"

"Don't touch the knob, Tony."

The child looked at him and continued to turn the control knob, her face defiant.

"Don't," Brad said quietly.

Tony ignored him. "I can make it go way up," she said, tilting the table. A set of blueprints began to move down the sloping surface.

Brad sighed, knowing what Tony was doing. The book said that children who escaped from abusive situations had a tendency to push the limits for a long time, testing their new environment to ensure that there wouldn't be violence, no matter how they behaved. But even though he understood the negative behavior, Brad found it tiring and deeply upsetting.

A year earlier, he thought with a weary grin, back in the days when he was a different man, there probably would have been some violence over a few of Tony's stunts.

Now he just crossed the room, picked Tony up and hugged her firmly, then reset the control knob without saying anything about her behavior and carried her back to sit on his lap.

"How long did Clara stay away, Tony? Did she ever leave you alone overnight?"

The child's calm blue gaze shifted up to him in mild surprise. "Lots of times."

Brad nodded, trying not to show his anger.

Over the past few days he'd learned quite a lot about Clara. The people at the child-welfare agency admitted that they'd been taken in by the young woman, who had appeared neat and presentable in their office when she'd applied for guardianship of Tony and had been granted the extra funds that went along with that responsibility.

Even during the infrequent home visitations, Clara's house had been reasonably tidy and her demeanor had not caused the social workers to be suspicious, although Brad learned that she'd always had warning of the visits.

"It seems monstrous," he'd said angrily to the director of the agency. *"How can someone just take a child, abuse and neglect her like this and get away with it?"*

"Mr. Carmichael," the woman had responded wearily, *"can you imagine what our caseload is like? At our level of funding and staffing, if every single one of us worked twenty-four hours a day, we couldn't give adequate coverage to the people in our care. The best we can do is scratch the surface."*

Gloomily, Brad balanced the child on his knee and continued to eat his unappetizing plateful of food, thinking that Tony was probably right. At her young age she'd already had so much experience in looking after herself that the normal rules for four-year-olds hardly applied to her.

Still, he knew that she needed to be managed with a firmer hand than his, made to recognize and obey limitations on her behavior. But how could he do that without resorting to the same kind of heavy-handed methods that Clara had used?

Brad remembered how skillfully Abby had handled Aaron, controlling the high-spirited little boy with humor and loving intelligence. It seemed to have been almost instinctive with Abby, when to give in and when to take a stand and hold fast to her position.

For the hundredth time, he wished that he could confide in Abby, tell her all about Tony and ask for her help.

But he was afraid.

There was some strange kind of tension in Abby whenever she talked about Aaron, particularly when Brad told her how he'd solved the mystery of the moving toys. Brad recognized an undercurrent there, something deeply troubling that was beyond his understanding.

He wanted to tell Abby that he had a permanent houseguest, introduce her to Tony and laugh about the whole thing. But he was afraid that Abby wouldn't laugh.

He thought about the woman he loved, about her slender body in his arms and the glow of her dark eyes gazing into his, and felt a surge of love and sexual desire that frightened him with its intensity.

Abby, he thought. *Abby, darling, I want you so much. I want you right now—*

"Eat your pickle," Tony repeated sternly, seeing his attention wandering once more. "*And* the carrot."

Brad lifted the dripping pickle obediently to his mouth, looking at Tony with sudden thoughtfulness.

"Tony..."

"What?"

"You used to play with Aaron at his house. Do you remember Aaron's mommy?"

"She's pretty," Tony said, reaching out a small sticky hand to touch the jar holding Brad's collection of drafting pencils. "She still talks to Aaron."

Brad looked at the child in surprise. "Don't touch the pencils, Tony," he said automatically. "What do you mean, she talks to Aaron?"

Tony frowned, still looking at the pencils, but she didn't touch them. "Once she came home when I was playing in Aaron's room and I didn't hear until she was way inside the house. I had to hide behind the door until she went away."

Brad felt a sudden chill. "Yes?" he prompted. "What happened, Tony?"

"She came into the bedroom and sat on the bed for a long time. She hugged the lion and talked to Aaron like he was there, but he wasn't."

"What did she say?"

Tony shrugged. "Just some stuff. She was crying. She said she loved him and he could come back and play anytime he liked. Stuff like that."

Brad nodded, then finished his meal in brooding silence. Tony kept a watchful eye on him until the last unappetizing mouthful had vanished, then gathered up the plate and fork and bustled off to the kitchen.

"Don't start the dishwasher unless I'm there!" Brad called after her, feeling more helpless than ever.

He listened to the distant clatter for a moment, then got up and went across the hall to wash his sticky hands before coming back to the office and returning to his papers.

On Brad's desk was a scanty dossier on Tony, all that the child-welfare agency had been able to supply him. He had copies of her birth certificate, the report of the social worker assigned to the case after Tony's mother had died and a few test results.

Tony's mother had been unmarried and nineteen years old when Tony was born. Her name was Shelley Bradley, and she apparently had no relatives who could be contacted to care for her child when Shelley had died of a drug overdose at the age of twenty-two. Only Clara Wahl, a casual friend of Shelley's, had come forward to offer shelter to the little girl. Still, the records indicated that Shelley, in spite of her personal problems and her life-style, had done her best to raise her little girl. At the time of initial contact, Tony was reported to be a cheerful, healthy child of three years, with above-average verbal skills and comprehension.

"Observation indicates that the child has apparently been played with and read to a great deal," the report stated. "She is familiar with several advanced concepts, including numbers, colors, and other cognitive skills. Her intelligence quotient is significantly above the normal range."

Brad's throat tightened and ached with sympathy when he thought of the poor dead woman, barely more than a child herself, reading stories and playing with her little girl.

And when Shelley had died, Tony had gone to live with Clara, abruptly transplanted into a brutal life of abuse and neglect that she was too young to understand. A year later she had few memories of her mother beyond a wistful vision of someone cuddling her, of a bedtime song and some books that she'd loved.

Reading this bleak history, Brad was amazed once more by the child's resilience. Tony seemed to have emerged relatively unscathed from the trials of her formative years, and maintained a cheerful, inquisitive attitude toward life in general. Occasionally, though, she was haunted by nightmares that would wake her in screaming terror and bring Brad hurrying into the room to hold her and comfort her until she drifted off to sleep again.

More than anything else, these disturbing nighttime incidents strengthened his resolve to keep Tony with him and do his very best to keep anything frightening from entering her world, ever again. But the whole situation was just so complex....

Wearily Brad swept the papers together into a file folder, locked them in his briefcase and went to look for Tony.

He found her in the living room, switching television channels.

"There's no cartoons on," she announced. "Just people talking."

"Well, we have to go out for a while, anyhow. Get your coat, Tony."

Tony brightened. "Will we see Gladys?"

"Yes, we will. We'll stop at the office on our way downtown."

"I drew her some pictures!" Tony shouted, running into the hallway leading to her room. "I'll get them right away!"

"Go to the bathroom first," Brad called after her vanishing form. "And wash your hands."

He shrugged into his leather jacket, picked up his briefcase again and waited by the door until Tony reappeared, racing down the hall with her jacket trailing from one arm and a sheaf of papers clutched in her hands.

Brad knelt to put the small coat on properly. He zipped it up to Tony's chin and put her hood in place while she stood patiently, arms spread wide as she waited.

"Can I work on the jigsaw puzzle at your office?"

"Not the big one," Brad said absently, struggling with the fastener on her parka. "It's too hard for you. There're a couple of smaller ones there that I bought for you, remember?"

Tony nodded. "I like the one with the bears on it. They're chasing a butterfly."

Still kneeling with his hands on the little fur-trimmed hood, Brad looked deep into those solemn blue eyes, then leaned forward impulsively to hug Tony and kiss her cheek.

She giggled in delight, then sobered. "I love you," she told him.

Brad smiled at her, his eyes suddenly moist. Despite her enormous energy, Tony was not a demonstrative child. This was the first time she'd ever spoken those words to him.

"I love you too, Tony," he whispered huskily, getting to his feet. "Let's go before Gladys leaves for lunch, okay?"

The child trotted down the hall in front of him and entered the elevator. By now Tony was familiar with all the workings of this fascinating device and refused to allow Brad to push any of the buttons. In the basement she bustled ahead of him to the car, then waited while he unlocked the door and lifted her into the new car seat.

"What pictures did you draw for Gladys?" Brad asked, squinting in the winter sunlight as he pulled out onto the street.

"Some cows," Tony said, looking with deep satisfaction at a page full of brown blobs and green smudges. "Eating grass."

"That's nice," Brad said. "She'll probably hang them on the wall with the other ones."

"I know. They're really, really good," Tony said placidly.

Brad grinned as he drove, thinking that despite her troubled background, Tony's self-confidence appeared not to have suffered in any significant way.

They chatted as they traveled, a conversation made up largely of questions from Tony and answers from him. Brad was getting more competent with this kind of interrogation, though some of her questions still defeated him.

"Why don't worms have faces?" Tony asked, peering thoughtfully at the passing cars.

Brad shifted gears and frowned at a truck edging toward the intersection. "Because they aren't people," he said.

"Cows aren't people, but they have faces."

"They're more like people than worms are."

To his surprise, Tony seemed willing to accept this feeble argument. She turned to him, her blue eyes wide and curious. "Why don't *shadows* have faces?"

Brad groaned in despair and parked next to his office building, deeply grateful for the distraction.

"Gladys!" Tony shouted, racing in front of him into the reception area. "Look at the picture I drew. It's cows!"

Gladys smiled at Brad and took the little girl onto her knee, cuddling Tony in a cozy embrace. "Cows, did you say? Well, I just *love* cows."

"I knew you would," Tony said, beaming with pride. Gladys unzipped the parka, looking over Tony's head at Brad. "I left the messages on your desk," she said. "You can deal with them now and I'll look after this little lady. I've got a whole pile of work for her today, too."

Brad nodded gratefully. "Thanks, Gladys." He paused at his office door, smiling as Gladys got the child settled at the typing table near her desk with a small supply of office equipment. Tony loved playing secretary, sitting next to Gladys and imitating her brisk, efficient actions.

He went into his office and closed the door, hanging his jacket away and settling in to deal with the work that was accumulating while he stayed home to look after Tony.

He heard a knock on the door and glanced up as Gladys entered, carrying a pile of requisition forms and a couple of rolled blueprints.

"Any problems out there?"

"She's just a little angel, Brad. I've never seen a child so well behaved."

Brad shook his head ruefully. "If you say so, Gladys."

The secretary looked at him with sympathy. "No matter how good she is, a four-year-old takes some getting used to."

"You're telling me. Why don't worms have faces, Gladys?"

She chuckled, then sobered. "Any luck with the nanny?"

Brad shook his head. "I've called every agency in the valley and contacted all the people who've advertised privately. Nobody wants to share a small apartment with a single guy and a four-year-old."

"That's just because they don't know how handsome you are," Gladys told him with a comforting smile.

Brad grinned wanly. "I'm not looking for a live-in girlfriend, Gladys. I've already got a girlfriend. I just want a baby-sitter."

Gladys hesitated, looking suddenly awkward. "Your girlfriend . . . she owns a house, doesn't she? It seems like the most sensible thing would be . . ." Her voice trailed off.

"It's just not possible. There's been . . . we've already got a lot of problems in our relationship. We're certainly not ready for a huge complication like Tony." Brad pushed his chair back with a restless gesture. "I just don't know what to do."

"Talked to the child-welfare people lately?"

"I talk to them all the time. I'm practically talking to them in my sleep."

"And?"

"And the latest news is that Clara is gone completely. The landlord said she took off in the middle of the night, left the place in a mess and four months' rent unpaid."

"So I guess her claim on Tony is no longer valid."

"Hardly. They're talking about long-term foster care, possibly adoption, but nothing concrete at the moment. If I give her up, I haven't the slightest idea where she'll be going. I just can't stand that, Gladys."

"How much time have you got?"

"Less than two weeks. If I don't have an acceptable living arrangement by mid-December, in addition to filing all the necessary paperwork, they'll take her back into their custody."

Gladys met his eyes for a moment, her plump face full of concern. "Something will come up," she said with forced cheerfulness. "I've got everybody in my family and all my friends out beating the bushes, looking for some kind of baby-sitter. I wish I could help, Brad," she added with regret. "But my place is even smaller than yours, and now with Stan's emphysema . . ."

"It's okay, Gladys. You've already helped so much. I can't tell you how grateful I am."

"Speaking of which, are we still on for Saturday night?"

"If you can," Brad said gratefully. "I've got a date," he added, his face softening. "Abby and I are going out for dinner, then over to see the new musical."

"Sounds nice. What time will you drop Tony off at my place?"

"About six. Is that all right? I'll make sure she's had supper before she comes."

"Good. And," Gladys added with a sudden mischievous smile, "you'll be bringing her pajamas, won't you? Just in case your date turns out to be, shall we say... longer than you expected, *again?*"

"You're a wicked woman, Gladys."

"Not a bit. Just realistic. Don't think I haven't noticed how much happier and more relaxed you're looking these days, even though you're worried sick about that little girl. Love," Gladys observed solemnly, "is good for everybody." She grabbed a handful of signed letters and ducked quickly out of the office before Brad could reply.

For a long time after she disappeared, Brad sat smiling absently at the door. His thoughts were faraway, rich with visions of starry dark eyes and shining hair, of silken skin and warm lips and melting sweetness.

"AT FIRST I WAS just drifting in a black, black void," the disembodied voice said on Abby's small tape recorder. "I'd never seen anything so black. Then I realized that the blackness was a kind of... like a laundry chute, sort of, but without a top. And it was getting brighter. The sides were glowing."

"A laundry chute without a top? What do you mean? Did it feel like a tunnel?"

"Not really. I think of a tunnel as being all closed in, like a pipe. This was open at the top, like a ... like a bobsled run, sort of. That's what it was like, sliding very fast down a bobsled run. Headfirst."

"Were you frightened?"

"At first I was, because I couldn't figure out what was happening and I thought I might have an accident or bump into something, you know? Then I started to understand that nothing bad was going to happen. I'm not sure how I knew that, I just had the feeling that nothing bad would ever happen to me again. I felt incredibly safe and wonderful and full of peace."

"What happened then?"

"Then this chute thing got brighter and brighter. But I realized that the light was coming from the other end of it. It was almost like the light was a magnet, you know, pulling me along? All of a sudden I wanted to see that light, more than anything in the whole world. I wanted to see what the light was coming from."

"And did you?"

"Just for a second. I had the feeling that the bobsled run ended, and I stepped out into a place that was flooded with light. It was a *different* kind of light. It was incredibly bright, but also warm and soothing. It didn't hurt my eyes a bit, didn't even make me blink. And it was so warm. I just wanted to walk into the light and never leave. Then I heard a voice, and I realized that the light was talking to me."

"You heard an audible voice?"

"Not really. I heard it with my heart, sort of, if you know what I mean. I knew what it was telling me, but thoughts were just being put directly into my head."

"What were those thoughts?"

"That I couldn't stay with the light. I had to come back and help my husband because he was sick and he needed me."

"How did you feel then?"

"I felt really sad. I didn't want to leave the light. I could feel so much love flowing toward me, and I just wanted to... I'll tell you what it was like. I was sixty-seven years old when this happened to me, but when I talked with the light I felt like a little girl again. I wanted to curl up and cuddle and be hugged, and never go away."

"Did you feel that you had a choice?"

"Sort of. I felt that I could probably stay if I wanted. But then I thought of Hal—that's my husband—and how hard it would be for him to manage on his own because he'd just been diagnosed with cancer. I knew that's what the light wanted me to think of, so I turned around, and right away I woke up in my hospital room and all the doctors and nurses were working over my body on the bed—"

Abby leaned forward and switched off her tape recorder, pausing to make some notes.

She ran the tape forward, checked the numbers, then switched the machine on again and settled back in her chair to listen to the next interview.

"I'm twenty-eight years old. I'm a boilermaker, so I travel all over the place to do my job. I was working at a resort in the Rocky Mountains last summer, and on Sunday afternoon I went with some other guys for a swim in the lake. I'm a strong swimmer, but I went out too far and then got a terrible cramp in my stomach. It hurt so much I couldn't even catch my breath, and before I knew it I was floundering and choking. I couldn't even turn over and try to float, because I wasn't able to extend my body. I thought, 'My God,

I'm going to die.' It was a terrible, suffocating feeling, like total panic."

"How long did that last?"

"I don't know. It felt like hours, but I'd guess it was about forty or fifty seconds. The next thing I knew, all the panic was gone. There was a beautiful warm light all around me, and it was talking to me."

"How did you get to the light? Did you have a sensation of traveling through a tunnel, or up into the sky?"

"No, I felt like I was still in the water, but I was just drifting. I didn't feel worried anymore, and there was no pain or panic. The light was telling me not to be afraid. It was showing me my life."

"Showing you your life?"

"Like a movie. It was very vivid. It started when I was a baby and moved forward with incredible speed, yet in total detail. I saw myself playing with things at kindergarten, winning a prize at Cub Scouts, running around with other little boys on the playground. And I wasn't just watching, I was feeling all those things, really vivid, you know. It was just like living through them again."

"How many incidents did you recall?"

"You don't understand. I wasn't just recalling incidents. I was living through my whole life over again, every single detail, but all speeded up. Later on, I mean after I recovered and went back to work, I could remember dozens of things from my early life that I'd forgotten all those years. I still can."

"Did you feel that your life was being judged?"

"Not at all. Even when I watched things I'd done that weren't so great, things I've been ashamed of, I had no feeling that there was any disapproval of those things. More like, 'Well, *that* wasn't such a good idea, but you learned something from it, didn't you?' And I'd say, 'Yes, I learned not to be so selfish,' and we'd move on."

"We?"

"Myself and the light. It was the light talking to me. The light was a person."

"Was it God?"

"I don't know. I've never really believed in God, and I still don't. Not in the sense of some old guy with a beard, wearing a nightgown, standing around condemning people to hell and all that. The light was different. It was warm and loving, as real as you and me, with all kinds of gentleness and even a sense of humor. Once we were watching when I'd gotten into trouble as a teenager by dating two girls at the same time, telling all kinds of lies to both of them, and I could feel the light was smiling."

"The light?"

"Yes. The person who was inside the light."

"What happened next?"

"I don't really know. I was still reliving my life and finding it really interesting. All of sudden I saw myself lying on the beach, and a man was giving me mouth-to-mouth resuscitation."

"You saw that or felt it?"

"I saw it. That was the weirdest thing of all. I remember watching it from behind. He was getting bald, and he had his hair all swirled around this bald patch on the back of his head. I was looking at the *back of his head*. There's no way I could have known about that hair, because I only saw the guy briefly after that and he had a hat on. I watched him trying to revive me for a while, then suddenly I realized I was back in my body. My lungs were burning and I was spitting up water, and people were shouting and running all over the beach.''

"How did you feel about this experience? Afterward, I mean?"

"For a long time I never told anybody. My buddies would have laughed and accused me of getting religion, although that's not true at all. I didn't tell anybody until I heard about this group. I was amazed to find out that all kinds of people have had the same experience. It feels good to talk about it—''

Again Abby paused the tape recorder, flipping to another section in her notebook. She advanced the tape, then switched it on again and sipped her coffee, waiting for the recorded voice to begin.

"I'm a speech pathologist, working in the school system. I was forty-three years old when I had open-heart surgery," a woman's voice began. "My vital signs went flat on the operating table and I was clinically dead for seven minutes. During that time I had a near-death experience."

"Can you describe your experience?"

"It started in the operating room. I was floating somewhere near the ceiling, in the corner. I was watching them trying to revive me, and I couldn't understand how I could be outside, watching this. Then I realized I was dead.''

"How did that feel?"

"It was strange. I don't think I was terrified or anything. I was just really confused. I had no idea what to do next. I kept hoping someone would come along and tell me where I was supposed to go and then suddenly I realized how ridiculous that was. I distinctly remember chuckling about it.''

''What happened next?''

''I watched the doctors and nurses for a few minutes, but it all began to look so silly. I didn't like to watch them working so hard over that body when I didn't need it anymore. After a while I went out into the hallway and down to the waiting room. My husband was sitting there with our two daughters. Amy was crying, and John dug in his pocket for a handkerchief, but all he had was this wad of pink tissue. He wiped her face and threw the tissue away in the wastebasket. Later when I told him about it he was amazed, because he'd just picked up those tissues that morning at my sister's house on the way over to the hospital. There was no way I could have seen them or known about them.''

''How did you feel when you saw your family?''

''I felt really sorry for them. I wanted to tell them not to worry, that I was fine. But when I tried to touch them they couldn't feel me.''

''Could you feel them?''

''Not really. My hands just sort of went through them.''

''But you had hands?''

''Oh, absolutely. I had a body. I was very conscious of it because my body had felt so weak before the surgery, but now my legs were strong. I felt as if I could run and dance. My body was so real that when I was near the window, watching my family, I was conscious of my left side getting cold, so I moved away.''

"Where did you go?"

"I just kind of drifted out of the hospital and across the grounds. It was summertime, and the sun was shining. Then suddenly the sunlight turned into this other light that shone on a kind of sunken pathway, and I felt so relieved. I finally knew where I was supposed to go."

"Did you have any feeling that the light was a person?"

"I felt that it was God. I had the distinct impression that I was almost in the presence of God. It was the most beautiful place I'd ever seen, and the light was so warm and comforting. Then I saw a man trimming a hedge. When he turned around it was my father, who died when I was a teenager."

"Trimming a hedge?"

"This was a real place. It wasn't like...pearly gates and harps and all that. It was a real place with grass and trees and sunshine. It all just felt so clean and beautiful."

"Did your father recognize you?"

"Yes. He smiled at me and said he loved me, but it wasn't time for me to come."

"Do you ever have the feeling now that this was a dream?"

"Not in the slightest. I sometimes dream about my father, but this didn't have any of that dreamlike quality, and it hasn't faded at all with the passage of time. It wasn't a dream. It was an experience."

"What happened after you saw your father?"

"I started seeing other people I recognized. There was my grandmother, who had died a few years ago, and a cousin I'd loved when I was a little girl, and even a baby daughter that I'd miscarried twenty years ago when I was five months pregnant. She was so beautiful."

"You recognized a baby that you'd never seen?"

"I didn't recognize people by the way they *looked*. It's really hard to explain. It's like I could see what the people *were,* and that's how I was able to recognize them. Does that sound crazy?"

"I've heard quite a few others say much the same thing. Please go on."

"All the people kept repeating what my father had told me—that it wasn't time for me to come. After a while I knew that they were right, that I had to turn around and go back. I started down the path in the opposite direction and quick as a flash I was back in my body. One of the nurses said, 'We have a pulse!' and I felt like crying. After that I don't remember a thing until I woke up in the recovery room."

"The experience was so positive that you regretted being alive?"

"Yes."

"This is something I've wanted to ask others who've had near-death experiences. Since you now look on death as such a positive experience, what's your view of suicide? Would you consider it as an option for yourself if you found your life getting difficult?"

"Not at all! I have the feeling, more than ever, that suicide is terribly wrong. I think there's a plan of some kind and it gets spoiled if we don't follow the plan. I believe it would be an awful feeling to walk up the pathway after having taken your own life. I feel so sorry for people who have to face that."

"How has this experience affected you?"

"It's changed my whole life. I'm a totally different person."

"In what way?"

"I value life a lot more. I don't get all stressed out over little things, because I know that's not what matters."

"What is it that matters?"

"Love. Nothing matters but love. Since this experience, I truly believe we're just put here to love others—that's what we're supposed to learn. I feel so full of love sometimes that I can hardly contain myself. And I enjoy every second of my life. It just feels so precious."

Abby switched the tape recorder off, made a few notes, then curled up on the couch, hugging her knees and resting her chin on them with a brooding expression.

There were significant differences in detail among the interviews, but many of them were also disturbingly similar on important points. For instance, she'd interviewed three people whose near-death experiences had been the result of suicide attempts. All of them reported a feeling of unhappiness and confusion, of going to a place that was "cold and lonely, kind of like a waiting room," and having the feeling that they would have to stay there a long, long time before they could move on.

Another similarity was the "tunnel," although it was variously described as a cylinder, a valley, a trough, a chute, or simply a path. People seemed to lack the vocabulary to describe the exact nature of the tunnel, the light, or the body that they possessed during their paranormal experience. But they all agreed on feelings of warmth, love, peace and happiness. And many of them, like the last woman on the tape, reported an enduring and life-transforming impact.

Abby thought of Brad, of his strange new tenderness, the loving gentleness of his hands, his consideration and empathy. She trembled at the memory of his lovemaking. He seemed so selfless and generous now, so intent on pleasing her, on giving her a feeling of being cherished and adored.

Had her wild reckless lover really been transformed by some kind of occult experience? Or had he just matured and strengthened as a result of a close brush with death and come to realize what was important in his life?

Abby shook her head in sudden impatience and stood up, then wandered restlessly across the room to switch on her computer. After all these weeks of research, she still didn't know what to think about the whole near-death phenomenon.

Her rational mind tended to accept a physiological explanation, that hormones and other chemicals released in the brain at the time of death resulted in an experience that had certain common elements, in rather the same way that all people see similar bright lights and shapes when they press hard on their closed eyelids.

After all, only a small fraction of people who approached or experienced clinical death had any kind of near-death story to tell. Most patients had no memory of any kind after they recovered.

But it was difficult to explain things like permanently changed lives and perceptions. Most of all, it was difficult to explain the way Brad was now, all the subtle differences in him that were so clear to Abby. She didn't know any of the people she'd interviewed, hadn't been acquainted with them prior to the experience they'd recounted. But she knew Brad Carmichael with every fiber of her body and soul, and she didn't know what to think.

All Abby knew was that for some reason, a deep hidden part of her resisted this phenomenon. What's more, she knew that she would stubbornly refuse to believe it no matter how convincingly the evidence mounted.

CHAPTER TWELVE

WILBUR STROLLED OUT from the direction of the hallway, examined the living room in gloomy silence for a moment, then approached Abby, who sat in front of her computer screen.

With the air of a king bestowing a knighthood, the big cat inclined his head briefly before stepping forward with delicacy to lower his fat body onto Abby's feet. Abby sighed at the feeling of substantial warmth and softness. "Why, thank you, Wilbur," she murmured in surprise. "That's very sweet."

Nothing personal, Wilbur's slitted green eyes told her. *It's just that the floor is too cold and the hearth is too warm. As soon as you make me uncomfortable in any way, I'm out of here, kid.*

Abby grinned down at him, strongly tempted to wiggle her toes and tickle his soft furry belly, but too pleased by the solid comfort of his presence to disturb him.

All at once the doorbell rang, shattering the peaceful firelighted stillness. Wilbur flashed his mistress a bitter "don't-you-dare" kind of look that made her waver helplessly.

"Wilbur, sweetie, I have to answer the door," Abby pleaded. "I'll be right back and then you can lie on my feet again. I promise."

The big cat glared at her, sighed and heaved himself erect, then stalked out of the room with a bristling look of hurt.

Abby went to the door, and smiled to see Joan on the darkened veranda.

"Is this a bad time?" Joan asked anxiously. "I mean, Brad isn't here or anything?"

"No, Brad's not here. But Wilbur was lying on my feet just now when I had to get up to answer the door. He won't forgive me for a week."

"He's such a pompous disgusting cat. Why don't you get a nice little budgie or something?"

"Because," Abby said cheerfully, "Wilbur would eat it. Joannie, don't you look pretty! What *is* that material?"

Joan touched her slacks in a self-conscious gesture. "It's a kind of shiny Lycra-cotton blend. I just came from my exercise class. Do you think this is too loud?"

"I think it's gorgeous. I'm really jealous. Is there a top to match? Quick, take off your coat."

Laughing in protest, Joan let Abby peel her coat away to reveal a two-piece exercise outfit of shiny cream and teal green. The rich colors made Joan's face glow, and the tight stretch fabric accentuated a figure that was trim and shapely.

"Wow! You look like somebody on one of those workout videos. I should join an exercise class, too, shouldn't I?" Abby said wistfully. "My god, Joannie, I feel like such a frump. Look at me, in these old jeans and Brad's sweatshirt."

"You look beautiful, Abby. You always do," Joan said loyally.

"Right," Abby said with a rueful grin. "Especially when I've been working for about seventeen hours and haven't even stopped to eat."

Joan gazed in concern at her friend's weary face. "Is that true, Abby? You've been working all that time without a break?"

"Not really. There was some leftover pizza in the fridge from when Brad was here the other night, and I heated that up a few hours ago."

"For lunch or dinner?"

Abby shrugged. "Lunch, dinner . . . it all runs together in my mind."

Joan put her hands on trim, shiny hips and shook her head. "Well, that's just no good at all. You finish what you're doing and I'll make an omelet and a salad, and then we'll settle down by the fire and have a nice long chat, just like old times."

"Joannie," Abby said with a sigh, hugging her friend, "you're an angel, you know that?"

She wasn't aware that her choice of words had possibly been less than tactful until she felt the other woman stiffen and turn away before hurrying into the kitchen.

"I just have a few more paragraphs to type," Abby called into the next room, where pots and dishes were already clattering. "Then I'll shut down and come out to help you. Actually, I could use a break, now that you remind me."

She finished the page, stored it to backup disks and switched the computer off, then paused to put another log on the fire and a quiet symphony tape on the stereo.

At last she presented herself in the kitchen, looking for work. "Can I break the eggs? Chop mushrooms? Dice onions—no, better not do the onions."

"Why not?" Joan asked in a harried fashion, rushing between table and counter.

"If I chop onions," Abby said, hoisting herself onto one of the kitchen stools, "then I'll probably start crying and never be able to stop."

Joan cast a quick glance over her shoulder. "What's the matter, Abby? Aren't things going well with you and Brad?"

Restlessly, Abby shook her head and reached for a block of cheese on the counter, then shredded it methodically. "Things are great with Brad. He's the most gentle, tender, considerate man you ever met. It's almost spooky, Joan. It's like he's had a brain transplant. Do you really think it's possible—such a complete transformation of personality? Could I actually begin to trust the man?"

Joan gave her a measuring look as she held a dripping head of lettuce over the sink. "I don't know. He says it's from having this near-death experience, right?"

Abby nodded gloomily. "Right. And other people who've had the experience say the same thing. But I don't know, Joannie." She got off the stool and wandered over to take the lettuce from her friend. "These people . . . it all seems to me like Looney Tunes time, you know? Angels and lighted bobsled runs and all kinds of contradictory confusing images."

"You mean they don't all see the same thing?"

"Goodness, no! Some of them see babies, even pets that have died. Some see traditional religious-type stuff—churches or mosques—or nature scenes or orchestras...it just seems to be a matter of what they've been programmed to see during their life. Personally I think the whole thing is mainly a combination of chemical phenomena and autosuggestion."

"I know," Joan said, beating eggs with a whisk, adding milk and seasonings and pouring the mixture into a dish. "You've said that before. But," she added after a brief awkward silence, "Abby, what about the children? Don't you think the children—"

"Look at all the brown stuff in this lettuce!" Abby interrupted. "It never fails, I buy a head that looks all green and fresh and then when I break it open it's got three layers of brown spots."

"Take it back and complain," Joan said mildly. "Assert your rights."

"Yeah, *sure*. Look who's become a personal-rights activist," Abby said with a grin. "The girl who refuses to complain when a horse is standing on her foot, for fear it might be an inconvenience to somebody."

"I complained," Joan said. "Just a little quietly, that's all. Nobody heard me."

Abby giggled. "And then I realized what was happening and gave that horse such a whack that he bolted and poor dear Kimberley had to hang on for dear life."

Both friends smiled at the memory of that ill-fated visit to a dude ranch during their high school years.

"Served her right," Abby said finally, picking through the spotted lettuce for enough green leaves to make their salad. "Kimberley was sitting up there acting so lofty and important, like we unmounted mortals weren't worth speaking to."

"Abby, why won't you talk with me about this?" Joan said gently. "After all, you still have to write the article. Wouldn't it be easier to bounce some ideas off me like you always do, just to help sort them out in your mind?"

"It's okay, Joannie. The article is shaping up all right—it really is. And thanks for your help, but I just can't stand—" Abby's voice broke, then steadied. "For some reason I can't stand talking about near-death experiences among children. I don't know why, but I just can't. So," she added with deliberate briskness, "let's talk about something else. How's your angel? I haven't noticed him on the street corner lately. I guess it got too cold and he flew south with the snowbirds. Say, Joannie," she went on, rummaging in the spice cabinet for her salad seasoning, "where do you think vagrants go in the winter? Do they spend all that panhandling money on condos in Palm Springs, or what?"

Abby turned around slowly, aware that a tense silence had fallen in the room. Joan stood clutching the omelet pan in her hands, her face drained of color, her blue eyes wide and miserable.

"Oh, Joannie," Abby whispered, putting the salad aside and crossing the room to hug her friend. "Sweetie, what is it?"

"I'm such a fool," Joan lamented. "Such a fool, Abby."

"You fell in love with this guy? Like really loved him?"

Joan nodded, gulping back tears.

Abby hesitated awkwardly. "Did...did anything happen?" she asked tactfully. "I mean, like anything you'd...?"

"No," Joan said. "Nothing happened. Except," she added with a bleak smile, "that I finally achieved my independence from Mom. I started lying to her all the time, Abby, so I could slip away and meet him in the evening by the lake. Now I don't even have to lie anymore. She acknowledges that I have a life of my own and we both understand that I'm free to come and go as I please. And you know what? Her arthritis is getting a lot better, and she's even started talking about getting a part-time job at the library."

At this moment Abby was not interested in Vera Holland's reluctant journey toward personal independence. "Joan," she said, "what happened? All those evenings you slipped out to be alone with him, did the two of you ever...?"

Joan smiled sadly. "We never even held hands. We just sat and talked." Her face was taut with emotion, "It was the most wonderful, glorious experience of my life. I fell so much in love with him, Abby, and now he's...he's just gone, and I think I'm going to *die*," Joan wailed.

She leaned against Abby's shoulder, and began to sob in earnest.

SEVERAL DAYS LATER the first snowfall came, muffling the world in white. Deep in the night the street lamps were circled with huge misty halos of pale gold and the bare tree branches glistened like shadowy lace against the black winter sky. There was no wind at all, and the snow piled up in smooth feathery mounds on every surface, topping fence posts and railings and parked cars.

Abby stood at the window of her darkened bedroom, looking out at the world. She hugged her body in the thin fabric of a peach silk nightgown, her face drawn and pallid in the ghostly light.

On nights like this she always missed Aaron so much. She knew it was ridiculous, but she just couldn't stop herself from worrying about where he was, wondering if he was warm enough.

It was totally irrational. Abby still believed the extinction of the body was the end of everything. But she could never completely overcome that haunting urge to hold him, to shelter him from the cold, to tuck the blankets up warmly around his little sleeping face and draw his curtains tight against the winter chill....

"Sweetheart?" Brad murmured drowsily from the bed. "Is something the matter?"

Abby turned and forced herself to smile at him. "It's snowing. It'll soon be Christmas, Brad."

He was silent, watching her in the darkness. She could see the dim glow from the street lamps glimmering on his face and the soft line of his mouth as she crossed the room toward him.

"Are you planning anything special for Christmas, Abby?" he asked finally, stretching his arms and sitting up against the pillows. "We haven't talked about it yet, have we?"

Abby shook her head, slipping under the covers and nestling close to him, grateful for his warmth. "Last Christmas was so terrible, Brad. The most dreadful time in all my life. I'd like this year to be a nice happy time, just the two of us here at home, and then maybe I can start to forget."

Again he was silent, as if weighing something in his mind. Abby looked up at him. "Brad? Is that all right with you, or was there something else you wanted to do? Did you want to go away skiing, or something like that? Because I could—"

"No," he said, shaking his head and gathering her into his arms. "A nice homey Christmas is just fine, Abby. It sounds good to me."

They were both silent for a moment. Abby was certain he was thinking the same thing she was—that this place still wasn't officially his home. She hadn't invited him to move back yet, although she was prepared to do so whenever he asked. She'd come to this decision just recently, realizing that she was ready to abandon all her fears and doubts just for the joy of having him back in her life on a permanent basis.

She loved him so much.

Abby sighed and snuggled closer to him, reaching up to kiss the warm hollow of his throat. "I love you," she whispered.

"Do you?" he murmured huskily. "How much?"

Abby smiled in the darkness. "I thought I showed you that earlier. Weren't you paying attention?"

"Oh, Abby, I was paying attention, all right. Girl, you can get my attention better than anyone in the world."

He began to caress the curves of her body beneath the silky fabric of her nightgown, stroking the long sleek line of hip and thigh, following the sweep of her narrow waist upward to cup her breast.

Abby shuddered and drew away, a little frightened by the fiery urgency of her response. "We just *did* this," she protested. "Let's get up and have some hot chocolate."

"Hot chocolate!" he scoffed, his mouth roaming hungrily over her face and neck.

Abby sighed and yielded briefly to pleasure, marveling at the wonder of him in her arms and in her bed. In some ways it felt as if he'd never left, as if this whole miserable year had been a bad dream from which she'd mercifully awakened.

But at other times the present situation itself had a strange feeling of unreality, as if Brad's lovemaking and her passionate response were tenuous wisps of feeling, not connected to real life, which could be swept away by the first strong wind.

"Brad," she whispered, drawing away from him again. "Brad, stop. I want to talk about something."

"Later, all right?" He bent his crisp dark head to kiss her breasts. "I'm not in the mood for talk."

She chuckled and pushed at him. "You're insatiable," she said. "Talk to me for a minute and then I promise you we'll get back to this. Okay?"

"Okay." He kissed her neck and breast once more, then touched them carefully with his fingers.

"What are you doing?"

"Marking my place," he told her with a grin, his white teeth flashing in the darkness. "I don't want to forget where I was."

Abby laughed again, loving him, her heart lifting with happiness.

"So." He stretched his long body and put an arm around her to draw her close, then tucked the covers carefully up around her shoulders. "What do you want to talk about?"

"The future. I really want to get some things decided, Brad."

"Good. So do I."

He'd spoken with such intensity that she was surprised and a little flustered.

"I mean," Abby went on, "we've just drifted back into this relationship, sort of, without ever really discussing it. I'd like to find out where we stand, Brad. I want to know where we're going."

"Me, too." Brad was silent a moment, while Abby looked up at his strong profile and his cheekbones washed with silver by the snowy outside light. "Abby, there's something I have to ask you."

She tensed, her heart beating fast.

Here it comes, she thought. *He was going to ask her if he could move back in, live here with her again. And she going to say yes, because she couldn't imagine living without him anymore.*

"But first," he went on, surprising her again with his seriousness, "there's something I have to tell you."

"What is it, Brad?"

"You remember the little girl I told you about? Tony, from up the street?"

"The one who was moving Aaron's toys?"

"Yes, that's the one."

"What about her?" Abby prompted when he hesitated.

"She didn't go away with her guardian. I took her home with me."

"*What?*" Abby leaned up on one elbow and stared at him, her eyes wide with shock.

"The day I found her here, I went up the street to talk to her so-called guardian," he said, a note of bitterness in his voice. "You should have seen the squalor that woman was living in, Abby. And she was drunk half the time, left the poor little kid alone, beat her for no reason at all.... Tony was covered with bruises and not getting enough to eat, absolutely no proper care or protection. I just couldn't stand it. The woman wasn't even any relation to her. Tony's mother died over a year ago."

"So you *took* her? Just like a . . . an abandoned kitten or something? Brad, how could you do that? I mean, it's not even legal to take a child from her guardian, is it?"

Brad smiled grimly. "Not without great difficulty. She's been living with me at my apartment for the past two weeks, and I've been negotiating with the child-welfare agency."

Abby's head whirled. She had the sensation that all her happiness was rushing away from her, spinning out of sight before her horrified eyes.

"Abby?"

She licked her lips and forced herself to look up at him. "What?"

"I want to keep her. I want to become her legal guardian, even adopt her if I can. But I need your help."

"My help?"

"I need to give her a home, Abby. I need to prove to the authorities that I can offer her stability, adequate shelter, a family environment. I want you to—"

"*No!*" Abby whispered, looking at him in panic. "No, Brad. Please don't ask me this."

She flung herself out of bed and started to pace around the room, her chest heaving, her heart thundering.

Abby had no idea why she was reacting so violently, why part of her recoiled so harshly at the thought of some strange child taking Aaron's place in her life. Another, more rational part of her mind was consumed with guilt, and an overwhelming helpless shame that made her cold and sick.

"Abby," he said gently, watching her from the bed, "I don't understand."

Abby turned to look at him. "This is so hard to bear," she whispered. "This is really unfair of you, Brad. You're putting me in an impossible position."

"How?" he asked, genuinely puzzled. "I don't understand, Abby. Tell me why you're so upset."

Tears stung her eyes and began to trickle down her cheeks. She paused by the window and turned to look at the man in her bed.

"Aaron was...he was my baby," she whispered haltingly. "He was...I loved him so much. He was the most precious thing in my life. Brad, how can you be so cruel, asking this of me? I can't love some other child just because you ask me to. I can't just replace my son with this little girl, as if Aaron were no more than...than a puppy who got run over on the street!"

She sank into the chair by the window, curled up and began to sob, her body heaving, her face buried against her knees. Brad watched her in alarm, then got out of bed to approach her.

"Abby," he began, reaching toward her. "Abby, darling, I didn't mean to hurt you. I just thought..."

"Go away," she sobbed, her voice muffled.

"Please, sweetheart, can't we..."

Abby raised her tear-streaked face to look at him. He seemed faraway and dim, obscured by the swirling mists of her terrible pain.

"Go away, Brad," she said tonelessly. "I'm sorry, but I want to be alone now. I need to think."

"But, Abby..."

"Please don't say anything more. Just leave me alone."

Abby watched as he gathered his clothes and walked quietly out of the bedroom. She sat in the chair, listening to the sounds of him getting dressed in the other room and leaving the house. Even after he was gone, his car dimming and vanishing in the falling snow, she continued to rock and stare out at the silvery night with wide haunted eyes.

She was oblivious to the chill in the room, to her bare arms and shivering body. All she felt was a wintry desolate pain that swallowed up the whole world.

THE SNOW CONTINUED to fall over the next few days, sifting gently onto the hills around the lake. When the clouds finally cleared away, the valley lay quiet and still beneath a blanket of white that sparkled with rainbows in the sun.

Abby walked up the curving path at the edge of the lake on Sunday afternoon, hands deep in the pockets of her winter coat. Her face was brooding and silent as she gazed across the shimmering water where tendrils of mist swirled up from the silvered expanse and frost crystals danced above the surface in dazzling prisms. In this gentle climate the big lake never froze completely, making it a haven for waterfowl, which often spent the whole winter swimming and feeding along the shoreline. Abby's face twisted when she thought about Aaron, who always worried so much when he saw the ducks and geese swimming in the icy water.

"Won't they get cold, Mommy? Look, they're even going right down underneath!"

Abby shook off the memories and turned back onto the path, her boots crunching on the fresh snow.

She was drowning in misery, as tormented as if Aaron had died just last week, instead of last year. And she had no real understanding of why she was feeling this way, why she'd tumbled so suddenly and terribly back into the depths of grief.

Of course, it had sprung partly from Brad's shocking announcement the other night. She could still remember how it had felt to hear him calmly telling her something so appalling and unexpected, when she'd been looking forward to a romantic, private time with him.

She knew she was being selfish and uncharitable. It was awful of her to treat him this way and, worse, to react so negatively to the little homeless girl. Brad had called several times since that dreadful night, but Abby had cut him off with brief monosyllables, telling him that she was busy and nearing her story deadline, that she had no time to see him.

Of course, that wasn't really the case. The simple truth was that she dreaded seeing Brad because she knew she couldn't face the child he'd undertaken to look after. That unknown little girl had invaded Abby's home and usurped Aaron's place there, as well as stealing part of Brad's affection. Abby wanted nothing to do with her.

Still, she was honest enough to recognize that it wasn't just hearing about the abandoned waif in Brad's apartment that had triggered this emotional relapse.

Her feelings also had something to do with the article she was writing, her concentration on death. All these months she'd forced herself to acknowledge the reality and finality of Aaron's death. But now, she found herself brooding about it all the time, as if it had just happened.

And, of course, the anniversary date was nearing. Everyone had warned her that anniversaries were the very worst times for grief, that the old emotions could leap out and ambush you even when you thought you'd fully recovered.

Abby shook her head impatiently, despising herself for being so predictable and weak.

She looked up at the bank of waterfront condos and wondered if Mitch was at home this afternoon. Maybe she could drop in on him for a visit. It would be so nice, Abby thought wistfully, to talk with somebody who had nothing to do with her emotional life, who made no demands on her.

She hesitated, still gazing up at the place where Mitch lived, then stared in sudden shock. A man was approaching her on the path, strolling along with a casual air as if deeply absorbed in the beauty of the winter day.

Abby recognized him as the vagrant who'd captivated Joan's attention during the past months. So he hadn't left the valley after all, she thought, noting that he was dressed much the same as always. Apparently his only concession to the frosty temperature was a ragged flannel shirt pulled on over the old denim one.

He came nearer on the path and gazed into Abby's eyes with a look of calm recognition.

"Hello," he said, his weathered face tranquil and quiet.

"Hello," Abby said brusquely, stepping aside to let him pass.

But he paused and continued to look at her, somehow holding her with the intensity of his gaze.

Abby shifted on the path and bit her lip, longing to be on her way, mysteriously unable to move.

"Why are you staring at me?" she asked abruptly. "What do you want?"

"Your pain is so great," he said. "Why do you cling to such pain?"

Anger welled up inside her and spilled over in a hot corrosive flood. "I *don't* cling to it," she shouted at him, her voice ringing on the still, wintry air, so shrill that she trembled in embarrassment.

The vagrant watched her quietly as she struggled to control her emotions.

"Look," Abby said finally in a lower voice. "I don't know who you are. And I certainly don't know why you think you're such an expert on human nature, when you can't even buy yourself a decent pair of shoes. And," she added, unable to stop the bitter flow of words, "when you've caused my friend so much misery!"

He looked at her in mild surprise, his gentle face suddenly full of concern. "Your friend?"

"You know who I mean," Abby told him.

"Yes, I know who you mean. Is she unhappy?"

"I guess she's worried about you," Abby said. She felt herself growing calmer, almost mesmerized by the man's eyes and the peacefulness of him. "She thought the two of you had . . . some kind of friendship. Then suddenly you vanished without a word. She's wondering where you are, and if you're all right. Joan's that kind of person, you know. She worries about people."

"Yes," the man said, still watching Abby's face. "She does."

Abby gazed at him. Her fury had ebbed and she found herself battling a distressingly childlike urge to ask him a flood of questions. She wanted to know who he was, where he came from, what he knew about the secrets of life and the universe.

What he knew about Aaron. . . .

But that was ridiculous, she reminded herself. He was a homeless street musician, nothing more. Whatever Joan's imagination had manufactured, there was no truth to it. That whole idea was just part of a lonely woman's fantasy.

Still, those eyes . . .

"Tell her I'll be here tomorrow evening at seven," the tall man said at last. "Please ask her to come and see me."

Abby hesitated, trying to be rational. By this time of the year, the park would be in starry blackness at seven o'clock. Did she really want to send her friend out to meet this mysterious vagabond on such a winter evening in this isolated place?

Once more, he read her thoughts without effort. "Your friend will be safe. I will not harm her."

Abby shrugged, suddenly anxious to be away from that serene, penetrating gaze.

"She's a grown-up woman. I'll just pass on your message, and she can make her own decision."

"Thank you."

The man smiled, a gentle luminous smile that warmed her like a blessing. Then he turned and moved off down the path, his ragged boots flapping as he walked. Abby stood watching him go, and tears burned in her eyes as she quelled a sudden and completely irrational urge to run after him and beg him for comfort.

CHAPTER THIRTEEN

JOAN PULLED her coat collar up around her ears and tugged on the ends of her long woolen scarf. The wind sighed through blackened tree branches, outlined in stark relief against the dull silver of the night sky. A waning moon was partly concealed behind a lacy drift of cloud, its frosted light spilling onto the snowy landscape.

She shivered and glanced around at the empty path, her eyes wide and dark in the moonlight, and wished briefly that she'd accepted Abby's offer to come with her and wait in the car. Joan wasn't at all frightened of the angel, but there was always the possibility that he could fail to arrive. And who knew what other kind of stranger might haunt this park on chilly moon-lighted nights?

She gazed up at the bank of condos, wondering idly which one belonged to Mitch Flanagan. The condo windows flared in cheery rectangles of light that spilled down over the snow and the darkened surface of the lake. People moved against the windows, looking small and cozy within their sheltered spaces. Christmas lights flickered gaily from around windows and balcony railings, and from Christmas trees already standing in some of the windows.

Joan turned and plodded on, calming her troubled thoughts by thinking in a determined fashion about Christmas. It was time to put a tree up and decorate the house, although she certainly didn't feel much like it this year. Vera, on the other hand, was showing more enthusiasm about the holiday than she had for a long time. Joan's mother had actually joined a bowling league and made several friends, and she wanted to have them over some evening near Christmas.

Joan shook her head, marveling at the rapid, almost miraculous change in her mother. Vera Holland didn't complain nearly as much about her health these days. She even walked with a brisker step, and the sleepless pain-racked nights seemed to be mostly a thing of the past.

Probably, Joan thought with a wry smile, because Vera was out so much in the daytime now, visiting and going for long walks instead of napping all afternoon on the couch.

"Are you cold?" a polite voice inquired at her elbow.

Joan tensed with alarm and looked up. The angel was walking beside her, his weathered face tranquil in the moonlight, his ragged clothes swinging soundlessly around him like ghostly rags.

"My goodness! You startled me," Joan said, trying to laugh. "I looked around just a second ago and there wasn't a soul in sight. Where on earth did you come from?"

"I was here," he told her. "You didn't see me, but I was here."

Joan nodded and fell into step beside him. The silence lengthened and grew awkward as they moved slowly along the curving path at the water's edge.

"I didn't...I haven't seen you for a long time," Joan ventured finally. "I wondered if you'd left the valley."

"I will be leaving soon," the man said in his gentle musical voice.

Joan tensed and looked up at him quickly. "You will? Why do you have to leave?"

He was silent, gazing out across the darkened water.

"Is it..." Joan began awkwardly, then paused. "Is it just because the weather's so cold? I mean, if you need a place to live, I know a couple who have this nice basement suite for rent, and they're looking for a caretaker for the building. If you wanted to..."

Joan's voice trailed off when she saw the way he was looking at her. His eyes were black in the moonlight, but she could still see their compassion and gentle understanding. As always, she felt that he was looking rather than listening, gazing into the depths of her soul and recognizing what she was feeling instead of what she said.

Her cheeks reddened with embarrassment. She turned away, grateful for the sheltering darkness.

The man walked quietly beside her, his torn boot sole flapping rhythmically on the icy pavement.

"I don't want you to feel sad," he told her unexpectedly. "There is nothing for you to be sad about."

"But I'll...I'll miss you," Joan whispered, her throat tight and aching with sorrow.

"I will be near," he said with calm matter-of-factness.

Joan stopped again and looked up at him, feeling a reckless surge of desperation. "Who are you?" she asked urgently, her voice rising a little. "I really need to know. Who *are* you?"

He shrugged and smiled at her. "I am whatever you want to think I am."

"I can't accept that." Joan paused, then plunged ahead. "I want to know if you're just...just some kind of peaceful nonconformist, or if you're...something more."

"Something more?" he echoed, sounding genuinely puzzled.

"Are you an angel?" Joan asked bluntly. "Or," she added after a brief hesitation, "are you some form of God?"

He smiled, his face washed with icy silver by the moonlight. "Of course not."

"Then who are you? Why do you know everything I'm thinking all the time? How did you know all about my mother before I told you?"

"Did I? Or did you just think I did?"

Joan paused, startled, and thought about his question. "But you're..." she faltered. "You always seem to know things that I..."

The man nodded gently when she fell silent. "Perhaps I just reflect what I see in you."

"But how do you see it? Other people don't see those things."

"People tend not to look too deeply," the stranger told her in that same quiet tone. "They are busy looking into their own hearts, and they seldom take time to examine the hearts of others."

"So you're nothing special at all?" Joan asked, too troubled and confused to frame her question more tactfully. "You're just a sensitive, unselfish person, that's all?"

The vagrant grinned, a distinctly human kind of grin, and turned around, taking Joan's elbow to guide her back along the moonlighted path. Joan trembled at the touch of his strong sinewy hand resting warmly and powerfully on her arm.

"If that's the case," she persisted, "then how did you know so much about my mother? Did you have some way of...of learning about my life?"

"How is your mother now?" he asked, ignoring her question.

"She's much better. In fact, it's almost miraculous. She goes out and does things without depending on me all the time. She's making friends and allowing me to have some freedom."

Joan fell silent, realizing that in some obscure fashion, by saying those things she had answered her own question.

He paused and gazed once more at the shimmering expanse of the lake. The water was so still that the reflections from the opposite shore lay long and brilliant on the surface, like fingers of light beckoning them forward and upward.

"What should I do now?" Joan whispered, feeling as bereft and frightened as a child. "What should I do after you've gone away?"

He smiled down at her, a shining boyish smile that stabbed her to the heart.

"You know what to do, Joan," he murmured. "You know perfectly well what you should do next."

Then, suddenly, he was gone.

Joan stood blinking in surprise, gazing at the place where he'd been. Had he plunged off into the darkness so abruptly that she hadn't seen him leave? No, that wasn't possible. The whole park was washed with a dull silver glow, shimmering in the frosty night. She could see clearly for many yards all around her, and there was no sign of him.

She shook her head, wondering if he'd hypnotized her somehow, put her into some kind of brief trance to give himself time to vanish.

Staring around feverishly, she refused to accept the crushing pain of this loss, hungry for another sight of his tall ragged form. She could search the snow for footprints, run back along the path and see if he was there behind the shelter, or over in the shrubbery near the water's edge . . .

"You know what to do, Joan," his voice said quietly in her memory. *"You know perfectly well what you should do next."*

All at once her desperate anxiety ebbed. She was left feeling tranquil and composed, filled with a deep peacefulness and a calm sense of purpose.

"Yes," she murmured aloud to the stars that danced across the wintry sky. "Yes, you're right. I know what to do next."

There was no sadness any longer, and no more pain. All she felt was an excitement and anticipation that rose within her as she turned and hurried off along the curving path.

MITCH FLANAGAN GAZED dubiously at the small potted fir tree in his entry hall. He knew that this was a good thing to do, environmentally correct and responsible. But it looked like such a scrawny little Christmas tree.

He thought about Abby's invitation to climb the cliffs with her and cut a live tree. That was really the strong, outdoorsy thing to do, Mitch acknowledged. But it involved all that red tape to acquire the permit, then a grueling three-hour hike through snow and freezing temperatures to get to the designated area where small trees were being carefully thinned.

Mitch shuddered, thinking about that hike.

Besides, he reflected, there was something not quite right about Abby's determination to cut her own tree this year. Her quest had a kind of obsessive element to it, something more like a mission than a pleasant weekend pastime.

She'd been on her way to cut a tree the year before, when Aaron died, he recalled. He sensed that her stubborn determination to finish the job this year amounted to some kind of personal pilgrimage. She was displaying a degree of zealousness about the tree cutting that made him a little uncomfortable.

"Probably I'm just lazy," he told the drooping little tree in its pot of earth. "The least you can do is perk up a bit and quit making me look bad."

Cheered by the sound of his own voice, he dragged the small fir tree, pot and all, into the living room, where a welter of boxes lay on the floor, spilling Christmas ornaments and tangled strings of lights across the carpet. He paused to switch on a tape of instrumental carols, grinning ruefully at himself.

Mitch loved Christmas, always had, even though he either spent the holiday alone every year or accepted one of the sympathetic invitations from friends to pass the day in the bosom of someone else's family.

"I'm just a sucker for sentiment, I guess," he told the scanty fir tree. "Now, do you want to stand here in the window, or would you be more comfortable over in the corner? I think probably—"

The doorbell rang.

"It's not locked. Come in," Mitch called, wondering what Ethel wanted. His new neighbor was seventy-two and recently widowed. In the month since she'd moved into the next condo, she had grown quite reliant on Mitch to help her adjust to a new world of loneliness and bewildering responsibility.

"So what do you think?" Mitch asked when he heard her come into the living room. He was still kneeling in front of the little tree, wrestling the heavy earthenware pot across the thick carpet. "Do you think I should put this thing in the window or hide it in the corner?"

"I think it should be in the window for everybody to see," a soft voice told him. "It's such a beautiful little tree."

Mitch sprang to his feet, staring in amazement at Joan Holland, who stood smiling in the doorway.

"You told me to come in," she said.

"I...I thought you were the old lady who lives next door."

"I can leave again if I'm intruding," Joan told him, beginning to look a little anxious.

"Intruding?" Mitch echoed. "You? Nobody has ever been more welcome in my house."

"Really? Well, in that case..." Still smiling, Joan took off her coat and scarf and handed them to her dazed host.

"Any boots?" he asked, holding her coat tightly in his arms, thrilled by the sweet fragrance that lingered around the collar.

"I left them by the door."

"Okay. Do you want some slippers?" he asked, looking anxiously at her stockinged feet.

Joan pretended to consider the offer. "Do they have eyes and whiskers?"

"Say again?"

"The slippers? Are they the kind with bunny ears, or big pink noses, or claws that flap?"

"Certainly not," Mitch said with dignity. "Do you consider me that ridiculously immature?"

"Actually," Joan said, looking around his apartment, "yes, I think you might be capable of slippers with eyes and whiskers."

He shouted with laughter and dropped an arm around her shoulder, giving her a joyous squeeze. "Joan, it's so nice to have you here."

She smiled at him and Mitch continued to hold her, closer to this delectable woman than he'd ever been. He could see the fine sheen of her delicate skin, the shy curving line of her mouth, a small vein that throbbed in her temple.

They gazed into each other's eyes for a long breathless moment until Joan finally turned aside and knelt to examine the Christmas ornaments. "Oh, Mitch!" she exclaimed in delight. "Look at these little ivory reindeer. I've never seen anything so beautiful."

"There's a whole set." Mitch knelt beside her, riffling through the boxes and wrapping paper. "They pull a little pink jade sleigh all filled with tiny gifts, decorated with gold leaf and semiprecious stones."

"It's just exquisite," Joan breathed, cradling one of the carved reindeer in her hands. "Where did you get them?"

"In Peru. I spent a couple of years there as a journalist."

Joan turned to smile at him, her eyes starry with pleasure. Mitch caught his breath, overcome by emotion. He leaned forward, put his arms around her and drew her into a warm embrace.

Joan trembled in his arms and nestled closer, hiding her face against his shirtfront.

His heart thundered and his world turned from gray to gold. Joy beat and throbbed within him like tiny wings, along with a soaring new hope that left him almost unable to speak.

"Joan," he whispered finally against her hair. "Joan, I'm sorry if I..."

She drew away and gave him a little misty smile. "It's fine, Mitch. It's so good to be here. I feel like..."

"Like what?"

"Like I've finally found a nice comfortable place to be," Joan said simply. "It's so comfortable being with you."

Mitch realized that if he gave expression to his feelings, their sheer intensity might frighten her. Instead, he nodded cheerfully and began to rummage through the wrapping papers. "See? Here's the little Santa, all carved from red carnelian."

Joan smiled and took the exquisite little figurine. "Keep looking, Mitch. I want to see the pink jade sleigh. Where will you set the Santa?"

"Well, let's see." Mitch looked around the room, considering. "The nativity scene should go on the mantel, right?"

Joan nodded solemnly.

"Well, then, let's put the Santa here on the coffee table."

"And we can wind this holly all around it," Joan suggested.

"Great idea. Would you like some hot chocolate or something?"

Joan considered. "Do you have marshmallows?"

"By the bushel."

"All right, then. Here, let me help."

They got up and strolled into the kitchen as casually as if they'd been spending evenings together all their lives.

Mitch felt dazed with bliss, hardly able to contain himself. He wanted to run and shout, to spring onto his balcony ledge and call to the neighbors and the traffic below in the street, to dance along the rooftops.

"So, Joan," he asked calmly, switching the kettle on and measuring cocoa into mugs, "what brought you here tonight?"

"A friend suggested I should visit you," Joan said with a dreamy smile. "Maybe he knew that you needed help with your Christmas decorating."

"'He'? Wasn't it Abby?"

Joan shook her head. "Not Abby. Somebody you wouldn't be likely to know. I doubt...I doubt that I'll be seeing him again," Joan added with a brief catch in her voice. "He's leaving the valley tonight."

But when Mitch looked up at her, Joan seemed tranquil and composed, as contented with the present situation as he was.

"Well..." he began awkwardly, "whoever this friend was, I hope he knows how grateful I am. Joan..." Mitch frowned, pouring boiling water onto the cocoa and adding lavish mounds of marshmallows.

"Yes?"

"Do you think there's any way on earth to make that poor Christmas tree look less like a miserable orphan?"

"I don't know what you're talking about," Joan said, carrying her mug of hot chocolate to the doorway and gesturing toward the little tree. "Just look, Mitch."

He crossed the room to stand beside her, a cup in one hand, the other resting warmly around her shoulders.

Both of them gazed in wonder at the tree. As if by some strange alchemy, its branches had filled and expanded, taken on life and symmetry and fragrance. The potted tree filled the whole window, rich and vibrantly green, waiting to be decked in loveliness.

Mitch even imagined he could see a veil of gold surrounding the tree, a faint aura of shimmering radiance that hummed with unearthly music.

"It's magic," he whispered.

"Yes," she agreed, smiling back. "It's really magic."

Their lips met in a long sweet kiss, while the frost shone like rainbows on the windowpanes and the air sparkled with gold dust and mystery.

BRAD STRODE UP the curving walk to Abby's front door, moving so briskly that Tony had to run at his side to keep up. When he stopped on the veranda and rang the bell, Tony stood beside him, holding a bit of his pant leg firmly in her mittened fist.

Brad grinned at that small urgent pressure. Tony was generally a fearless child, but when situations were new or threatening she liked Brad to be somewhere nearby, comfortably within reach.

He wished for a brief moment that somebody very large and capable was next to him, so he could grab hold of a pant leg and stand behind a safe sheltering figure. But he was the biggest person here, and it was his job to protect everybody else. That, as he'd told Tony a number of times, was what it meant to be a grown-up.

The door opened suddenly and Abby stood in the entry, wearing jeans, hiking boots and a multicolored heavy sweater. She was silent as she gazed at them with haunted eyes.

Brad studied her face with aching love. She seemed thinner, probably because she hadn't been eating and sleeping well. And the old guarded look was back, the blank screen that she drew between herself and the world to shield her from pain.

"Abby," he said, as her gaze flickered briefly to the silent wide-eyed little girl beside him. "I need to talk you to for a minute. May we come in?"

"I don't have much time. I'm leaving right away for the north valley cliffs."

"By yourself? Abby, you shouldn't hike alone in the wintertime."

"I'm going to cut my Christmas tree. That's where Aaron and I were going last year when he had his accident. I don't like unfinished jobs."

There was a brittle, tense look about her that troubled Brad. "Look, Abby," he began gently, "let's just talk for a minute, all right? I'd really like to talk with you."

She nodded abruptly and stood aside to let them into the house, then watched without speaking while Brad knelt to remove Tony's boots, snowsuit and mittens.

Stripped of her bulky outerwear, Tony seemed small and vulnerable, partly because she was gazing up at Brad with a tense look of wide-eyed appeal.

Brad gave Abby an apologetic glance. "She wants to go play with the toys," he murmured.

Abby's body stiffened and her face tightened with pain. He watched her for a moment, reached out a gentle hand to touch her cheek, then looked down at Tony.

"It's all right, honey" he said. "You can run and play with the toys, but be careful, and remember to put everything away afterward."

"I always do!" Tony shouted over her shoulder, already racing down the hallway and into the room.

"She certainly seems to know the way," Abby observed coldly, walking with Brad to the living room and sinking into the rocking chair.

"Abby, I need to say some things to you."

"Do you?" she asked wearily. "Can't you just leave me alone?"

"No, I can't."

"Why not?"

"Because I love you. And even if you never want me again, if you kick me out of your life forever, I still feel a responsibility to tell you what I think."

She nodded, clutching a pillow against her chest and gazing at him over its tasseled edge.

"Abby, it's not like you to be cold and rejecting of a child. I've got all her things packed. Did you know that on Monday morning I have to turn her over to the child-welfare authorities? And then God knows what will happen to her. Do you care about that at all?"

Abby was silent, gripping the pillow so tightly that her knuckles were white against her skin.

"This just seems so out of character, Abby. And it's also not like you to cling selfishly to a roomful of toys that belonged to a child who'll never use them again. Do you want to know why I think you're doing this?"

Brad could see the taut line of her mouth, the dreadful tension in her body. He hated pushing her like this, but he knew he couldn't stop.

"I think you can't let go of Aaron. That's what I believe, Abby. I think you've got an idea that his spirit is still nearby, hovering between this world and the next, and that he may still come back to you somehow, or at least in some form."

"That's . . . that's ridiculous," Abby murmured in a low, choked voice. "It's not even rational. I don't believe in life after death."

"Not even after all the research you did for your article?"

"I'm afraid that plan didn't work, Brad. I finished the article and sent it off yesterday, and then I put it completely out of my mind. I'm just glad it's over."

"Okay, Abby. If you don't believe in life after death, then why won't you give his toys away? And why were you so upset when you found out about Tony?"

"I don't know," she whispered, feeling a mounting apprehension.

"Well, I do. You didn't *want* a rational explanation for the toys moving. You wanted it to be Aaron. And that's why you won't accept the reality of the near-death experience, either. If our experience is valid, if there's really something so wonderful out there, then chances are Aaron's moved on into that realm and left you behind, and you're just not ready to give him up. Is that right, Abby?"

"You're..." She looked up at him, her eyes black with pain. "Please leave me alone," she whispered.

"Abby," Brad said, aching with sorrow and concern. "Abby, darling, I don't want to hurt you. I love you with all my heart. But I want you to find a way to let Aaron go. He's dead. Let him go, and then you'll come back to us. Life is for the living, Abby. We need you, all of us. Not just me and Tony, but Mitch and Joan and all your other friends...everybody needs you. You have to let Aaron go and come back to us."

She wavered, clutching the pillow and staring at him with a steady, unfathomable look. At last she stood up.

"I'm sorry, Brad. I can't let Aaron go. I love him, and I just don't know how to let him go. I've never really believed in any kind of life after death, but you're right, I *do* have the feeling that he's nearby, that he needs me somehow. I can't give up that feeling, no matter how hard I try."

"Sweetheart," Brad whispered, his heart aching. "Abby, you'll never recover if you can't stop feeling this way. You have to come to terms with it."

Gradually he saw her pain and unhappiness beginning to harden into anger. She moved across the room, reaching into the closet for her parka. "I have to go now. I want to catch the best of the afternoon light. Please make sure that Aaron's room is tidy before we leave."

Brad nodded, painfully aware of her standing stiffly in the living room while he went down the hall to extract Tony from Aaron's room. The little girl lingered, gazing wistfully at the array of beloved toys. But she was obedient, helping Brad to restock the shelves and cupboards.

"Can I come back and play again?" she whispered, rearranging the tea set and touching the kettle with a loving finger. "Soon, Brad?"

"I don't know, darling." Brad gathered her into his arms and gazed over her shining head with a sad brooding expression. "I just don't know."

When the room was tidy he led Tony down the hall and put on her bulky winter clothes, while Abby waited in silence. The three of them left the house together.

Brad stood on the curb, holding Tony's hand, and watched as Abby got into her old car and drove off in the direction of the cliffs without a wave or a backward glance.

CHAPTER FOURTEEN

THE TWO TRAILS on the north valley cliffs were familiar to many residents of the area and were well used during most of the year. One was an easier, more gradual path, suitable for children, the other a shortcut up the cliff edge that was considerably tougher.

The latter climb was a pleasantly challenging trek in the summertime, beginning with a fast-rising set of switchbacks that traversed the lower base of the cliffs, then ascending gradually into some rugged uphill pulls that were the next thing to rock climbing. Near the top, the weary hiker came out onto a beautiful rolling plateau, starred with trees and shrubs and offering a breathtaking panoramic view of the Okanogan Valley far below.

Abby parked her car at the base of the trail, checking her backpack for equipment. She had a thermos of hot tea laced with sugar, a package of trail mix, a metallic ground sheet and first-aid kit, her tree permit and a small hatchet, extra socks and glove liners, a flashlight and a box of waterproof matches.

"Not bad," she murmured, grinning at herself, "for a three-hour hike in broad daylight. You'd think I was trekking to the South Pole or something."

Still, Abby was an experienced outdoorswoman, and she tried to follow the counsel she gave others—

that it was always foolhardy to venture into the woods without proper equipment. She set out on the steeper trail, her boots crunching in the icy drifts of snow that lay across the path and rustling in the dense carpet of pine needles. At first, the climb was easy, giving Abby time to think about Brad's final words just an hour or so ago, and his accusation that she was crippling her life by refusing to let go of Aaron.

Brad Carmichael was hardly the person to be lecturing about a crippled life, Abby thought bitterly, living the way he did. He was wild and reckless, disappointed people all the time, drifted from job to job without meaning or purpose....

But he's different now, an inner voice said. *He's become a responsible man.*

An image of Tony slipped without warning into Abby's mind and she recoiled with shock. She could see the big blue eyes, the tense face and anxious hands, the sudden luminous glow when Brad had told her she could play with Aaron's toys.

"No! Not Aaron's toys," Abby whispered in agony. "She can't have Aaron's toys. They're *his* toys. He loves them so much. Oh, Aaron," she murmured, seeing her son's dear chubby face, his grave dark eyes and shy smile. "It's been a whole year, Aaron," she told him through her tears. "Did you know that, baby? A whole year ago today since Mommy saw you last. I love you, sweetheart. I miss you so much, every single day...."

While Abby was absorbed in her thoughts the trail was rapidly growing steeper. She had to scramble over fallen tree trunks rimmed with ice and hack away tangled branches obscuring the path. The trail tilted to become almost vertical in places, a treacherous icy slope that could only be navigated by hanging on to nearby tree limbs and cutting footholds in the rocky soil.

Abby panted and struggled, forgetting all about her problems in the sheer effort to make the climb. At one point, inside a long chute that wound upward in spiral fashion, she lost her balance near the top and slid all the way back to the lower trail, landing in an ignominious heap, muddy and chilled.

She picked herself up and started over, working with grim determination and choosing more reliable handholds. By the time she'd regained the lost ground, the sun was starting to fade away though the ranks of tall pines, leaving the trail in deep shade.

Feeling a brief chill of concern, she squinted upward, trying to gauge how much longer it would take to reach the top.

It couldn't be more than another half hour to the plateau, she calculated. If she was careful and didn't have any more time-wasting accidents, she could get there, select a tree, strap it to her back and make the return journey just before full darkness. Coming down was always twice as fast.

For a moment she hesitated, toying with the idea of abandoning the project and trying again another day. For some reason, she was so tired.

Then she thought of Aaron's death, exactly a year ago today. Abby squared her shoulders, set her jaw and started toiling upward again, her eyes on the distant ridge that was her goal, dark and sinister against a graying sky. The final upward pull was the worst. The trail was very steep, and studded with rocks that were both tempting and treacherous. Abby never really knew until she committed her weight to one of those rocks whether it was going to hold her. She eased her way forward, trying to stay at the rough edge of the path where there were more footholds, concentrating on placing her feet safely among twisted tree roots and large boulders.

She was sweating with effort despite the gathering darkness and the bitter cold, panting and puffing as she toiled upward. She reached ahead for a projecting branch, placed the toe of her right boot securely on a flat piece of rock, and then it happened.

Simultaneously, in a sort of hideous slow-motion routine, the branch came away in her hand and the rock slipped from under her boot, sending her sprawling. She began to roll downhill, tumbling and bumping across the slope, past the steep trail and into the trees, unable to do anything but curl up like a hedgehog and tuck her head deep in her collar to keep it from being battered on the rocks.

Then, with terrifying abruptness, the world changed. There was no resistance any longer, no bumps, no pain. Abby was falling through space, as light and free and graceful as a bit of thistledown. She hardly had time to enjoy this delicious sensation, before she landed with a vicious thump that knocked the air from her body for several seconds.

Rubbing a sore elbow, massaging an aching knee, Abby sat up to assess her situation. She had slipped over the cliff face onto a roomy ledge, perhaps ten- or twelve-feet wide at its outermost curve, and thirty feet long. The ledge was littered with rocks that had tumbled from the cliffs overhead, some of them larger than her body. Abby gazed up nervously toward the sheer cliff face, where tons of rock seemed poised to come crashing down at any moment.

The distance back up to the edge of the cliff over which she'd tumbled wasn't all that great, possibly about fifteen or twenty feet, but it was smooth rock and the light was fading. She couldn't make out secure handholds. She shook her head and edged cautiously over to look down, then gasped.

The perpendicular cliff face fell away beneath her in dizzying fashion, hundreds of feet to the bottom of the gorge. She could see parts of the trail she'd come up on, winding around like a narrow ribbon far below. And off in the distance, so small that it was just a speck, she could even see the waning sunlight glinting on her tiny car parked in the woods at the base of the trail.

"All right," Abby said finally, with another rueful glance at that sheer face above her. "Looks like I'll have to stay here for a while until they send out a rescue vehicle. Stupid of me, causing all this trouble."

She continued to talk aloud and move around on the ledge, determinedly keeping herself busy. She pulled and tugged at twigs growing from the rock face and in among the tumbled boulders, coaxing enough of them to build a fire. The damp green wood burned slowly, warming her bruised body as she ate the last of her trail mix and drank her lukewarm sweet tea.

The night sky deepened and grew menacing. The stars winked down at her, indifferent to whether she lived or died.

Abby had the same irrational feeling looking down at the houses in the valley below. She could see the warm pinpoints of light where people lived, watched television, ate their evening meals and put their babies to bed without a thought to the woman trapped in the blackness far above them.

"Except that I'm not in any danger, thank you very much," Abby told the silent brilliant sky. "I'm just fine. I have food, and a fire, even though it's so smoky that nobody can see it. And I have no injuries to speak of. You're not getting me."

Through the night she even managed to sleep a bit, curled up in her metallic sheet near the smoldering fire. Animal calls sobbed and quivered through the frosty air, dropping to her from the forest above, laments of sorrow and loss that were unspeakably chilling. By the time the morning sun glimmered pallidly through banked clouds, then vanished again, Abby wasn't nearly as confident about her situation.

There was no sign of a rescue vehicle, no air traffic at all. Maybe Brad hadn't alerted anybody. Probably he'd been so annoyed by her coldness and selfishness that he'd washed his hands of her and hadn't even bothered to call and check if she was home safely.

She felt an icy chill running along her spine. Nobody but Brad knew exactly where she was. Maybe Mitch had some idea that she was coming up here to cut a tree, but she hadn't been specific. It could be hours, even days, before somebody missed her. And she was getting so cold....

Abby ran around on the ledge, searching frantically for more wood to supplement her dying fire. She slapped her arms against her chest, hopped and danced on chilly feet, fervently grateful for the warmth of the space-age materials of her hiking clothes.

All her fingers and toes seemed to work, and there was no sign of frostbite. But she knew if she had to spend another day and night on this cramped ledge, especially without a fire, liquids or food supplies, she was in real danger of hypothermia.

Finally, in desperation, she cast her eyes over the upper cliff face again, assessing its strength and stability. There were a number of sturdy vines growing out of the rock, and it looked rougher in the clear light of day, affording more footholds.

"If I try it," Abby murmured, hoping that the sound of her own voice would keep her spirits up, "the worst that can happen is that I'll slide back down onto the ledge. That's all. And that isn't so bad."

Suddenly her imagination supplied her with a vivid picture of that sheer lower face, tumbling downward into the dark valley far below. She shivered, then drew herself erect. "I'll keep the ledge directly beneath me. Besides, I won't fall," she said.

She cast a last wistful glance at the heavens, searching for rescue planes of any kind. But the sky was leaden and ominous, and snowflakes were beginning to swirl around the higher elevations, drifting gently onto her face and arms. "All right. Better start now before it gets too slippery," Abby muttered, pushing her gloves into a side pocket and seizing a gnarled root projecting from the rock face. She found a toehold, pulled herself up and reached for another root, a jutting rock, anything. By slow torturous degrees she worked her way upward, going limp with relief every time a hold proved secure enough to take her weight. She was crawling like a fly up the icy cliff face, aching with weariness, her fingers bleeding and numb with cold. Her mouth filled with dirt as she climbed and every muscle in her body ached and throbbed with effort.

About five feet from the top, she was clinging in utter exhaustion to a tiny gnarled tree limb when she heard the helicopter.

It flew in out of the gray sky to the west, circled behind her and lifted up onto the plateau just above her. "Stay there if you're comfortable," a voice called down from a megaphone. "Or keep climbing if you have secure footholds. We'll be down to you in a minute."

"Oh, thank God," Abby sobbed. "Thank God." She let herself go for a second, her body weight hanging limply, and the tree branch gave way in her fingers. She felt herself tumbling, scraping, grabbing for handholds. Suddenly she landed facedown with a sickening thud on the mass of boulders that littered the narrow ledge. Her chest hit the corner of one of the rocks with crushing force, driving the breath from her body on impact.

Thought, memory and feeling all ceased at that instant. Abby Malone fell into a void that was vast and bottomless.

OUT OF THE DARKNESS she felt herself being lifted and carried, wafted as light as a feather up the face of the cliff.

"They've got me in one of those stretcher things, on ropes," Abby murmured, enjoying the sensation. It was so good to be in capable hands, to know that she was safe and cared for.

She flexed her fingers and knees, pleased to discover that nothing seemed to be broken. In fact, she felt strong and confident, and there was no more pain in her fingers. The bleeding had apparently stopped, as well.

"I can't believe how smooth the ride is," Abby said, delighted by the sound of her voice in the morning stillness. "This is fun."

Gradually she became aware of other noises, of shouts and confusion. Four men were on the plateau, working feverishly over something lying on the ground. Three of the men wore powder blue ski suits with a red logo on the arm. The fourth man was Brad.

Abby watched curiously, then moved closer to hear what they were saying.

"Her heart stopped," one of the men muttered. "When she landed she must have taken a blow like a knockout punch, right at the juncture of the aorta. Look at the damage to the skin."

Another of the uniformed men pushed close to the stretcher, filling a syringe from a small labeled bottle. Abby stared in confusion, wondering who the men were talking about. Was there another woman lost on the cliff face? What was happening?

Brad turned toward her, his shoulders heaving. Abby saw the tears on his face and felt a chill of fear.

She moved over to stand beside him, gazing down at the pale, dirt-smeared woman who lay on the stretcher.

It's me, she thought in confusion. *This is ridiculous. How can it be me?*

"Brad," she said, reaching for his hand. "Brad, don't cry, darling. I'm all right. Really I am. Look, I'm just fine."

But he ignored her, kneeling again beside the stretcher and touching the woman's cold face. Her muddy jacket was unzipped and her sweater and shirt had been cut open above her breasts. Abby could see the mass of discolored skin on the woman's chest, which appeared briefly when the paramedic paused in his rhythmic massage.

"Abby," Brad murmured. "Abby, darling, I love you. I'm so sorry...."

Abby yearned to comfort him, to put her arms around him and cradle him until his grief passed, but there seemed to be no way to reach him. She stood back, watching as the three paramedics labored frantically over the woman's still body, their faces taut with concern in the chill light of morning.

"It's partly the cold," one of them panted, "and the exertion of climbing. A blow like that, landing directly on an overworked heart, can cause instant death."

"If we'd only been a little sooner," Brad muttered in anguish. "We wasted the whole night searching on the other side of the cliff." He choked briefly, then went on, talking mostly to himself. "I thought she'd be using the easier trail. I never dreamed she'd come this way by herself...."

All at once, to Abby's alarm, their voices began to fade. She was drifting away from them, up along the cliff edge. She looked back, still longing to reach Brad and comfort him, but she could hardly see him any longer. He was growing small and indistinct, swallowed up in the swirling gusts of snow.

She yielded to the urge that drew her upward, into the mists above the tree line.

"I'm dead," she whispered, trying her voice again. "I must be dead. It's so confusing. I don't have the slightest idea what you're supposed to do when you're dead. I just feel so silly."

Saying the words aloud had a comforting effect. She felt absolutely normal, fully in control of her body and her mind. In fact, her mental processes were amazingly clear and lucid.

She found herself thinking about the past, about all the things that had happened in her life to bring her to this point. She had a nagging sense of incompletion, of things not being quite right, but it was hard to isolate the cause of her concern. While she frowned, still concentrating, Abby became aware of a different feeling in the air around her.

She wasn't walking up the cliff through snow and mist any longer. She seemed to have entered a different sort of atmosphere, a place that was small and tightly enclosed. She felt herself being drawn in, separated from her surroundings and propelled forward at great speed. No wonder people had difficulty describing the tunnel, Abby thought as she traveled. *This isn't really a thing at all. It's more like a feeling. It's like being...channelled, or something.*

Now she was hurtling through blackness so intense that it was unlike anything she'd ever known. But there was nothing frightening about this dark place. The blackness had a velvety, caressing feel, warm and comforting against her face and body. She felt a gentle wind brush her cheeks and then, gradually, light began to blossom.

The light was somewhere ahead, drawing her on. Abby's heart lifted and soared with happiness. There was something so wonderful about the light, so richly sweet and welcoming, that she felt tears beginning to flow down her face. Nothing in the world had ever been as important to her as reaching that light, being gathered up and enfolded by it.

Nearer, nearer…the world brightened and warmed all around her. Eventually she began to lose the sense of being confined and of traveling at great speed. Her body felt light and free, and she found herself able to walk again, to move about in a casual way.

Abby looked around curiously, awed by the beauty of the place. She was entering an unspoiled wilderness with towering forests, lush green meadows and a stream that glittered and plunged over rocky cataracts. Birds flew everywhere, lovely exotic creatures that Abby didn't recognize. In the middle of the stream the water foamed and danced against the rocks, sending bright sprays of rainbows into the sun.

A man and a small boy sat on the bank of the stream, near a tranquil pool where the water was calm and deep. They were talking together quietly, and Abby recognized the man's voice. She held her breath and moved closer.

"Dad?" she whispered. "Dad, is that you?"

Her father turned and smiled at her. "Hello, Abby," he said calmly, as if he'd seen her only hours ago. "Look what this young fellow made."

The boy stood proudly and drew up a glistening wooden boat attached to a long string. "Hi, Mom," he said, waving cheerfully at Abby. "Grandpa, my mast is tangled again. Can you get that little piece of string loose?"

Abby gazed hungrily at her son. Aaron seemed older than when she'd seen him last, strong and sun browned and happy.

Your son lives in love, a voice echoed distantly in her mind. *He is surrounded by love and he is happy.*

Who was it who'd told her that, Abby wondered, looking at Aaron's shining dark hair, his beautiful agile body and smiling face. And why had it been so hard for her to believe?

"You can't stay, dear," Abby's father told her gently as he worked the boy's mast free of confinement and lowered the boat tenderly back into the stream. He watched the little vessel bob away on the water, then made a slight adjustment to his own larger ship, which was moored nearby. "It's not time for you to join us."

Abby's heart filled with sorrow. "I can't?" she whispered. "Why not?"

"It's not time," her father repeated.

"Hey, Mom!" Aaron shouted, taking the roll of string from his grandfather. "Watch this!" He flicked his wrist and set the small boat bobbing off into midstream.

Abby smiled mistily, her heart aching with love and pride. She wanted to tell Aaron how wonderful he was, how happy she was to see him, but she felt herself being drawn farther on, closer and closer to the warmth and sweetness of the light.

"You see?" a voice said. The voice came from all around her, but also seemed to emanate mysteriously from somewhere within her. "There was nothing at all to worry about."

"I'm sorry," Abby whispered humbly. "I didn't know."

"Did you think I would take him and then not care for him?" the voice chided gently, almost teasing.

"Who are you?" Abby asked, turning toward the light. She felt herself being smiled at, picked up and cuddled, wrapped in gentleness and comfort.

"You're not ready to be here, Abby," the voice told her tenderly.

"But I want to stay," she said in childlike sorrow. "It's so beautiful here."

"You will come when it's time. Just now you are needed elsewhere."

"I'm needed?"

"Look, Abby."

As clearly as if they were standing in front of her, Abby saw Brad and the little girl he was looking after. They seemed cold and alone, small beings threatened by dark mists and untold dangers, things that were no part of this beautiful place where she found herself. She looked at the two of them and felt her heart aching and swelling with love. She hungered to take them in her arms together, Brad and the little girl, to hold them tight and pour all her energy into protecting them and surrounding them with happiness.

This love that sprang and flowed from her was so powerful it was frightening. She'd never felt such intense love, not even for Aaron when he was a helpless newborn baby.

"That is all that matters," the voice told her gently. "The love that you feel now is the only thing that exists in the world. Love is what makes the beauty all around you."

"Can it be beautiful there, too?" Abby whispered. "Can it ever be like this?"

"If there is enough love," the voice told her. "When love exists in completeness, there will be no difference between there and here."

Abby nodded, trying to understand, to absorb the marvelous truth that was being given to her. But all she could really feel was the need to see Brad again, to hold him and kiss him, to gather up that little homeless girl and pour enough love into her to make up for all the loneliness and suffering.

"I...I need to go back," she said in a halting voice. "Please, may I go back now?"

Again she felt herself enfolded and hugged, bathed in warm approval and tenderness. Then, in the merest fraction of an instant, she was lying in the cold with snow falling on her closed eyelids and a smothering, aching pain in her chest.

"My God," one of the paramedics breathed. "There's a pulse! Look, we've got her! There's a pulse!"

All the men shouted, but Abby was conscious only of Brad. Her eyes flickered open and she saw him kneeling above her, gripping her hands. His tears flowed unheeded, while a wondering joy dawned on his face.

EPILOGUE

IN FEBRUARY, the temperature plummeted and the earth drew in upon itself, locked in a bitter chill that was unusual for the Okanogan Valley. Snow piled everywhere, drifting silently across the orchards and onto the empty beaches, and frozen tree branches cracked like rifle shots in the stillness of the winter night.

Far-off in the darkness, somewhere among the distant icy stars, Abby heard a child crying. She sat bolt upright, her heart pounding with alarm, then reached for her robe and slippers.

Had it been just the wind howling around the eaves? No, she heard it more clearly now as she hurried down the hallway.

"Tony," she whispered, running into the other room and approaching the small rumpled bed. "Tony, darling, what is it?"

Abby gathered the warm little body into her arms, wrapping the blankets cozily up around Tony's chin and cuddling the child as she sobbed.

"I had a bad dream," Tony sobbed, her fingers in her mouth. "I had such a bad dream, Abby."

"Well, it was just a dream," Abby soothed, kissing the little girl's soft, fragrant hair, nuzzling her flushed cheek. "Just a silly old bad dream. I'm right here, and so is Brad, and all your toys are safe, see? Nothing can hurt you.''

Tony gazed up in the muted light, her wide blue eyes still cloudy with sleep.

''Abby?'' she murmured, nestling cozily in her arms.

''Yes, dear?''

''Can I call you Mommy?''

Abby drew her breath in sharply, trembling with emotion. Here it was at last, the moment they'd been waiting for, though she and Brad had agreed not to rush it, to let it happen naturally.

''Of course you can, sweetheart,'' Abby murmured, kissing Tony's soft temple and trying to sound casual. ''I'd like that very much.''

''And Brad? Can I call him Daddy?''

''Certainly. He'd love it, too. Tony, do you remember just after Christmas, when Brad and I got married?''

''Joan and Mitch were there, and Gladys, too,'' Tony recalled with sleepy satisfaction. ''Everybody laughed and danced, and Joan caught the bouquet, and I got to serve the cake.''

''That's right. Well, the wedding means that Brad and I are husband and wife now, and we've applied to adopt you, sweetheart, so we'll be your mommy and daddy forever. So if you want to call us that, we'd be really happy.''

''Mommy,'' Tony murmured, gathering up a handful of Abby's soft robe in her little fist. ''Mommy,'' she repeated with drowsy pleasure, obviously trying the word out, liking the sound of it. ''I love you, Mommy.''

Abby's heart swelled richly with happiness.

Tony looked up at her. "Why are you crying?"

"Because I just love you so very, very much. Now, go back to sleep, dear."

Obediently Tony curled up in the bed again, gripping the old stuffed lion in a fond embrace and closing her eyes. Abby stood looking down at her for a moment, her eyes still warm with tears, smiling mistily at the plump sleeping face before she turned and padded down the hall to her room.

"Any problems?" Brad asked drowsily from the bed. "Do you need me?"

Abby shook her head. "Just a bad dream." She gazed down at him, amazed as always by the succession of miracles that had brought the three of them together.

By tacit agreement, Abby and Brad never spoke of their near-death experiences. Knowing that they shared such a wondrous thing was too awesome to speak of, though that knowledge strengthened the deep foundation of their love and their life together.

"Is she all right now?"

"I think so," Abby said, slipping into bed and cuddling up to her husband, smiling privately.

He was going to be so thrilled in the morning when Tony called him Daddy.

"Brad, it's so *cold!*" she said aloud. "Here, let me..."

"Not the feet!" Brad shouted in mock.outrage. "Ow! Not the feet!"

Abby giggled, then sobered when she felt his hand tracing the outline of her face with a slow gentle touch.

"Abby," he said.

"Hmm?"

"Let's make a baby."

"Brad..."

"Come on, Abby. It'll be great. It'll be company for Tony, and it'll be so much fun for both of us. Let's do it."

"A baby's a lot of work, you know, Brad. And a huge responsibility."

"Well, I'm a real responsible guy. I'll help all the time, Abby. I'll clean her up and keep her in the garage and brush her. I'll take her for walks and keep her food dish filled all the time. Please, Abby?"

Abby chuckled, knowing that in spite of his teasing, Brad was telling her the truth. There was no more reliable and helpful husband than Brad Carmichael, and she knew from the depths of her soul that she could depend on him completely for the rest of her life.

"Well..." she murmured, beginning to respond to his caresses.

"Well what?" he whispered huskily.

"Well, let's just let nature take its course and see what happens. How's that?"

And so it happened on a starry winter night, in the northern latitudes of a blue-green planet whirling around a lesser sun, that another speck of being detached itself from the celestial light and began its perilous journey into the thrilling, wondrous mystery known as life.

My Valentine
1994

Celebrate the most romantic day of the year with
MY VALENTINE 1994
a collection of original stories, written by
four of Harlequin's most popular authors...

MARGOT DALTON
MURIEL JENSEN
MARISA CARROLL
KAREN YOUNG

Available in February, wherever
Harlequin Books are sold.

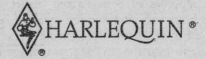

HARLEQUIN ®

VAL94

Relive the romance...
Harlequin® is proud to bring you

A new collection of three complete novels every
month. By the most requested authors, featuring
the most requested themes.

Available in January:

They're ranchers, horse trainers, cowboys...
They're willing to risk their lives.
But are they willing to risk their hearts?

Three complete novels in one special collection:

RISKY PLEASURE by JoAnn Ross
VOWS OF THE HEART by Susan Fox
BY SPECIAL REQUEST by Barbara Kaye

Available wherever Harlequin books are sold.

Where do you find hot Texas nights, smooth Texas charm and dangerously sexy cowboys?

NEW WAY TO FLY
by Margot Dalton

New Look—Texas Style!

Rancher Brock Munroe is smitten with Amanda Walker. But he hates what she does for a living. Amanda is a personal shopper. To Brock it's a ridiculous career—dressing people who have more money than sense. Still, Brock can't quite figure this lady out. It seems that with Amanda what you see is much less than what you get.

CRYSTAL CREEK reverberates with the exciting rhythm of Texas. Each story features the rugged individuals who live and love in the Lone Star state. And each one ends with the same invitation...

Y'ALL COME BACK...REAL SOON!

Don't miss *NEW WAY TO FLY* by Margot Dalton
Available in January wherever Harlequin Books are sold.

When the only time you have for yourself is…

STOLEN *moments* ™

Christmas is such a busy time—with shopping, decorating, writing cards, trimming trees, wrapping gifts….

When you do have a few *stolen moments* to call your own, treat yourself to a brand-new *short* novel. Relax with one of our Stocking Stuffers— or with all six!

Each STOLEN MOMENTS title is a complete and original contemporary romance that's the perfect length for the busy woman of the nineties! Especially at Christmas…

And they make perfect **stocking stuffers**, too! (For your mother, grandmother, daughters, friends, co-workers, neighbors, aunts, cousins—all the other women in your life!)

Look for the STOLEN MOMENTS display in December

STOCKING STUFFERS:

HIS MISTRESS Carrie Alexander
DANIEL'S DECEPTION Marie DeWitt
SNOW ANGEL Isolde Evans
THE FAMILY MAN Danielle Kelly
THE LONE WOLF Ellen Rogers
MONTANA CHRISTMAS Lynn Russell

HSM2

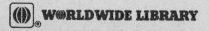 **WORLDWIDE LIBRARY**